VENTURA HELLWAY

CALIFORNIA DEMON, BOOK 3

DEBRA DUNBAR

CHAPTER 1

"Is he…is he drunk or something?" I squinted at the man in eight-thousand-dollar clothes whose hands were shaking as he tried to snap a magazine into his pistol.

"Fuck if I know." Telaney leaned forward to better eye the man. "He's *got* to be drunk or high. I expected him to send a hit man, or a hit squad, not show up to a fight all by his lonesome decked out in a bespoke suit."

"Maybe that's his fighting suit." I snorted.

"It's gonna be his burial suit," Telaney added.

Two months ago, Telaney had been late to a scavenge at a yoga studio where a man we'd called Big Studio Dude had killed his wife for screwing around on him with an equally Big Dude with the Palisades Militia. The militia had retaliated by bombing BSD's limo. The bomb killed the driver as well as BSD's friends who had borrowed the limo; the blast had turned the vehicle into twisted bits of blackened metal.

Telaney's intel was that BSD was going to make a move on the militia—step three in this escalating mini-war.

I'd assumed Big Studio Dude would hire someone to do

this job, but as I watched the fool swagger up to the chain-link fence of the Palisades Militia compound like he had steel balls, I thought differently.

"Is he gonna climb that fence?"

Telaney's question was rhetorical, but with this guy, who knew? I wouldn't be surprised if he rang the fucking bell and asked politely to be let in. What I didn't expect was him ripping the enormous iron gate off the hinges and tossing it aside into the decorative bushes.

"Holy fuck," Telaney muttered.

I nodded in agreement with Telaney. Normal humans couldn't do *that*. "He's heading up the walk. We better move in closer."

"Not too close," Telaney warned as we carefully made our way toward the gaping opening where a metal gate had once been. "Do you think he's a shifter or something?"

I shrugged. These days, who knew what anyone was. The man didn't look or act like the descriptions I'd been given of elves. I was ruling out mage, since I doubted Big Studio Guy would have the time or patience for that level of craft. Were there super-strength amulets? He clearly could afford one, judging from that suit, but this guy had a suicidal confidence that I wouldn't think a purchased magical device could give.

"Shifter, or maybe demon," I suggested.

"Demon?" Telaney turned wide eyes on me, then peeked around the rhododendron toward the retreating figure. "Shouldn't he have horns or a tail or lizard-skin or something then?"

"Sometimes they just look human," I told her.

Bishop had told me some demons were better at camouflaging themselves than others. Although if BSG was a demon, why hadn't he taken care of his Palisades Militia problem before now? Maybe the guy had sold his soul to a demon who'd taken up residence in the last few weeks, and this pending bloodbath was part of the deal. But the one-percent rarely made stupid deals like that. If one of them was going to sell their soul, it wouldn't be to get revenge against a group that blew up their limo. No, they'd just hire people to take care of that minor inconvenience, not go all Rambo themselves.

Still, if he was a demon, or anything not-human, we'd soon know. He'd either go furry or sprout horns.

Or get shot full of holes and die on the pavement.

"Just be careful," I warned, not wanting anything to happen to the woman who was quickly becoming one of my best friends.

We snuck through where the gate had been, darting behind trees and statuary as we followed the man up the drive. No one usually messed with Vultures like us. We weren't there to fight, just to sort through the bodies after it was all over. We scavenged. We didn't get involved. It was relatively safe. Occasionally someone would take a pot shot at one of us just out of general dislike, and there was always the danger of a stray bullet, but we tried to keep out of the way of projectiles.

Midway up the drive, a man approached. He shouted for BSG to "drop it" and "keep his hands where he could see them."

Telaney and I halted our advance, dropping low because shit was about to get real.

I expected BSG to start shooting, but instead he gently put the gun in his pocket and stood, hands raised. Then he grabbed a nearby statue and heaved it at the man. The concrete Athena flew through the air, knocking the man backward and to the ground before he could get off more than a few wild shots. He certainly wasn't getting up with a four-hundred-pound statue on him, but BSG wasn't taking any chances. He grabbed the statue's base with one hand, casually walked over to the guard, and bashed his head in.

Telaney sucked in a breath.

Kirstin VanMarten had decided to screw around with some man with the militia, when she was married to *this*? Girl should have left the state to get her business on because this wasn't the sort of husband a woman cuckolded and lived to tell the tale. I was surprised BSG had put a hit out on her instead of just caving her face in with one blow himself. This guy was scary. Note to self—don't mess with Big Studio Guy. And definitely don't marry him and cheat on him. Or blow up his limo.

The sound of a rifle shot had both Telaney and me flattening ourselves to the ground. Peeking up, I saw BSG spin around, drop to his knees, then get up and continue moving forward. Three more shots did little more than slow him a step or two.

"Fucker's got some serious armor on under that pricey suit," Telaney commented.

My friend Bags owned a similar vest, and it had saved his life at least once that I was aware of. But no matter what sort of flak jacket this guy was wearing, he was seriously badass to keep moving. Military-grade protection might keep a person alive, but getting shot still felt like someone had swung a baseball bat at your chest.

The shooter must have given up trying to snipe the intruder, because the gunfire stopped. Instead, a dozen guys poured out the front door, dropped to their knees, and opened fire. BSG shrugged off the hail of bullets and began launching statuary at the line of militia.

Second note to self: Never fill my front lawn with large concrete sculptures. Or small concrete sculptures.

Telaney and I kept low, sheltering behind one of the few statues BSG wasn't using as a projectile. After taking down half of the militia, the remaining six fled back into the house. BSG did his head-smashing version of the double-tap in zombie video games, then walked up to the front door.

Palisades Militia must have had a dozen locks on that thing, because it took BSG ten seconds longer to rip it off the hinges than it had taken to do the same thing to the front gate. He entered the building.

Even from across the spacious lawn, we could hear the screams and gunfire.

When it stopped, I turned to my friend. "Want to go in and pick through what's left?"

She let out a slow breath, then shook her head. "Let's wait until we're sure everyone's dead, and we're not going to be impaled by a stair-rail javelin or bludgeoned to death by a sofa."

"Good plan."

Telaney and I waited outside, standing but still remaining alert in case we needed to hit the ground again. I was glad we'd held off on scavenging when I saw the shadow of a figure by where the front door had once been. A long, high-pitched scream rent the air. Seconds later BSG walked outside, dragging a man behind him. The man's limbs were twisted at strange angles, sliding along the ground as if he no longer had use of them. His screams were hoarse and gulping.

We stared as BSG lugged the man over to a red Ferrari, hauled him up onto the hood, then shoved the man's head clear through the windshield. Blood sprayed, and the screams were abruptly silenced.

BSG wiped his hands on the dead man's pant legs, then walked down the driveway.

I wasn't sure if we should run for it or not. Not that we could outrun any statuary the guy might want to launch at us.

The man smoothed a hand over his hair, then winked at us. "Happy pickings, girls. Oh." He pulled the pistol out of his pocket and tossed it on the ground. I jumped a little, because firearm safety is a pet peeve of mine. "Here. You gals can keep this. I ended up not needing it."

He continued down the driveway, whistling a cheerful tune as he turned onto the street.

CHAPTER 2

Telaney followed me back to my house to celebrate our salvage, and so she could see my new digs. As usual, half the neighborhood was outside, watching as we drove up the road, parked in the driveway, and walked into the house.

"Wow, this is amazing." Telaney did a slow spin as she took in the first floor of my house. "I'm kinda jealous."

"You wouldn't be if knew my neighbors." I dropped my keys on the counter, still feeling that little thrill run through me. My house. Mine. And I loved it, even with the nearby weirdos who seemed to scrutinize my every move.

"Holy shit. That view!" Telaney moved into the living room to stare out the bank of windows that made up the entire back wall of the house.

It *was* an incredible view. The cliffside house overlooked the LA basin. At night it was all twinkling lights below and into the distance, as if I were some god on high surveying my people.

I smiled to myself as I pulled a bottle of white wine out of the fridge and two glasses from the dish drainer. There wasn't much here to offer guests. I picked up non-perishables every now and then in an attempt to stock up, but most times I forgot that I lived alone now and needed to buy food for myself that wouldn't spoil if the power went out. Half the time I got home too late to bother cooking. More than half the time I ate dinner over at Bea's with her and the girls, crashing on her couch for the night.

I was lonely. No one clued me in about that when I was all gung-ho to claim this place for myself. Nevarra still felt guilty for taking my bedroom. The more I slept on the couch there, the worse I made her feel. The girls were growing and deserved their own rooms. And me moving out meant more space for them. I needed to stop camping out on Bea's couch and really try to consider this place as my home.

"I'm surprised Bea and the girls wouldn't move in here with you," Telaney commented. "There's tons of space. It seems like a nice neighborhood. It's close to the park."

I winced, thinking about the argument I'd had with Bea over this very topic. Not that anyone ever argued with Bea. She listened, said her piece, and that was that.

"She's proud of the fact she bought that house in Sun Valley and had it paid off even before the demons came. She loves the neighbors there. It's home. It's *her* home. And this isn't."

Bea's home was my home as well, and this place still felt strange to me—like I was temporarily living in a model house and pretending to be independent until the real owners came back and I had to leave.

"The girls come over once a week to spend the night," I continued. "And I've still been spending the night there two or three times a week." I probably saw them more now than I had when I was on the run from the Fixers.

My new place was gorgeous, but sometimes I wasn't sure it would ever really feel like home. Was this something everyone went through the first time they moved out of their parent's house? Being here elicited a strange mix of excitement, fear, and loneliness, and I wasn't sure if that was something that would ever change.

I walked into the living room, handed Telaney the wineglasses, unscrewed the top on the wine bottle, and poured. It was white wine. That was it. White. For three bucks a bottle, I wasn't going to complain.

"Well, I think your house rocks." Telaney toasted me with her wine glass. "And unlike my house, you didn't have to patch up drywall, toss out pee-stained rugs, and buy all new furniture."

This place had come mostly furnished, and it hadn't been the slightest bit trashed. It was one of the few benefits of all those weird neighbors.

Telaney and I sat on the white couch—which I'd covered with a blanket, because who the hell can manage to keep a white couch clean, especially with my job? We sipped our wine, looking out at the city.

Telaney shook her head. "I sometimes wonder why more people didn't leave two years ago. Crazy ass people with six-figure a year jobs and million-dollar condos. I get that that's hard to leave behind, but they *could*. They've got mutual funds back in the states, probably vacation homes in Colorado. They could get jobs somewhere else, or get their big corporate employers to transfer them to another location. Why the fuck are they still here?"

I shrugged. "Because they still have six-figure a year jobs. And houses. All that shit the demons and monsters cause? That's happening to someone else. Yeah, maybe there's a dead body on the pavement when you're leaving work on a Wednesday, or someone a block over got their house broken into and their entire family disemboweled by something with claws and fangs, but that's *other* people. They'll carry a pistol and pay one of the militias or gangs for protection, and get a little rush, feeling like they're some badass in a spaghetti western. If there's a shop with a door smashed in on their way home, maybe they'll go in and steal something because they can. They don't give a shit about anyone else. They *won't* give a shit until it's their house that's broken into, and their friends and family being disemboweled."

Telaney snorted. "So basically, not much different than it was before the demons came?"

I thought about that for a second, about the violence, the haves and the have-nots. That safety and justice only seemed to be available to certain people who didn't look like us. "It's worse than before for some of us, for a lot of us. And not a whole lot different for others, sadly."

"Think that'll ever change?" she asked.

I felt as if I were standing on a ledge, looking over one side toward cheery optimism and the other side toward a gritty realism.

"I don't know." I shook my head. "I honestly don't know."

We continued drinking for a few moments, silent and looking out the windows. Did I think things would get better? Easier for the humans who couldn't afford all the magic, private militias, and the other stuff that insulated them from monsters around them? Was the solution to fight back? Or to save up and get the hell out of New Hell, which had been my plan for the last two years.

I had no idea.

"Good haul today," Telaney finally commented.

"Mmmm," I agreed.

If it had been accounting day at the militia, we would have scored more. Even so, it had been a big job. The dead guys had cash on them, and some jewelry. We found cash in the house, cash in the cars, cash in between the sofa seat cushions. Telaney had grabbed a nice set of lamps for her house, and I took all the cell phones, an Instant Pot still in the box, and a vacuum. There had been a few other things of value as well—two laptops, an iPad, and a virtual reality system. All the stuff would go to Bags's pawnshop tomorrow, and the cash would go to Bishop.

I was thinking about keeping the Instant Pot. Might be nice to throw food in before I left for the day so I could come home to a hot meal.

"That Big Studio Guy was freaky weird," Telaney commented. "Are you still thinking he might be a shifter? Or a demon?"

"He sure as hell is *something*, and that something isn't human," I replied. "His expensive suit was all ripped to shreds, but it didn't look like any of the blood decorating it was his."

"And he wasn't walking like a man who'd been shot—even one who'd been wearing a flak jacket when he'd been shot." Telaney shook her head. "Guy whistled as he left. And winked at us."

"And never shot one bullet himself. I doubt he even pulled that pistol from his pocket during the fight." I frowned, remembering what we'd observed. "Bulletproof skin. Super strength."

"Definitely not human," Telaney agreed. "My money is on shifter."

I thought back on the cougar in the customs warehouse, and how a week later HB was still scarred. "I don't think bullets bounce off shifters. I think they're hard to kill, and they heal wounds in hours or days, but not instantly. *Instantly* makes me think demon. And that cocky attitude—the whistling and the winking—makes me think demon as well."

Telaney shrugged, then took another sip of her wine. "You'd know better than me, girl. You've been up close and personal with a few demons, where I've only seen them a block or two away. See them, turn around and get the fuck outa there. That's my philosophy."

"It's a good philosophy," I agreed.

"As far as shifters," she continued. "I've got no idea if I've ever met any. Probably have. Seems like they keep to themselves, and if they don't, they pretend like they're human."

"That's true." I thought about Bishop's bar where shifter gangs, or packs, or whatever they called themselves hung out. I thought about my neighbors. I thought about Javier down the street from Bea's, who had a crush on Nevarra and who'd once picked up the front end of a truck with one hand while changing a tire.

"They're often good people. Shifters, that is," I told her.

And they were, except for those racist assholes I'd met that first night I'd been to Bishop's bar, Suerte. My neighbors might be nosy and suspicious and not-so-secretly dislike me, but they let me be. Javier was a good kid. And I trusted HB with my life.

I also trusted Bishop with my life. Thinking of him, my gaze strayed to the glass bud vase that held a large feather. Its colors were like the sun setting over the ocean, and it was unusually soft. I *felt* it—felt a strange electricity from it that vibrated through my body, down to my very soul. An angel? The thought still terrified me, but Bishop had once told me, "It doesn't matter what other people call you. The only thing that matters is what you are." I tried to keep that in mind, not just in regard to myself and my weird powers, but also about him.

And about my neighbors.

What we did, who we were day-to-day, *that's* what mattered. Not labels.

"Think your split from today is enough to pay off that Bishop guy?" Telaney asked, as if reading the train of my thoughts.

"I hope so." I'd been giving him about seventy percent of every haul I'd made in hopes of finally paying him off sometime this century. Today, I might have just made that dream come true.

Then I could start saving again to get Bea and the girls out of here. I'd given up hope that I'd ever be leaving. I'd cut a deal with the tax demons. I owed Desiree-the-demon a job, and maybe even my soul. If I left and skipped out on that, I'd end up endangering my family once more, and that wasn't something I was ever going to allow to happen again.

"Your weirdo neighbors will definitely know if you start screwing him," Telaney commented. "Gossipy busybodies."

I'd told her about how they'd watch from their windows and lawns every time I came and went, how sometimes I'd catch them standing in the street, staring at my house. I'd told her about the fight-me ritual I'd needed to take part in before they let me claim the house with squatter's rights. They *were* gossipy busybodies.

"I answered the door once in a shirt I'd stolen from Bishop's house, and the woman about had a heart attack," I told her. "Linda, three houses down on my side of the street. Said she'd come to borrow a cup of sugar, but I know she was just being nosy."

Telaney looked at me over the rim of her wine glass. "Who the fuck borrows sugar anymore?"

"Exactly." I pivoted on the couch to face her. "She obviously knew it was Bishop's shirt, and that really surprised me. It was clean. I'd taken it out of a drawer, not the laundry. Maybe the guy needs to rethink his detergent brand."

Telaney's eyes widened. "How did she know? Are his shirts that distinctive? Monogrammed?"

"She's a shifter," I admitted. "The whole neighborhood is shifters. That's why they had a total shit-fit when I tried to claim this house, and why they forced me to do that weird trial-by-combat HOA crap before they gave me the keys."

My friend stared at me openmouthed, then gulped down the rest of her wine. I refilled her glass, glad that I had the girls' beds I could use for guests if need be.

"Werewolves?" Her eyes darted furtively around the room, as if she expected one to jump out at her from the shadows.

"Fuck if I know." I shrugged. "I've never seen any of them in their animal form—at least I don't think I have. If they're hawk shifters, or coyote shifters, or stray-dog shifters, then maybe I have. They're secretive. They don't trust others. They watch me like I'm the wolf too close to the herd of sheep."

"That's fucked up." Telaney looked out the window at the view. "I'm still glad you kicked that guy's ass and won the right to live here, though."

"I didn't, though," I admitted. "He beat me. He could have killed me. I left with my tail between my legs—pun intended. Then the neighborhood leader, or pack leader or whatever he is showed up at Bea's house with an apology and the keys to the house."

My friend's smile was smug. "Bishop. The guy wants in your pants, and he intervened. I thought he was a myth until you told me you'd met him. Talk about secretive. But he clearly wants to bang you, and wants you to have your own house to do said banging in."

I frowned. "I don't think he intervened, or that he even knew about my interest in the house *or* the fight. Even if he did, I doubt he'd want the neighbors here knowing his personal business. I *do* think they let me move in because of my relationship with Bishop. I just don't think they know exactly what that relationship is. Neither do I, to be honest."

Telaney leaned over and clinked her wine glass against

mine. "You answered the door wearing his shirt. I think they're getting the idea."

A stolen shirt. And not even one he'd worn recently either.

One of the neighbors had seen me working in Bishop's bar that night I'd been hiding out from the Fixers. I assumed someone had mentioned it to Kevin Wong, who was clearly their leader, and he'd let me move in so as to curry favor with Bishop.

I wondered what would happen if Bishop and I never got intimate, if we drifted apart once my debt was paid? Would Wong kick me out of the house if he felt there was no advantage to my being here?

"Do you have any idea what the word *Ksatrei* means?" I asked Telaney.

Her brows knitted together. "Satay? Like the Indian appetizer? I love that stuff. Actually, I love the peanut sauce, although chicken is always a yes in my book."

"Not Satay. *Ksatrei.* The leader-alpha dude called me that, and it sounded like it was a title."

She shrugged. "I know some Spanish, some Tagalog, and some Urdu, but I've never heard that word."

My imagination went on a flight of fancy, thinking the word might mean queen or something connotating respect and admiration for my abilities and power.

Right. It probably meant shithead. Or stupid-chick-we-tolerate-until-we-realize-she's-a-nobody.

My phone beeped, and I dug it out of my pocket to check, thinking it might be a text from the girls or Bea.

"Sebastian?" I blinked at the screen, rereading the text. He wanted to know if I could meet in the morning for breakfast, or tomorrow night for dinner.

"Who's Sebastian?" Telaney looked at the text over my shoulder.

"He's with the Gray Dogs. He's an ex," I added a bit reluctantly.

"So, is this meeting business? Or pleasure?" Telaney elbowed me with the last question.

"It better be business." I shoved the phone back into my pocket. "We split up four years ago, and I've got no intention of going there again."

The fond memories of our relationship weren't so fond that I wanted an act two with Sebastian. Being the girlfriend of a major player in the Gray Dogs came with a whole lot of rules and responsibilities that weren't my thing.

Besides, Sebastian had a girlfriend. Even if he ousted her and publicly chose me, she'd still be pissed, and I didn't feel like having to fight and possibly kill another woman—especially over Sebastian.

"Is he hot?" Telaney asked.

"You really want to be a gang girlfriend?"

She laughed. "No. I just want the deets, girl. Living vicariously, here because the last time I got laid was when dinosaurs roamed the earth."

I shrugged, thinking a few details were the least I could do for a best friend. "He's not really handsome, but he's got presence. Average height. A little more muscular than most guys, and stronger than he looks. He comes across all manly and tough. He'd do anything to defend his woman and his family —which includes his gang family. He's respected and feared."

"But?" Telaney grinned.

I grinned back. "He's a good guy. He likes to cuddle. Dude is a serious cuddler. He likes to always have his hand on you. And it's not an ownership thing with him, it's more a connection thing. He won't eat pork because one of the few books they had when he was a kid was Charlotte's Web, and he says even the smell of bacon makes him think of Wilbur."

Telaney's smile softened. "You sure you're not interested in a round two with him?"

Bad memories tended to fade, leaving the good ones in the forefront. There had been good times with Sebastian, but we'd had more than our share of fights as well. We wanted different things from life, from each other. And I'd quickly discovered that I wasn't cut out for membership in a gang. Too many rules. Too many restrictions. And it was too... people-y. Talk to this person, don't talk to that person, say the right thing here, say something else there. I was always fucking up, and if I was always fucking up at seventeen, I'd really be fucking up at twenty-two.

I drank another gulp of the cheap wine and decided to share. "I caught him screwing around on me. I don't turn a blind eye to that. I mean, casual sex is totally my thing, but if you're mine, then you're *mine*. Sneaking behind my back really pisses me off."

Telaney grinned. "Did you shoot him? Knife him? Put a bottle of laxative in his energy drink?"

Good grief. My friend was worse than I was. "No. But I did key the words 'dickhead' and 'fuckboi' all over his car."

What I didn't tell my friend was that I hadn't used a key, I'd used my magical electrical abilities to burn the words through the paint and halfway through the steel.

Telaney choked on her wine. "You *what*? You vandalized his car?"

"Big time," I admitted. "I was seventeen, and he was eighteen but he had this sweet tricked out Charger that he loved more than life itself. I was furious at the time. We'd had a huge fight about him screwing this other girl where he basically told me him banging other women didn't mean anything and I needed to get over it if I wanted to be his girlfriend."

Telaney gasped. "Girl. I'm surprised you didn't kill him right then and there."

"I was tempted." I took a sip of my wine, remembering how hurt and angry I'd been. "I told him that he was shitty in bed and a loser, and that I could do better. Later that night I came back and keyed-up his car. And that was the end of me and Sebastian."

"Good job." Telaney held out her hand for a high-five and I smacked it. "Not all heroes wear capes," she informed me.

I saluted her with my wine glass. "Exactly."

We settled back on the sofa. "I had to go meet up with him a month ago to exchange some information, and everything was fine between us. I even got the impression he was kinda nostalgic about our past."

Telaney snorted. "I'm guessing he wasn't nostalgic about you ruining his car's paint job."

I laughed. "No. But he's a grown man. I'm a grown woman. We're not high school kids anymore. That all feels like forever ago."

She settled back on the sofa. "So you gonna meet with him in the morning or for dinner?"

I eyed my wineglass, knowing any hangover would be gone the moment I started my bike. I'd be stone-cold sober without a trace of alcohol in my weird, probably-not-human body. If I met him in the morning, I could get it all over with and get on with my day, but it would be awesome to get a decent meal out of this whole thing. "Tomorrow night. Might as well eat steak on his dime."

She chuckled. "Twenty bucks says you'll bang him in the back room. And be keying up his car by dawn."

I laughed. "Nope. Not going back there. That is one relationship I'm not interested in reviving."

Not with Sebastian, and not with the Gray Dogs either.

But I'd still meet with the man and see what he had to say. I'd still let him wine-and-dine me.

And if sparks flew, I *might* be open to a quick roll in the sheets. My mind shot back in time to memories of Sebastian and me together. Okay, maybe a *not-so-quick* roll in the sheets.

CHAPTER 3

The next morning Telaney and I ate the remains of a loaf of French bread for breakfast, then we loaded up her car with our salvage and drove to Bear State Pawnbrokers, me following her on my bike.

I loved my ancient Yamaha Fazer. It was rock-solid mechanically, easy for me to repair, and was able to weave around Los Angeles traffic with ease. The downfall was it absolutely limited what I could salvage. Lately I'd found myself annoyed at not being able to transport a microwave and an extension ladder on my bike. I was beginning to think I should be looking for a car or a truck to boost and use as my main ride.

In the beginning none of that had mattered, since I'd focused on grabbing cash, guns, and bullets and most of that could fit in the pockets of my cargo pants and my backpack. We hadn't planned on staying here for long, so I'd only salvaged what was portable, and easily converted into cold hard cash. But now it looked like we'd be here to stay for at least another year or two. Maybe longer. And each job seemed to have less and less available to grab.

Yesterday aside, the take from scavenging had gotten smaller over the last few months. Bullets were harder to come by. Guns didn't fetch as high a price as they once had. People didn't carry as much cash on them as they once had. And there were ten times the licensed Vultures, all trying to eat out of the same food trough.

Cash was the first thing everyone took. Bullets the second. Sometimes that left me picking through small appliances and damaged electronics. I'd even taken to eyeing dead people's shoes and belts.

Maybe it was time to think about another line of work—either to supplement the Vulture gig, or to replace it entirely. I liked scavenging. I was good at it, and aside from the sometimes lengthy stakeouts it required, it was a fun way to make money.

And yes, it was probably strange for me to think about watching people kill each other while I hid in the shadows, waiting to swoop in and pick the pockets of the dead as fun.

Telaney parked in front of the pawnshop, and I pulled in behind her. It felt so good to roll up to the front door like this instead of parking blocks away and sneaking around to make sure no one was waiting outside the store to jump me.

Nevarra was home, safe and healing emotionally from her ordeal. Sadie was healing as well. I no longer had a bounty on my head. And that bell on the front door of the pawnshop that chimed as Telaney and I dragged our haul inside sounded like a Halleluiah chorus to my heart.

"Hey, Bags!" I called out as we passed the rows of weed-eaters, bicycles, and power saws. The smell of mothballs, motor oil, creosote, and Windex tickled my nose and made me smile. Home. Just like Bea's house, this pawnshop was also my home.

A dark-skinned man in his mid-seventies rounded the counter, his arms outspread. Once he was within six feet of me, what looked like it might be an embrace turned into a clap on the shoulders. I wasn't a hugger unless it was Bea or the girls. Bags wasn't a hugger either. This was our welcome. No one else got a clap on the shoulders. Not even Telaney, who instead received a friendly smile and a nod.

"What ya got for me today, Eden?" Bags looked over our haul. "An Instant Pot? You're kidding me."

"Hey, that thing is amazing, and it's brand new, in-the-box. If you don't give me a good price for it, I'm going to keep it," I told him.

He snorted. "And do what with it? Use it as a planter? Catch water drips from a leaky roof?"

"I can throw some food in it before I leave in the morning and come home to dinner. No need to cook, just toss my keys on the counter, dish it into a bowl, and eat." I patted the box. "Cooking convenience for busy professionals coming home tired and dirty from a Vulture job."

Bags folded his arms across his broad chest and gave me his signature raised-eyebrow look. "Power goes out midday, and you're coming home to half-cooked, spoiled chicken, that's what you're coming home to. And no one is gonna want to waste running a generator all day while they're at work just to power this thing. Unless someone has solar panels, this Instant Pot might as well be called Salmonella Pot."

He had a point.

"Two bucks," Bags announced. "And I'll give you three for that vacuum."

And thus began our time-honored ritual of bargaining. When we finished up, I didn't have much more cash than I'd walked in with, but every little bit counted. And I probably got the better end of the deal with the Instant Pot. Bags ended up paying me five bucks for it, and the thing would probably sit in his window gathering dust for months until he sold it for seven—if he was lucky.

Telaney made out better than I had done, but she sold the majority of the bullets she'd grabbed, while I kept most of mine. I'd gotten into a lot of shoot-outs in the last few months, and I'd been in a lot of situations where I absolutely didn't want to run out of ammo. My mind drifted to memories of the fight in the customs warehouse, of Desiree. I only had a couple of those anti-magic paintball bullets left, and I had a feeling I was going to need every one of them in the near future, along with several boxes of non-magical firepower.

When business transactions had been completed, Bags brought us each out a mug of hot tea and we all sat around the back counter, exchanging gossip and news. The pawn-broker liked to stay current on everything happening in the county, and in the Valley in particular, and I often came to him for information. Bags seemed to know everyone, and if he didn't know someone, he knew of a guy, or gal, who did.

"This was a good haul for you girls," Bags commented. "Better than usual."

"Yeah." Telaney snorted. "And weirder than usual."

We told Bags about the one-sided fight between Big Studio Guy and a dozen of the Palisades Militia, including his oddly cheerful parting gift.

"Think he's a demon?" I asked the pawnbroker.

Bags shrugged. "Could be. Bullets kill some of them, but not the higher-level ones. From what I heard, they like to let the bullets hit them, so they can keep coming all gory and zombie-like. Adds to that freak-out factor, I guess. Never heard of one being bulletproof, just able to survive a whole lot of damage, fixing it all before their body dies."

There had been recent bullet wounds that I'd uncon-sciously healed within hours or a day. I grimaced at the reminder that I had more in common with demons than I wanted to admit.

"Maybe he felt that bullets bouncing off his skin was freakier than the zombie thing," Telaney commented. "Either way, I really don't want to run across that guy ever again. He had his wife killed for cheating on him, then when her lover retaliated, he killed him and a dozen of his co-workers."

"Do demons have wives? Husbands?" I frowned at the idea.

"I don't know." Bags shrugged again. "They supposedly like sex, and I've heard they're violently possessive about things and people they think belong to them. I could see a demon maybe taking a lover, and then killing him or her if she cheated. Maybe she was a demon as well?"

I shook my head. "I'm positive she was human. We saw her body. He'd had her killed when she was heading in for a yoga class, and he didn't do it himself."

"I'd think a demon would want to handle that personally, given how much they like the whole pain and torture thing, but I've never had more than a passing conversation with one or two of them, so I don't really know. I see them coming, and I go the other way."

I chuckled, remembering Telaney had said almost exactly the same thing.

"What's going on this week?" I asked, changing the subject. "Any talk about a hit or a gang scuffle that we can get in on?"

"Southside Militia's making noises about another move on the Gray Dogs, but nothing concrete so far. There's rumored to be a new gang settling in around Glendale, so that might cause problems if they start taking Gray Dog business. Oh, and there's some fools calling themselves the Righteous that are trying to take back LA from the demons."

"*That's* gonna end well," Telaney drawled.

"Probably won't be anything left to salvage, though," I reminded her.

We chatted for a while about how long these Righteous people were going to last. I finished my tea, told Bags that I'd see him soon, then Telaney and I walked out.

"Let me know if you hear of a job and want help," she offered as she opened her car door and climbed in.

"Likewise," I told her. "I could use another haul like the one yesterday. A whole lotta cash, and I didn't even get shot at."

She grinned. "Yeah, a girl could get used to that. There might be something happening tomorrow. I'll call you."

"Thanks." I watched her drive off, wondering what I'd ever done to deserve a friend like Telaney.

Then I got on my bike and headed northeast. There was one more errand I needed to run before I went to see Bea and the girls. I needed to go to Suerte, hand a wad of cash over to Bishop, and hope it was enough to wipe that ledger clean.

Then maybe there could be something between us besides business and debt.

CHAPTER 4

I pulled into Suerte's parking lot just before noon. The usual half dozen or so vehicles were there, but the lunch crowd was very different from the evening crowd.

The first time I'd come here I'd seen a biker bar whose clientele had racist leanings. Over the last few months, I'd gotten a much clearer picture of the place. Suerte catered to shifters—groups as well as individuals. Packs, or whatever they called themselves, had designated nights to be social, hold meetings, and maybe even do trivia games and karaoke with another group. I got the impression any human patrons were quickly scooted out the door and on their way. So while the harsh reception I'd received my first night here had definitely been due to racism, it had also been because I wasn't a shifter.

I wouldn't say the shifters who came to Suerte had grown hospitable toward me, but they did seem to regard me with a sort of wary tolerance. Bishop had given me his blessing, and so had HB, so the shifters left me alone.

After parking my bike, I walked into the bar and paused

so I could assess the risk. The patrons probably wouldn't attack me, but after the last few months I'd had, it always paid to be cautious.

Four women in jeans and T-shirts sat at a corner table, talking over beer and burgers. Two men and a woman sat at the bar—all of them scrolling through something on their phones as they ate. I recognized the bartender from a few weeks ago—a short, round woman with curly dark hair held back in a low messy bun. I think her name was Carrie or Terry or something.

HB came out of the back room, wiping her hands on a bar rag and smiling. I walked up to the bar to meet her, and Carrie-Terry slid me a glass of iced tea. I had no idea how this had become a ritual, but every time I came in, someone served me iced tea. Every. Time.

"What's up, Eden?" HB stood opposite me, leaning her elbows on the bar.

"Is Bishop here? I've got some money for him." I pivoted around as I talked, expecting him to suddenly appear behind me, like he always seemed to do.

"He's off on business," HB said. "I don't expect him back until tonight. I can take the payment and give you a receipt, though."

I don't know why I felt a crushing disappointment at her words. Actually, I did know why. There had only been a few times when Bishop hadn't either been here or showed up right after I arrived. Seeing him had become the major highlight of my week—or my day, since I'd taken to showing up even if I only had a fifty to give him. It was more than physical attraction. I liked being near him. I trusted him. I felt safe around him. With him by my side, I got the impression we could take on any baddie in the world and win. I was positive he was the angel who'd swooped in and saved me when I'd gone over the side of a high-rise and had been seconds from splatting on the ground.

The idea that he was an angel was downright terrifying. Angels were supposed to help us when the demons arrived, but all they'd really done was further wreck the place in a handful of battles, then abandon us. Demons were brutal, lawless, and cruel. Angels were otherworldly and impersonal. Of the two, I'd rather face a demon.

Bishop was an angel. I still couldn't quite get my head around the idea, and I certainly had never confronted him with that, or confirmed my suspicions with HB. Bishop didn't *seem* like an angel. He seemed like…Bishop. Which left me very conflicted about what sort of relationship I wanted or didn't want with him.

It doesn't matter what other people call you. The only thing that matters is what you are.

At the end of the day, I needed to accept him as he was, without labels. He'd done that with me, and I wanted to return the favor. It was a good philosophy, one I was trying to keep in mind as I navigated this new world we lived in.

HB must have seen the disappointment on my face, because she sighed and waved a hand for me to follow her. We went into Bishop's office. She closed the door, then touched a second switch on the wall. No additional light came on, but I felt a static wave zip along my skin and my ears popped.

I pulled a wad of money out of my backpack while HB grabbed the receipt book from Bishop's desk. Her eyebrows went up when I handed her the cash.

"Is that enough? To pay off what I owe him?" I asked once she was finished counting.

"Yeah." She gave me a twenty back and started to write out the receipt.

Relief washed over me. Done. Paid in full. I'd cleared my

huge debt to Bishop. I'd paid off the tax demons, except for the ten jobs I owed them. I still owed Desiree a favor if she ever managed to find me—which I hoped she wouldn't. Technically I'd bargained my soul away to her, but there were some loopholes in that whole deal that I didn't really understand. The cash side of my obligations had at least been resolved, though. Now I could start saving to get Bea and the girls out of here.

And now I might be able to get Bishop into bed and bring to life these hot fantasies that were causing me lots of sleepless nights.

HB handed me the receipt, then paused. Her eyes narrowed, then she gestured for me to sit down. I stuffed the receipt into my backpack and plopped onto the couch, feeling like I was about to get a lecture.

I wasn't wrong.

"Look, I like you," she began, sitting down beside me. "I count you as one of my friends, which is why I'm going to tell you right now to get Bishop out of your head. Go date some nice human boy. Bishop's not...he's not boyfriend material. He's not anything material."

It was easy for me to have this sort of conversation with Telaney, but HB *knew* Bishop. She'd known him long before I had. I wasn't sure what sort of relationship they had, or their history together. So sitting here, talking about me lusting after her boss, or friend, or lover, or whatever was super awkward.

"Are you guys... Do you know this because of something personal between you?" I squirmed on the ratty couch, not sure if I wanted to hear the answer to these questions or not.

She laughed. "Uh...no. I mean, we've never been romantically or physically involved with each other. Bishop was like a father figure to me growing up. We've always been close, but not like that."

Bishop looked to be in his late twenties. HB looked more like she'd be a sister of his than someone young enough for him to have been a father figure when she was a child. I'd suspected Bishop was way older than he appeared, just because people like Bags talked about hearing about him for decades. When I'd first come to Suerte, I'd expected a guy in his sixties or seventies, and had wondered whether Bishop was the original Bishop's son or something. Clearly that was not the case.

"He's old." HB gave me a knowing look. "Really old."

"Like a hundred years old?" I asked, wondering how long shifters lived. But I was convinced Bishop was an angel. "A thousand years?" I amended. "Tens of thousands of years?"

"Older. Like before the ice age, older. Like asteroid wiping out the dinosaurs older. Like dawn of the earth older."

"Shit." I stared down at my hands.

So much for my fantasies. I definitely felt a strong attraction between us, though. And he had made that comment about not sleeping with me until the debt between us was gone. But how much of my interpretation of that one comment was wishful thinking on my part?

"He's different," HB went on. "He's secretive about his private life. I'm pretty sure he's had some physical relationships over the ages, but I've only heard rumors of one or two in my lifetime. They were short. Very short. As in, don't-let-the-door-hit-you-on-the-ass short. There are a whole lot of women who would give their left paw to have even one night with him. None that I know of even get that."

What I got out of this whole lecture was that at least I had some tiny, infinitesimal hope for a one-night stand. If that was all I got, I'd take it. I hadn't even had *that* lately. And maybe one night with Bishop would get him out of my mind. Maybe that was all it would take for me to stop obsessing about him, so I could go back, as HB had said, and find a nice human boyfriend.

"I like you." HB repeated as she put an arm around my shoulder and squeezed. "You're a friend. You're like the little sister I never had. I don't want to see you hurt."

"Thanks. I appreciate the head's up."

If Bishop so much as cocked an eyebrow in my direction, I was so going to hit that. Sorry, not sorry. I might wind up hurt, but at least I'd get a good night of sex out of it.

She sighed. "You're not going to take my advice, are you?"

"Nope." I grinned at her. "If I've got any chance at getting naked and sweaty with Bishop, I'm taking it. Sorry, not sorry."

She lifted her hands in the air. "I tried. If he ghosts you and you need me to run a rescue mission with ice cream, wine, and a Netflix login, you call me."

"Deal." I laughed, not because I wanted that scenario, but because it was good to know HB would be there for me. Her. Telaney. My best friends. And thinking about them made me realize I needed to have a girls party at my new house. HB, Telaney, ice cream, booze, and Netflix—but without the break-up sorrow.

"Can I ask you something?" I pivoted on the sofa to face HB and waited for her nod. "Do you know why Kevin Wong's group in Los Feliz let me move into their neighborhood, even after I lost the fight and pissed them off? And what's a Ksatrei?"

HB burst out laughing. When she was finished, she wiped her eyes. "He called you that? Kevin called you Ksatrei?"

I nodded. "When he came by to give me the keys to the house. And to apologize for rudeness, or some shit like that."

"Ksatrei...it kind of means pet."

"Pet?" I frowned. "*Pet?* Like a dog, pet?"

"Yeah. But more than just a dog. It's a term someone

would use to describe a favorite pet of an important person. Like your grandmother's chihuahua that you secretly hate, but that you respect and kowtow to because your grandmother might otherwise beat your ass."

I must have looked horrified, because she laughed again.

"Hey, don't be insulted. People love their pets, sometimes more than their friends or family."

"So Bishop is the grandmother, and I'm his *chihuahua?*" I really wasn't liking this comparison. I'd hoped it meant mate, or lover, or adored girlfriend or something, but no.

Chihuahua. Lovely.

"Kind of." She stood. "Ksatrei is an old term used among clouded leopard shifters."

"So my neighbors are clouded leopard shifters? Kevin Wong is a clouded leopard shifter?" I'd avoided asking who was what since it felt rude, but if they were going to call me a chihuahua, then I wanted to know what to call them.

"Kevin is. They're all big cat shifters in that neighborhood, though. Big cats don't operate the same way the other shifter groups do. They're much more independent and less pack oriented. They strongly value individual territory. They're more chill about members coming and going."

Big cat shifters. I shivered, wondering if I'd made the right choice moving there. I could always go back to Bea's, to my familiar, comfortable home.

No, I couldn't. That wouldn't be fair to Nevarra, or Bea. I was a grown woman. I could love my family, be there for them, help them, but still start to have an independent life of my own.

An independent life of my own, surrounded by big cat shifters who saw me as a tiny, annoying, yappy dog.

"Are you…?" I hesitated, not sure if this crossed a line into prying about personal stuff or not. "Do you live there too? As part of their group?"

"No, I don't." HB smiled. "Some big cats prefer to walk alone."

I absolutely understood that.

HB walked over and flicked the non-light light switch. We left the office. Instead of staying at the bar, she walked with me across the floor and out the door to the parking lot.

"Where are you headed today?" she asked.

"To visit Bea and the girls. I'm meeting someone for dinner." I wasn't sure why I told her the last bit. Maybe because I didn't want her to see me as some pathetic loser, pining after Bishop with no other dating options on the horizon.

"A guy?" She smiled approvingly. "Or a girl? I don't want to assume…"

"A guy. He's an ex," I added. "I needed to go to him for something last month, and that was the first time I'd seen him in four years. Then last night, he texts me out of the blue, wanting to meet for dinner."

Or breakfast, but adding that option put me back in the pathetic territory. I mean, what sort of guy would romance a girl over breakfast? Unless it was breakfast in bed, naked, after having had epic sex, that is.

"Cool. Good luck with the ex. I'll make sure when Bishop gets back he knows you're all paid up on the debt."

Not "I'll have him call you" or anything like that. No, she'd just let him know I was paid up and that I wouldn't be hanging around the bar every day or so, like some sort of lost puppy dog.

Like a chihuahua.

Would I ever see Bishop again? Ever hear from him? I didn't owe him money. I didn't have any reason to hire him right now. It would be weird for me to just start showing up at his shifter bar.

I'd wait a few weeks and see if he called or came by or

something. If he didn't, I might need to actually swallow my pride and call him. Maybe I could pretend that I was checking to make sure he got that last payment, and that we were squared up. Yeah. Perfect excuse.

"Thanks," I told HB. "I guess…I guess I'll see you around? Call me? Don't be a stranger?" Just like I had with Bishop, I wondered what my friendship with HB would morph into now that my debt to Bishop was paid.

"Sure. We'll do lunch sometime. And not here either."

I put my helmet on, bemused at the idea of HB and me hanging out. Lunch. Or I could always invite her over to my place for cheap wine and whatever I had in the fridge that wasn't moldy. Or do that girls' night with Telaney I'd been considering earlier. I wondered what my neighbors would think about the three of us? A cougar shifter, a human, and a…a demon.

My chest constricted at the thought, not wanting to even admit that to myself.

Waving to HB, I pulled out of the parking lot, and headed toward Sun Valley.

It was a gorgeous Saturday afternoon. Turning down our street, I felt the familiar zing of magic as I passed the runes that Genevieve Planteaux had painted in a line across the asphalt. I'd always doubted her abilities, but in the last month, her street art had started delivering a noticeable effect. It did nothing to keep me out of my own neighborhood, though. I wasn't sure if the visible runes deterred those who wished us harm, or if it was the magic, but her contributions along with the neighborhood watch had done a lot toward reducing petty crime on our block.

In all honesty, my moving out had probably done more to deter threats more serious than petty crime. Yes, there was no longer a bounty on my head, but I had made enemies, and my family as well as the others who lived here were probably safer with me gone.

My new neighbors could take care of themselves. Any idiot who came into that area intending to steal or worse would find themselves mauled by a bunch of shifters.

I waved to Linda and her son as I drove by. The pair were tending a garden in front of their house that grew a mixture of flowers, vegetables, and herbs. Bea had been making noises about doing the same in our yard—somewhere that the chickens wouldn't have access to.

Fresh eggs. The chicks we'd gotten from Linda for weren't quite at the egg laying stage yet, but they'd soon be. Four hens meant we'd have a steady supply of eggs to rely on if things got lean again.

Things wouldn't get lean. I wasn't about to let that ever happen to my family again. I might have moved out on my own, but Bea and the girls were still at the top of my priority list.

I pulled in the driveway and got off my bike, noting that Nevarra was down the street, sitting next to Javier in the back of a pickup truck. The boy had a rifle beside him, and I was pretty sure there was also a pistol nearby. Nevarra waved when she saw me. She hopped out of the truck, picked up her own pistol, and jogged over to greet me.

I hugged her one-armed. "How are things?"

"You mean in the last forty-eight hours since we've seen you last? Or in the twenty-four hours since you called?" she scoffed.

Smart ass. I couldn't help the frequent visits, calls, and texts. I missed them, and I constantly worried that they'd need me. The events of two months ago had made me incredibly paranoid when it came to those I loved, and even the vigilance of our newly formed neighborhood watch couldn't completely alleviate my fears.

"Any trouble?" I asked, just to make sure they were okay.

Nevarra rolled her eyes. "None in the past day. Unless you count Dave Rickard nearly shooting one of Linda's chickens last night thinking it was a demon."

"Hmm." I didn't blame Dave Rickard. Linda's chickens were free-range, and they tended to roost in low tree branches and bushes at night. I could see where one stirring in its sleep on a moonless night might give someone a start.

"Other than that, we're good. Bea's got some extra sewing work she's doing for a co-worker. Sadie is painting her room —Javier gave us half a gallon of paint left over from one of his dad's jobs. 'Seafoam Spray,' the color is called. I'm in charge of dinner tonight. Are you staying?"

We walked toward the front door. "Nope. I'm meeting someone tonight, and I want to be good and hungry so I can eat big on his tab."

Nevarra stopped on the porch to face me, her expression downright excited. "A date? Who? Is it that Bishop guy? He's hot. And scary. Is it weird for someone to be hot and scary at the same time?"

That certainly seemed to be the combination that I liked, but I hoped my sister had better sense. "It's not Bishop. It's an ex of mine from years back. Remember Sebastian?"

Nevarra made a face. "Yeah, I remember Sebastian. Didn't he cheat on you? Didn't you boot his ass to the curb four years ago?"

"Yes, and yes." I looped my arm in hers. "I can see you're not a fan. Don't worry. I'm not getting back together with him. I'm just going to hear him out over steak, lobster, and a bottle of wine. That's it."

Nevarra planted her feet and refused to move as I tried to tug her forward.

"I *am* worried," she informed me. "You're a sucker for people who need you, Eden. If he's coming to you with a problem, or he's throwing himself at your feet to tell you what a fool he was and that he can't survive without your help, you'll give in."

I experienced a split second of outrage before I realized she was right. I liked to think that I didn't forgive easily, that once lost, my good opinion could never be regained. But in all honesty, I had a hard time letting go of those few people I let inside my heart. And if they needed my help, I struggled to say no.

Who was I kidding, I couldn't say no. And that needed to change. Sebastian was a mover and a shaker in the Gray Dogs. He was powerful. He was strong. If he had a problem, he was absolutely in a position to take care of it himself. Any plea for my help was manipulating bullshit. Nevarra had just reminded me I needed to stay strong against that.

So much for me being the older sister.

I put my arm around her shoulder and squeezed. "I'm not getting back with Sebastian. I did have to see him last month over something, but it was purely business. Maybe that sent the wrong message, and if that's the case, I'll set him straight. But if he needs some information from me, I do at least owe him that. Plus, I'm not turning down a good meal."

Nevarra glanced over toward the truck where Javier still sat. "I'm all for a good meal, especially if someone else is paying."

I itched to ask her about the neighbor boy who was probably a werewolf, but I kept my mouth shut. Teasing Nevarra was my prerogative as her older sister, but I knew better than to push too far. Things seemed to be going well between the two of them, and I didn't want to mess up what could be a wonderful first romance for her.

We walked to the door, and I stood at the threshold for a moment, taking it all in. I'd been here two days ago, but now that I'd moved out, the sense of home that washed over me each time I walked through this doorway was a poignant reminder of all the blessings I had in my life—blessings that would destroy me if they were ever lost.

Shaking off the strange mixture of morbid nostalgia, I walked into the kitchen to greet Bea who was busy sewing at a table filled with pinned pieces of fabric. Nevarra got started on lunch, and waved me away when I tried to help, telling me to go spend some time with Sadie while she put food together for us.

Leaving her, I thought about how quickly she'd assumed the elder sister role and went back to the front of the house and down the hallway to the bedrooms. I heard Sadie singing softly to herself, and crept up to the doorway to watch her a moment before announcing my presence. The lower half of the right wall was a lovely shade of light blueish green, and she was busy working on the back wall, carefully brushing paint next to the white trim around the window. She shuffled, awkwardly moving to the paint can and holding one leg at a sharp angle as she bent to dip her brush. Sadie had been cleared to put weight on her injured leg, and the crutches sat unused in a corner of her room, but it was clear she still had a ways to go before she regained full use of that limb.

Fear shivered through me as I wondered if she'd ever be able to run again, or even walk without a limp.

"Hey peanut," I said softly so as to not startle her.

Sadie turned, a wide grin on her face. Her straight, golden brown hair had been pulled back in a ponytail, but wisps had escaped to frame her round face. Dark eyes sparkled with joy, as if she hadn't just seen me two days ago.

"Eden! Are you staying for dinner?"

"Not tonight." I crossed the room to kiss her cheek, then reached down to pick up the paint roller. "I'm meeting an old friend for dinner. I might be back tomorrow though, depending on what comes up work-wise."

Sadie went back to painting the wall around the window. "Can we come to your house this weekend? Maybe spend the night? I like your new place."

"Absolutely." I pulled a chair over, climbed up, and started painting the top half of the wall where Sadie hadn't been able to reach. "I like this color. It reminds me of sea glass and mermaids. I'll keep my eyes open for some ocean-themed paintings for you to put up, if you want."

"Ones with dolphins," Sadie suggested. "Or maybe seagulls. I like seagulls."

I didn't. Damned rats with wings, always swooping down and trying to steal your food.

"Is Nevarra going to paint her room as well?" I asked. There wasn't enough paint in the can for both rooms, but maybe Javier would score another gallon in a color my other sister might like.

"She wants to keep it like you left it." Sadie turned to look at me. "Like a shrine."

Her words hit me hard. I stopped rolling and faced Sadie. "It's *her* room now. I moved out. She needs to have a room of her own. You do, too. That room was Drew's before it was mine. And now it's hers."

Nevarra and I had shared a room for those years when Drew had still been here, then I'd taken the smaller room when he'd left, and Sadie had come to share the larger room with Nevarra. Thinking back to those days, I remembered how uneasy I'd felt moving into what had been Drew's room. I'd felt like a usurper. As much as I'd wanted my own room, I'd wanted him to come back and live with us again more. And the whole thing had been made even more awkward by the fact that Drew and I had been physically intimate in that very bedroom.

He'd left. He'd walked out on the day of his eighteenth birthday and never returned. He'd left our family. He'd left me. And every night I lay in that bed had been a reminder of those facts.

But eventually it had truly become my room, and those memories of Drew had burned down into smoldering coals of resentment. Maybe what Nevarra was going through wasn't too different from what I'd experienced, except *I* still came back every few days to visit, and Nevarra's and my relationship had been strictly as siblings.

"She misses you." Sadie suddenly sounded far older than her years. "She loves having her own room, but she wants you to come back and have things the way they were. Change is really hard for Nevarra. And I think…I think she feels safer when you're here."

She'd been through so much in the past few months—Sadie had too. Honestly, I struggled with not being right here to protect and defend them, but now that I'd resolved my tax situation, the neighborhood wasn't as dangerous as it had been. I still owed the tax demons service, still owed Desiree if she ever found me. Honestly, they were safer here without me.

I turned back to the wall and kept painting. "The neighbors are all watching out for you. I'll be here if you need me. And what happened two months ago isn't going to happen ever again. Ever. You and Nevarra don't need to be afraid."

"I know. I feel it. I feel the protection over us like a blanket. I don't really understand it, but I feel safe. I think Nevarra will eventually too. She's just…worried."

Nevarra was always worried. And that meant I worried as well.

"I'll bring some paint and stuff to decorate her room next time," I told Sadie. "Maybe if I help, she'll feel more like it's her own space. What color should I get? What sort of decorations? Does she still love horses?"

"Horses and sunflowers. Oh, and she's really into the chickens. And bright colors. Maybe yellow paint? Or yellow pillows?"

I had a sudden vision of cream-colored walls with pictures of sunflowers and abstracts or horses, yellow and red throw pillows, maybe even a matching comforter. I didn't often have a salvage where home décor items were up for grabs, so maybe I'd need to put aside a little money from this week and buy a few things as a present. Anything to make Nevarra feel like that room was truly her own.

And part of that might be my not spending the night here anymore, or maybe having them over at my house more often, to drive home the fact that I was a grown woman who had a place of her own. That might be a good idea for me as well as Nevarra.

Sadie and I painted until Nevarra announced that lunch was ready. I walked behind Sadie as she made her slow and painful way down the hall and into the kitchen where Bea had cleared away her sewing and Nevarra had set up a lunch of potato salad, sandwiches, and glasses of iced tea. Outside the back door, our young chickens pecked for insects in the yard. Maybe I should get a few chickens of my own for my house. Except I didn't have much of a yard, and I didn't know if my neighbors would eat them. Did big cat shifters eat chickens? They probably did, as well as other things.

It's not like I had time for chickens anyway. It's not like I had time for any of these things Bea and the girls were doing to normalize their lives here in a post-demon world.

Just like the Instant Pot, none of this was for me. And that thought wrenched my heart.

CHAPTER 6

*A*fter lunch, we cleaned up the dishes, refilling water bottles and buckets since the stars had aligned and all the utilities were simultaneously on. There was a knock on the door just as we were putting the last glass away.

Sadie grimaced. "That's my physical therapist, Stan. I'm ready for my hour of torture," she called out as Bea went to answer the door.

I was just grateful our mysterious benefactor had arranged for this service. Sadie was alive and walking thanks to Dr. Mwangi and all the meds and tests we hadn't even been billed for, but this cheerful middle-aged, balding physical therapist who came three times a week would make sure Sadie recovered as much of her leg's function as medically possible. There had been some muscle damage to her calf, but both Dr. Mwangi and Stan were convinced other than an ugly, misshapen scar, she'd be back to normal. It was just a matter of time—and hard, painful work.

Bea led Stan into the kitchen where the man immediately started grilling Sadie on her compliance with his regime of daily exercises.

As he spoke, Bea turned to Nevarra and handed her a twenty. "Why don't you and Eden run down to the market and see if there are fresh vegetables for tonight. If not, look around and see if there's anything you think we might need. Pick up a box of donuts for you and Sadie if there's enough money left."

Nevarra's lips thinned, but she nodded and headed toward the door. I followed her out. She paused halfway down the walk, turning to glance back at the house.

"It hurts, and Sadie cries. I...I don't like to be in the house when she's got therapy. Guess that makes me a coward."

"That makes you a teenage girl who loves her sister and doesn't want to see her in pain." I motioned for her to keep walking. "Did you ever think that maybe *Sadie* doesn't want you there? Maybe she's feeling like a bit of a coward herself, and she would rather go through this without you there to see her cry."

She nodded, and we continued on, headed down the street.

"What happened to the bush?" I asked, noticing that the hedge at the corner of our property was now a bunch of blackened sticks.

"That kitten from hell," Nevarra replied. "It's been here three times in the last week. The thing sits on the sidewalk and meows at the house. Bea makes sure we stay inside near the kitchen so we can run out the back if it tries to burn down our home, but up until yesterday it would just sit there and yowl for an hour or so, then hiss a bunch and leave."

"What was different yesterday?" I swiveled my head to glance back at the burned bush.

"No idea. I think it's pissed that you're not here, got fed up, and set fire to the bush. Thankfully, it left, and we were able to put the fire out before it spread." Nevarra scowled. "You shouldn't have pet it, Eden. It used to leave us alone."

I felt a wave of guilt over that. I had no idea why the Hellkitty that I'd impulsively named Mittens liked me. As far as I knew, I was the only one who'd ever been able to touch the thing. And now that I'd moved away it was evidently terrorizing my neighborhood. I wasn't sure what to do about that. Maybe I could trap it, but then what would I do with it?

For a second, I thought about bringing Mittens to my new home. The neighbors would probably have a fit, but what could they possibly do? Big cat shifters versus laser-eyed kitten from Hel? I was pretty sure that would be a horribly uneven fight.

It would be funny, but I had enough problems with my neighbors without antagonizing them further.

"The neighbors here are pissed, Eden," Nevarra went on. "They kinda blame you for all the bounty hunters and what happened two months ago, even though Bea's told them over and over it wasn't your fault, that you were set up. But that, and now this kitten. People saw you petting it, and they're saying you're the reason it's coming around again. They're scared it's gonna burn down houses and cars...or kill people."

Honestly, that hadn't been my fault either. Yes, I had petted the kitten when it had come up and sat on my lap that one evening, but before that it had snuck in through my bedroom window and slept on my bed. The thing had attached itself to me, and I wasn't sure why.

And I wasn't sad about it either. I was worried that the kitten might harm one of my family or a neighbor, or damage their property, but I didn't regret petting it one bit. It had been soft, purring under my hand and kneading my leg with careful paws. I could swear it was self-aware, intelligent, and...lonely.

I got that. I was lonely, too.

"Cassie Hoang said you're a weirdo for being able to touch it and not get killed," Nevarra continued, her voice becoming strained and tight. "She said you probably sold your soul to a demon, and that's why the kitten likes you. I punched her." Nevarra's grim smile was full of satisfaction. "I punched her hard. No one says that about one of my sisters. No one says that about you."

Pride in my sister defending my reputation warred with dismay that she was getting into fist-fights over me. "It's okay, Nevarra. It doesn't matter what Cassie Hoang says. Don't start any neighborhood feuds on my behalf."

She snorted. "Too late. Cassie is dead to me now. Dead."

I eyed her in shock, and she laughed.

"Not literally dead. I mean, I was tempted, but she's not worth it. Javier said he was going to shoot the kitten, or dismember it or something gross like that. I told him he was gonna end up with a laser hole through his chest and every hair on his body singed off. He said he didn't care, that someone needed to protect the neighborhood. That's when I told him if he hurt your kitten, I was gonna shoot him myself. And that I'd never kiss him ever again."

Wait…what?

"You kissed Javier?"

Her head dipped, eyes focused on the pavement as we walked. "Yeah. A few times. I…I like him. I think. I'm not sure if I *really* like him, or I feel this way because it's nice to have someone who obviously likes *me*."

We kept walking in silence for a moment while I tried to think of the right thing to say. I wasn't exactly the best role model when it came to relationships.

"Just give it time," I finally told her. "I know I almost shot him that one day he was fixing our door, but I think he's a good guy."

The silence stretched between us for another block. I was thinking about changing the subject, when Nevarra finally spoke up.

"I told him," she whispered so quiet that I barely heard her. "I told him what happened. I wanted him to know in case it was a problem. I didn't want to get attached to him only to have him dump me when he found out."

I knew exactly what she was talking about, and held my breath for a second, realizing the agony Nevarra probably suffered having that conversation with a boy she might, or might not be romantically interested in.

"What did he say?" I finally asked.

"That he wished he'd been the one who killed the bastard. That he wanted to claw the guy's liver out and eat it while he slowly died. It was some pretty graphic shit, Eden, but he didn't seem to like me any less after I told him."

Good boy. "I'm glad. And I'm glad *you* were the one who shot that fucker, not me."

She nodded and we kept walking one block. Two blocks.

"I lied," Nevarra said out of the blue. "I lied when I said that he never touched me, that he never...you know. I didn't want to tell you or Sadie or even Bea. I didn't want anyone to know. I just wanted to pretend it never happened, that he didn't do those things to me."

"Oh, honey." I reached out and put my arm around her shoulder. She stiffened for an instant, and then relaxed against my side.

"I told Javier exactly what happened. Because he needed to know that I'm not... He needed to know before we did anything more than just kiss in the back of his dad's pickup truck. I'm not pure. And I wanted him to know."

Damn it all to fucking hell. Why did girls have to grow up thinking their only value was in some freaky virginal freshness seal?

"You *are* pure," I snapped, furious that she'd think otherwise. "That had nothing to do with sex, Nevarra. It was all about violence and control, not sex. It's never about sex."

"I'm so ashamed," she whispered. "I don't want anyone to know. Just Javier and you. I just want to pretend it didn't happen."

I took a deep breath and blinked back tears. "I understand, and I won't tell anyone. I promise. But what he did is the same as if he'd hit you. If you'd come home with a black eye and a broken arm, you wouldn't feel ashamed of what happened, would you?"

She drew in a shaky breath. "I *wish* he'd hit me. I can take that. This…I didn't try to stop him, Eden. I didn't even try. I was so scared, and I just let it happen. The only thing I'm proud of is that I didn't cry when he did it. I didn't cry. I didn't."

God, my heart was breaking for her. Nevarra had been through enough in her young life. She didn't need to add this onto the shit she'd dealt with and fought to overcome.

"I'm *proud* of you. You did what you needed to do." I stopped walking, turned to face Nevarra and held her gaze. "You did the right thing. Use every weapon you've got. Every weapon. If that means you need to play innocent and compliant, then do it. If that means you have to pretend you like someone, do it. You never have to feel ashamed of doing what you need to do to survive. Never. Sometimes you use the blade of a knife, sometimes you use the handle. It's still a weapon. And at the end of the fight if you're the one standing, then what you did was justified. You survived. That's strength, not weakness."

The girl swiped angrily at her eyes. *Good,* I thought. *Let her be angry.*

"My brain knows I did the right thing, but I still wish I'd kicked him in the balls." She was quiet for a moment, looking over at a burned-out, boarded up house as we walked past. "I hated it. I hated him. I hated that he did those things to me. I hated myself for being his 'good little baby' and *letting* him do those things to me. I thought if he saw me as a scared little girl, he'd relax, and I'd have a chance to get away." She glanced up at me, her smile wry. "Of course, I *was* a scared little girl."

I was so proud of her that I could hardly stand it. My sister. Mine. My *badass* sister.

"You were smart," I reminded her. "You used the weapons you had. And you used the most powerful weapon of all— your brain."

Now I sounded like Bea. We crossed another street, and I saw the little market ahead.

"I'm glad I told you, Eden," Nevarra said. "I feel better. I knew you'd make me feel better, but it…it was hard to let you know what happened. It was hard letting Javier know, too."

"I'm glad you told me as well," I said. "But never be ashamed of the battles you've fought, of what you've survived. Never."

She sniffed, and as she looked up at me, her smile held a confidence and toughness that was all Nevarra.

We turned the corner at the end of the block, walked into the market, grabbed a hand basket, and headed toward the rear of the store where a truly sad selection of fruits and vegetables dotted empty bins.

"I never in my life thought I'd be saying this, but maybe we should start a garden," I commented, picking up a small, dented zucchini and putting it in my basket.

"The chickens would eat all the plants. Our yard isn't big enough for chickens *and* a garden." Nevarra eyed a tomato with yellow spots, then turned to a display of six apples.

"Maybe the neighbors can band together and make a community garden," I suggested. "There's that empty lot one block over. If everyone clears out the rubble, it might make a good-sized garden."

Nevarra snorted. "We can barely coordinate the neighborhood watch. Can you imagine trying to figure out whose turn it is to weed or water or who gets what vegetables? We'd all end up shooting each other over a cantaloupe."

"Mmm." I'd been only half listening to Nevarra, instead watching a woman who'd come into the store. She weaved down the aisle to the produce section, nearly knocking over a display of dried soups. Her clothes were dirty, torn and stained with blood, her straight hair damp and matted. It wasn't all that uncommon to see people walking around with dirty, torn, and bloody clothing, and there had been plenty of times I'd been so tired that walking straight had been a challenge, but there was something off about the woman.

"What do you think about these bananas?" Nevarra asked. "They're kinda ripe. Ugh, I hate overripe bananas, but I guess we can make bread or something with them if we don't eat them in time."

"I like banana bread." I edged between Nevarra and the woman, just in case.

The woman was muttering something, gripping the edge of the produce rack with shaking hands. Her grip tightened and the metal squealed, denting and folding under her fingers.

"Should we get— Eden? What are you doing?" Nevarra asked as I backed up, pushing her farther from the woman.

Every now and then a demon showed up in our neighborhood. Sometimes, like that Low a few years back, they broke into cars, stole stuff, and jacked off on our lawns, leaving brown and dead vegetation that never seemed to recover. Sometimes they trashed homes and stores, killing the humans in a truly horrific manner. There were demons who liked to torture, those who liked to kill. There were those who spread horrible disease with a touch, killing dozens of people as they watched. The last few months had shown me that some demons looked just like humans, flying under the radar and far more subtle in their actions, but the other kind were more prevalent.

This woman…something was wrong about her. And all I cared about at this moment was making sure Nevarra was safe.

"Eden!" My sister shoved me, refusing to budge further. "Stop it! She's just sick. Mentally ill, or on drugs, or traumatized, or something. You didn't used to be so insensitive."

That was before the demons came.

"Turn around and walk all the way to the other end of the store, down the aisle, and out," I whispered to her.

"Why?" Nevarra's voice was loud. It attracted attention.

The woman bending a steel produce stand with her bare hands was also attracting attention.

I turned to look at Nevarra, still trying to keep the woman in my peripheral vision. "I think she's a demon."

"Demon!" The woman shrieked. The metal rack twisted in her hands, spilling over-ripe produce everywhere. Lifting the eight-foot rack upward, she launched it at me.

I threw up my hands as I scrambled backward, trying to protect Nevarra. The rack deflected away only inches from me, shoved by my telekinetic ability. A piece of the thing caught me on the leg, tearing my jeans and slicing a gash across my calf. I felt the hot blood gush down my leg into my shoe.

Customers screamed and ran. I waited for Nevarra to make a break for it so I could cover her, but she was boxed into a corner. The woman grabbed another, smaller metal rack and advanced, cutting off any avenue of escape. I needed to get my sister out of here, and the only way I could think of doing that was my engaging this demon one-on-one.

And hopefully surviving.

"When you get an opening, run," I told Nevarra. Then I stepped forward and grabbed the other end of the metal rack the woman was wielding like a bat. Before I could summon my electricity and zap her, she swung the rack with inhuman strength. I lost my balance and my hold on the weapon, and flew across the aisle into a display half-filled with boxes of crackers.

Nevarra went to run, but the woman blocked her escape and reached out to grab her. My sister cried out, evading the demon and scurrying back into the corner once more.

"Come here, little girl. Come here," the woman dug in one of her pockets for something with one hand as she stepped toward Nevarra.

Shit.

"Hey!" I yelled, trying to draw the woman's attention again. I couldn't zap her without running the risk of electrocuting my sister, so instead I threw a box of crackers at her and dashed forward, trying to tackle her to the ground.

It was like trying to wrestle a truck. I hit her hard and bounced off onto the floor. Then the woman brought the rack down on me, swinging it with one hand while she still dug in her pocket with the other. I rolled, but not fast enough to avoid taking a hit to the shoulder. On her next swing, I grabbed the end of the rack and sent a jolt of electricity through it as she swung me along with the rack. The electricity danced along the outside of her skin for a second. The woman cried out, but it didn't seem to affect her—it certainly didn't affect her enough to keep her from continuing to swing the rack around. Centrifugal force wasn't my friend, and my grip slipped. I flew into the stand of bananas, slipping on the bloodied and fruit-strewn floor as I scrambled to my feet.

Duh. I was immune to electricity. Navy Seal Guy was

immune to electricity. I should have realized any demon would also be immune. But she hadn't absorbed the energy like me and Navy Seal Guy. It had flowed on the outside of her as if her skin had shielded her from the blast.

Nevarra made a break for it, but the woman dropped the rack and shot out a hand to grab her. Her other hand came out of her pocket, spilling syringes and three little drug bottles to the floor.

I hesitated, not wanting to hurt Nevarra. It gave me a second to realize that the woman was bleeding. The hand that held Nevarra shook, her grip faltering. Her pupils were huge, swallowing up her irises. Her breathing was shallow and ragged. She reached for the syringes, crying out in frustration and…pain.

"I'll help you. I'll help you," she chanted. "I'll protect you. I drew the short straw. I'm the one. I'm the one. No demons ever again. No demons are gonna hurt you. I just need…I just need more—"

The blast of a pistol firing cut off her words. I stared in horror at the hole in the woman's forehead. Nevarra screamed, the sound muffled in my ringing ears. The woman slumped to the ground, and I spun around to see the store owner standing a few feet behind me, a pistol in his outstretched hands.

In less than a second I was beside Nevarra, checking her for any injury. Blood splattered her clothing, but she only seemed shaken. Relieved, I turned back to the store owner.

"You *fucking* idiot," I snapped. "You could have hit my sister. What the fuck were you thinking shooting when she was so close?"

"Is she dead?" The owner ignored me, edging closer to the woman with the bullet hole in the middle of her forehead. "Usually, it takes more than one shot to kill demons."

I edged Nevarra aside. The guy was clearly a good shot,

but I didn't trust him not to decide we all needed to die, just in case.

"She's not a demon, you moron." She wasn't, even though up until a few seconds ago, I'd also thought the woman was a demon. "She's a junkie."

I nudged the syringes with my foot. They were empty, although one of the vials appeared to still have more than residual liquid in it. Kneeling down, I picked it up. It was the same sort of dark brown bottle with the rubber-sealed cap I'd seen dozens of times in my life.

The store owner hesitated, then lowered his gun, eyeing the dead woman with growing fear. "A junkie? But she picked up those racks and threw them, bent one. She was tossing you around like you were a piece of driftwood."

"I weigh all of one-thirty," I told him, shaving nearly twenty pounds off my real weight. "And these racks aren't that heavy, especially to someone who's juiced up."

He flipped the safety on the pistol and slid it into his waistband, bending down to look at the woman. "Are you sure? I heard someone shouting 'demon,' and then she bent that rack."

"And how old are these cheap-ass racks?" Nevarra asked. "This woman was the one shouting 'demon' not us. You killed her. You killed some poor junkie who thought she was trying to protect *us* from a demon."

I pocketed the vial, realizing that Nevarra was right. This woman thought *I* was the bad-guy, the demon. She'd been trying to protect Nevarra from *me*. I couldn't completely blame the store owner for shooting her, though. The times we now lived in necessitated quick action, and sometimes that action got innocent people killed.

"I'll call the police." The man leaned down and closed the dead woman's eyes. "If she's a demon, they'll have some way of telling, won't they? And if she's not…"

I patted his shoulder, still pissed that he'd shot the woman so close to Nevarra, but knowing that I might have done the same.

"If not, you still did what you had to do," I told him. "You did what you had to do."

CHAPTER 7

*N*evarra and I stayed around until the police arrived, giving our statements and watching as they took the woman's body away. I hadn't remained for completely altruistic reasons. The store owner was suddenly afraid he might face some sort of prosecution, and he wanted us there to tell police how unhinged the woman had been. In return, he gave us free veggies and fruit—and a dozen glazed donuts.

While we were waiting, I searched the woman's pockets, trying to get some sort of clue as to what the hell had been going on with her. Her torn and bloody clothing aside, she'd been clean and injury free—aside from the recent cuts on her hands and the bullet wound. How had she survived whatever the hell had happened to her clothing and gotten through it without a scratch? And in spite of what I'd claimed to the police and the store owner, the woman's physical abilities were far beyond what I'd expected even someone drugged out on PCP to be. Plus, I'd hit her with a jolt of electricity that should have at the very least knocked her on her ass, but it had done nothing.

Her license had been issued to a Lindsey Allen. I typed the name and address down in the notes section of my phone, putting the wallet along with the ID and the twenty it held back in her pocket. As a licensed Vulture, I had every right to take the money, but somehow it felt wrong to rob this particular dead woman. That twenty probably wouldn't be there by the time the body made it to the morgue, but I wasn't going to be the one who took it. I left the two empty vials of whatever she'd been on, but I kept the full one. This woman had sent my senses into full-on warning the moment she'd walked into the store, and it wasn't because she was strung out on drugs either. She might not be a demon, but there had been something off about Lindsey Allen, and I had a feeling I needed to figure out this particular mystery.

The store owner needn't have worried.

The police took everyone's statement, and then they left as soon as the body was wheeled out, not taking the man into custody or even bringing him in for questioning. Two years ago, this would have been a big deal, but now it was hardly a blip on their daily radar. Another person dead. A junkie who'd been trashing the place and threatening customers. The dead woman wasn't someone rich or influential, and the store owner and witnesses all agreed that they'd thought she was a demon.

Just another day in New Hell.

I walked Nevarra home and stayed to see how Sadie's physical therapy went before heading out. I thought about going back to my house to clean up and change in preparation for my dinner, but instead turned my bike toward Artemis Books. It wasn't like my dinner with Sebastian was at all romantic. It was probably a good idea for me to show up somewhat dirty with a torn bloody pant leg and bruises. Dressing up for him would give him the wrong idea, and I really didn't want to give Sebastian the wrong idea.

Besides, Alfie, the guy who ran the esoteric Artemis Books, was a fount of knowledge. He tended to know about the supernatural, the mythic, and the magic, but he also knew his way around a computer. I was betting he might recognize what this drug was that Lindsey Allen had been taking or at least point me in the right direction.

I shouldn't care. I had enough to do just keeping food on the table, paying my debts, and staying alive. Some addict wrecking a local grocery and raging about demons shouldn't be something I spent more than five seconds thinking about. But that woman haunted me. I'd jumped to conclusions and thought she'd been a demon. I'd been terrified that she might hurt Nevarra. But her last words…

She'd drawn the short straw? She'd protect Nevarra? She'd fight the demons? What the hell had Lindsey Allen been doing, and what was that drug she'd been on?

Artemis Books was oddly packed for a used esoteric bookstore in the Valley, even on a Saturday. I browsed the racks while I waited for Alfie to get a long enough break to talk to me. I'd been slowly making my way through the giant demonology book I'd finally paid off, and the last time I'd been here, I'd picked up a book on what I referred to as Magic 101. Alfie had recommended it, but I was beginning to think even the most basic of how-to magic books were useless without some sort of personal instruction by a mage who knew what the fuck he was doing.

The first problem had been the spell ingredients. Most of the stuff listed wasn't the sort of thing I could find in my front yard or in the local grocery. I'd had to go back to Mathias's Magics and Oddities to get the herbs, stones, and special parchment, spending money I really didn't have for something I hadn't even been sure would work.

The second problem was time. I just hadn't had more than a few moments here and there to work this spell. This was all complicated because certain things needed to be done when key astrological events were occurring.

Third, even if I had managed to get all the right shit combined under the right moon, I still had no idea if I was pronouncing the incantation correctly. After half-heartedly messing around with this stuff for a month, I'd realized I really wasn't temperamentally suited for this kind of magic. It was too much work, where the magic that I'd been born with required very little effort at all.

I wanted to be able to do more than electrocute someone, swat shit out of the air telekinetically, super-heal, and occasionally move a bit faster than a human should be able to move, but at the end of the day, I just didn't want to put in all the time and energy it seemed to take to do things like raise the dead, make myself invisible, create a teleportation device, or make someone dance until they dropped dead.

The last spell was particularly appealing, but still too much trouble to make it worth the bother.

If anything sealed my decision to abandon my tentative study of magic, this big-ass spell book I was leafing through in Alfie's shop did. The dancing spell or even the ghost one was a pain in the butt, but these seemed close to impossible. What the fuck was an Aeroga, anyway? And how was I supposed to know if Leo was in the seventh house or not? Seventh house of what?

"Hey, Eden!" Alfie rounded the corner of the aisle only to come to an abrupt halt, wincing when he saw what I had in my hand. "I can't sell that one to you. It's a matter of public safety, you understand. Those spells in the hands of the uninitiated can go very wrong."

I put it back on the shelf. "Don't worry. I'm still trying to get the ghost-away one to work. At this rate, I'll be eight hundred years old before I even make it halfway through the beginner book you sold me."

He sighed. "Sadly, the best mages tend to start when they're children. Even then, it's a full-time practice. Those who make it to the sorcerer level have truly dedicated their lives to the magical arts."

"I think I'd do better if I had an instructor." I waved at the books. "Maybe if all this came with a semester at a magical academy or something, I'd actually be making progress."

His lips twitched. "I doubt a magical academy could help you, Eden. Few people truly have the talent for magic, although we all have the ability. As much as I'd like to sell you additional books, maybe you should stick to Vulturing."

But I *did* have magical abilities—abilities that it seemed from my roundabout questioning of the mage Mathias, no other human magic user seemed to have. But Alfie was right, and I honestly didn't have the money for this hobby anyway —even if I had managed to get that ghost-away spell to work.

"Actually, I'm here about something else." I pulled the vial out of my pocket and handed it over to Alfie. "Have you heard anything about this drug?"

I told him about the woman at the market and what had happened this afternoon.

Alfie eyed the bottle. "There's no label at all. Usually stuff in these vials that gets sold on the black market still has labels. There's no reason to bother trying to take them off. In fact, it adds to the authenticity to have it on."

"I was thinking maybe angel dust based on how she was acting," I suggested. "Or maybe special K?"

PCP wasn't a commonly used drug anymore, and neither was Ketamine, but they were the only ones I knew of that caused hallucinations and violent behavior.

Alfie shrugged and handed the bottle back. "PCP is usually sold in powdered form. Ketamine might come in a vial if someone lifted it from a veterinary practice, but I can't see them taking the label off. You'd need to get this tested at a lab to figure out exactly what it is."

That's what I'd figured, but I hadn't known the extent of Alfie's knowledge or skills. For all I knew he had a lab set up in a back room somewhere, or could tell what drug it was just by eyeballing it.

PCP or Ketamine would explain the woman's behavior, and both numbed a person to the sensation of pain, making them able to power through gunshot wounds or stabbings, but neither one gave someone superhuman strength or the ability to resist electrocution. I'd originally thought the woman was a demon, and both her actions and her unusual abilities fit with that description, but if she was a demon then why had she been absolutely triggered by the idea that *I* was one? And why was she so determined to protect Nevarra? And if she was a demon, then why the drugs?

"Do demons do drugs?" I asked Alfie.

"Demons do whatever they like. They're all about chaos and sensation, so it's not unusual to see one drunk or high. But they can clear it from their system instantly if they want or need to, and they don't get addicted."

I thought about my weird ability to clear alcohol from my system, and quickly decided I didn't want to go there. Nope. I was going to stay in absolute denial about all the signs pointing to what I was. Human. I was a human. Sort of, anyway. I'd been abandoned as an infant, and I was a human —weird abilities aside.

"How about shifters?" I asked.

He wrinkled his nose. "I really don't know much about shifters. They tend to self-isolate. Even with detection spells they show up as human as often as they show up as 'other.' They're stronger and faster than humans, but that varies depending on how diluted their Nephilim genetics are, and their specific shifter abilities. And advanced healing doesn't always mean they are invulnerable to substances that affect humans. If I had to guess, I'd assume they'd be just as susceptible to drug and alcohol addiction as any human."

That fit the situation. A shifter with extra strength and some inborn protection against electricity, who hated and was afraid of demons, and was a drug addict taking stuff that sent her into a spiral of hallucinations and violence. The perfect storm, right there in a neighborhood market.

Poor woman. I only wished the shop owner hadn't shot her, that we could have calmed her down and gotten her some help. Did she have a pack out there missing her? A family? Was she a regular at Bishop's bar like other shifters?

I'd never know. I pocketed the vial, thinking I should probably meet up with Juke, my police detective friend, and hand it over eventually. Whatever it was, it didn't need to be sitting around my house, or even in my backpack, but I also didn't want to just throw it in a dumpster where a desperate person could find it and overdose.

I'd get rid of it later. For now, I needed to hustle, so I wouldn't be late for dinner. Torn, blood-stained pants aside, I was starving. And admittedly I was curious what Sebastian wanted that he'd invite me out to dinner. Maybe it was him wanting to rekindle our old relationship, or have one last night together for old times' sake.

Or maybe it was something else.

CHAPTER 8

J sat on my bike for a while in the restaurant parking lot, trying to decide whether I should go in or just bail on the whole thing. I was tired, dirty, and although the cut on my calf had speed-healed to a raised pink line, it still ached. I wanted a shower and bed more than I wanted food, and honestly, I wasn't feeling up to dealing with whatever bullshit Sebastian was going to send my way tonight.

Plus, Matelli's was a bit swankier than I'd expected. The thick, carved walnut doors had scroll-shaped brass handles, and the building was faced with old-world, faux-aged brick instead of the usual stucco. I yanked the elastic out of my hair and tried to finger-comb the worst of the snarls out. Were they going to let me in wearing bloody, dirt-stained cargo pants and a tank top?

But this was a restaurant in Gray Dogs' territory, in a demon-run New Hell, and I was meeting Sebastian. I could have been naked and covered in cow shit, and they probably would still let me in.

Figuring my hair was as good as it was going to get, I got

off my bike and walked to the door. Sebastian must have given them enough of a description to identify me because they ushered me through the bar to a little out-of-the-way booth where the Gray Dog already sat.

Sebastian poured me a glass of red wine as I took off my backpack and slid into the booth across from him.

He pushed the glass over to me. "I'm surprised you agreed to come."

"Why?" I'd gone to meet him just last month to ask him about a Gray Dogs member who'd died under some unusual circumstances. Our meeting had gone well, without any more than some understandable faint emotional undertones. There was no reason I could think of that would lead him to believe I'd refuse to see him.

"You made it clear last month you weren't interested in trying to revive the past. I figured you'd assume I was trying to make a move and just blow me off."

I took a sip and made an appreciative noise. Sebastian had always had a thing for good wines. Food. Wine. Women. Fast cars. Nostalgia rolled through me like a warm ocean wave.

"You saw me when *I* asked. I'm not going to refuse to return the favor. And I didn't assume you were trying to make a move," I added hastily, just in case. "You've currently got a woman. I thought you wanted to see me for some other reason."

"Yeah, I got a woman." Sebastian's mouth thinned, as if he wasn't particularly happy about that fact. "You got a man?"

For a second, my mind went straight to Bishop. "No. I don't. There's someone I'm kinda interested in, but…it's complicated."

Sebastian snorted. "Ain't complicated. And since when has any guy said no to you?"

Uh, since forever. I cleaned up nice, but it wasn't like I had guys fawning all over me. Most guys wouldn't turn down a hit-it-and-quit-it if I offered, but they were plenty eager to say no to more than just sex.

And then there were the guys who I couldn't even manage to get into bed. Once again, my thoughts strayed to Bishop.

The waiter saved me from having to reply. I knew Sebastian was either picking up the tab or the restaurant was comping us as part of their payment for Gray Dog protection, so I ordered a chopped salad and linguini with salmon and pesto sauce. Hopefully the portions were big, and I could take some of the pasta home to stick in the fridge for breakfast tomorrow.

"You were a partner, Eden." Sebastian looked me over once the waiter had left. "Dolled up you were pretty enough for arm candy, but if shit went down, you were *there*. You had my back. You fought at my side. Fuck, the guys were scared of you. I miss that. I was young and stupid and thought it would be easy enough to find another like you. I want you back, Eden. I want us to try again."

His eyes met mine, and I felt that zing, but if I was honest, that feeling was rooted in our past, not in the now.

"I...I can't." Crap, this was awkward.

"It's this other guy, isn't it?" he asked.

It would be easier on his ego if I said yes, but Sebastian deserved the truth.

"No, it's that I'm not the same person I was back when we were together. I'll never be her anymore. I've changed. And you have too. We're both different people now, Sebastian." I searched for the right words to say. "It would never work out between us romantically—not in the long run. Trying again..."

"We'd both probably end up killing each other," he agreed. Then he laughed. "Actually, you'd probably end up killing me."

"Nah." I grinned, thankful he wasn't pressing the issue. "You're faster with a knife."

"And you're a better shot." He held out a hand.

I shook his hand. "So? Why am I here?"

A little flirtation with an old flame wasn't exactly a high price to pay for a decent dinner and some really good wine. But clearly there was some other reason he'd invited me here—some other reason besides trying to rekindle the past.

I couldn't deny that the idea didn't have some appeal now that I was sitting across from him. Sebastian looked good—really good. Like I'd said to Telaney, he wasn't conventionally handsome, but he had that confident, dangerous air about him that had always drawn me. It wouldn't be a problem at all to flirt with him for a few hours. It wouldn't be a problem at all to more than flirt with him, except I didn't want to have to deal with an angry girlfriend, or a persistent Sebastian who'd surely read more into sex than I wanted him to.

Sebastian reached for his wineglass, then pulled his hand back. "Why don't we eat first? Catch up. Talk about the old times a bit. Then I'll tell you why I wanted to see you."

I leaned back against the booth, eyeing him. "That bad?" My mind went through all the horrible things he could be trying to delay telling me. Had a mutual friend of ours died? Did he have cancer? Was I in trouble with the Gray Dogs for something or another?

He fidgeted for a few long minutes, and I waited, knowing he'd eventually tell me.

Finally, he cleared his throat and spoke. "I need you to do something for me. I'm asking for your help with…something."

That wasn't what I'd expected at all. Sebastian didn't ask for help. The whole time we'd dated, I couldn't recall him ever asking me to help him with anything. There'd been a whole lot of him telling me what I was going to do and where I was going to go. At first that had been kind of sexy, but I'd quickly gotten tired of that dynamic and started to rebel—which had started the spiral downward that led to the end of our relationship.

"It's Anton," he continued. "He's gone missing. I think…I think he might be dead. If he's not, then something's definitely wrong. If he is…" Sebastian shrugged, trying to look casual and failing. "If he is, then I want to know. Either way, I want to know."

"Anton?" What the hell had Anton gotten himself into that Sebastian needed *my* help? I hadn't seen Sebastian's little brother in four years—which meant he wouldn't be so little anymore. Eighteen, I calculated. He'd been fourteen when Sebastian and I had broken up, and a total brat. Sebastian had always adored his kid brother, and while I hadn't exactly felt the same way, I understood what it meant to be family. If Anton was missing, Sebastian must be losing his mind.

So why he was here, eating dinner with me and asking for my help instead of turning the Valley inside out looking for Anton?

The waiter put our salads in front of us. Sebastian picked up his fork and toyed with his while I took a few bites and waited for him to continue.

"Anton's done some work for us off and on over the last few years, but he never went all in with the Gray Dogs," Sebastian finally said. "He was a stick-up boy for a while, and a caller. I thought he'd eventually join up all the way, but the kid was always looking for something else, some way to make it big fast, and you know things take time in an organization like the Gray Dogs. People gotta prove themselves, work their way up, gain the respect of the rest of the guys."

I nodded, shoveling more salad into my mouth and wondering how long it had been since I'd had fresh vegetables. We occasionally got cabbage or carrots or some potatoes, but salad fixings didn't keep all that well, and they were pricey. Now that I was on my own…well, fresh vegetables spoiled quickly, and I wasn't home enough to waste the money on lettuce that would rot before I had a chance to eat it. If someone had told me two years ago that I'd be eating a salad like it was a lobster, I would have thought they were crazy, but here I was, scarfing the stuff down like I was two seconds from a case of scurvy.

Sebastian took a few more bites of his salad as well, then nudged the bowl away and continued. "Last month, I found out Anton had been going down south of the city. I warned him. Told him he better stay in the Valley, but he said he was working on something big."

I paused with my fork halfway to my mouth. "Where south?"

The Gray Dogs were a Valley gang, and as with most gangs, they had a very specific territory. Trespassing into another gang's territory could get a person killed. Even if Anton wasn't fully a Gray Dog member, he was still Sebastian's brother. He might not get shot, but he'd definitely get the crap beaten out of him to send a message that the Dogs and their affiliates needed to stay in their own lane.

"Inglewood."

I put my fork back in the bowl. Inglewood was near the airport—and thus near the customs warehouse where I'd gone to rescue Nevarra from two months ago. Inglewood was Disciple territory—although pretty much everywhere was Disciple territory nowadays.

Every Disciple I'd come across while I was hunting for Nevarra was dead except one—one plus the demon, Desiree, who had used Disciple members in her human trafficking business. Chances were good that no one would recognize me and put two and two together about the gang deaths in the Valley or those in the warehouse and connect those with me, but I was still nervous.

"I can't really go there right now." I chose my words carefully. "I had a bit of a run-in with a few people in that area, and don't want to stoke the fire, you know?"

Sebastian frowned. "I haven't heard anything about you being in trouble, beyond that issue with the tax office. You resolved that, right?"

He knew about that? Had Sebastian asked questions and dug around after my visit to him, or had he been keeping tabs on me all along? I hoped it was the former. Actually, I hoped it was neither one since I didn't need him poking his nose into my business. But there was no other way to explain how a Gray Dog would have known about an ex-girlfriend's tax trouble.

"Risk mentioned there was a bounty on your head after you came to see me. He thought I should know just in case… well, just in case," he explained.

Bunch of gossips, that's what they were. Just as bad as my damned neighbors. I was sure within five seconds of my visit, the whole gang was buzzing with the news. I'm sure they all thought there was a whole lot of "personal" behind the business nature of our meeting. Half the Gray Dogs were probably betting on whether or not I'd be moved in with Sebastian by the end of the month.

"The tax problem is taken care of, and my license is good," I told him. "But I had some issues with the Disciples and someone else south of the city a few months ago. It's best I stay clear of them for a while."

"Shit." A muscle twitched in Sebastian's jaw. "I really need your help, Eden. Are you sure you can't run down to Inglewood for a day and just ask around?"

Guilt gnawed its way around my middle. Sebastian and I might no longer be close, but we once were, and that history meant something to me. But it didn't mean enough to me that I was willing to risk my ass nosing around Inglewood.

"You don't have to get involved," he assured me. "If Anton's dead, then just let me know. If he's alive, tell me what's going on, and I'll handle the rest. I don't wanna go down there myself and stir up a whole lot of shit, only to find out Anton's run off with some piece of ass and didn't charge his phone."

"I can't." I grimaced, because saying that to Sebastian was harder than I'd expected. "I know it wouldn't be wise to send one of your Dogs down there to ask around, but there's got to be someone else you can ask—someone not affiliated with the Gray Dogs."

"Not anyone I trust," he countered. "Especially not anyone I trust as much as you. You're smart, strong, and a hell of a good shot. And you're a woman—a damned hot woman. Those guys down in Inglewood aren't going to know what hit them."

"I know they won't, because I'm not going down there."

Aren't going to know what hit them?

Suddenly this was sounding more like a fight and less like a reconnaissance mission, and I definitely wanted to avoid a fight in the middle of Disciple's territory. I didn't need to give that gang any reason to connect me with what went down two months ago. Sebastian could sweet-talk me all he wanted with his compliments, but this hot woman was *not* going to Inglewood.

"It's Anton, Eden. My little brother." He must have seen me waver at that, and hit me in my weak spot. "He's family. If he's in trouble, I need to know so I can help him. If he's dead… If it was one of your sisters that had gone missing, you'd be worried too."

I would, and I'd be down in Inglewood in a shot. I understood Sebastian's worry, and his dilemma. He didn't want to start a gang war unless he really needed to. Anton might be fine, but if he wasn't… I thought about the smart-ass fourteen-year-old, and knew deep in my heart that Sebastian's fears were valid.

"What about if I pay you?" he added. "And you'll be considered a friend of the Gray Dogs. You need a favor? We'll be there."

The money would be nice, but it was the whole family responsibility thing that had me rethinking my refusal. His little brother.

And money aside, the friend of the Gray Dogs designation would be really useful. All the shit I'd dealt with in trying to find Nevarra, plus dealing with bounty hunters the last few months had made me realize the importance of alliances. My family and I could do a lot on our own, but it didn't hurt to have resources. The Gray Dogs had intel that I couldn't get from Bags, Detective Juke, Bishop, or even Alfie. If I needed protection, influence, or even a small army the Gray Dogs were the ones to turn to in the Valley. What Sebastian was offering was no small thing.

He must *really* be worried. And I understood. Family was family. There was nothing I wouldn't do for those I loved, those I cared about. And I knew Sebastian was the same. It was one of the things that had drawn me to him years ago.

Well, that and his six-pack abs.

I sighed. "Okay. How about six hundred plus expenses? That ought to cover my lost time on Vulture jobs. And I'll gratefully accept that 'friend of the Gray Dogs' status."

His grin held a sexy edge to it that made me wonder if his offer didn't have a few invisible strings attached to it. Oh well. I'd deal with that later—after I found Anton.

"Thanks, Eden. I owe you one—more than you know."

He refilled my wineglass. As I went to take a sip, his eyes met mine, and the heat in his gaze stirred something down low. It had been a long time since I'd had sex, but this wasn't just lust. Sebastian and I had history. When I cared about someone, I never stopped caring, even if that relationship had ended in a lot of screaming, thrown dishes, and a keyed-up Charger. My acceptance of this deal wasn't about the money or the alliance with the Gray Dogs. It wasn't even really about my sympathy for family issues. It was about Sebastian.

I cared. I'd always care. But that didn't mean I was going to slide back into a relationship that would be even more of a bad fit now than it had been four years ago.

I set down the wine, lowering my gaze and fiddling with the stem of the glass. "So, what do you know about this mess Anton is in? What do you suspect happened?"

He leaned back in the booth, and I could feel his eyes still on me. "He had that business he was into south of the city. He wouldn't tell me exactly what it was, but he claimed it was going to be big—big money and big power. He said if this went down, the Gray Dogs would be the dominant gang in the county, or even in the state."

I winced, because there was only one way that was going to happen and it involved a lot of bodies on the pavement. "He was talking war? I'm guessing this deal had something to do with big weaponry and ammunition?"

He held up his hands. "I don't know. I told him to stay out of it. We're not in any position to do a territory grab. Hell, we're barely holding on to the neighborhoods against the Southside Militia. A tank or a bunch of rocket launchers might help us there, but even that kind of weaponry isn't going to suddenly make us kingpins."

But Anton might not have thought the same way. As a kid, he'd always played his hand as if he'd held all the aces. I doubted he'd changed much in four years.

"I'm thinking the Disciples *might* have something to do

with Anton's disappearance," Sebastian said. "If they caught him doing a deal in their territory, they wouldn't just let him walk away. I warned him about that, and he laughed it off. Told me he was working with one of them—a guy named Tape. Said the guy was connected somehow and would cover for him if they got caught."

I grimaced. "Right. Sure."

Anton was a fool. If they got caught, that Tape guy would totally throw him under the bus. I didn't care how connected the guy was, the Disciples wouldn't just shrug off a member going rogue and cutting a deal outside the gang. Tape would be in big trouble, and to lessen that trouble, he'd serve up Anton like breakfast.

And how the hell could Anton trust anyone named *Tape*? Sometimes people had the weirdest nicknames. Was this guy particularly sticky? Held things together in the gang? Or was Tape short for Tapeworm, meaning the guy was thin as a rail and ate everything in sight?

"Here's the last text I got from him." Sebastian pulled out his phone, opened the text, and handed it to me. "Yesterday morning. He was supposed to check in late afternoon, but he didn't. When he didn't respond to my texts or calls, I knew something had gone wrong. That's when I texted you."

I read the message. *Big money coming our way, Bas. This guy, Tape, has what I need to make it all happen. Today it's all going down!*

"Do you mind?" I asked, pointing to the phone.

Sebastian nodded, an unusual gesture of trust given that we hadn't been close for years. I scrolled through the texts between him and his brother as he watched, careful not to glance at anything else on his phone. I didn't need to get mixed up in Gray Dogs business, and I especially didn't want to intrude into Sebastian's private life.

"He doesn't specify if this deal is weapons."

It was the only thing that made sense, though. Anton had talked about what this deal would mean for them, how rich and powerful they'd all be, but he was careful not to mention either the Gray Dogs or the deal specifically. *No wonder Sebastian is worried,* I thought as I handed the phone back. This whole thing set off all my alarm bells, too.

"The texts aren't super clear on exactly what he was doing," I commented. "And who is this Aries guy he's talking about?"

Sebastian shrugged. "No idea. I know a handful of the Disciples—mostly the ones who do business up here in the Valley—but I've never heard of a guy named Aries. Or Tape, for that matter."

"I'm assuming it's unusual for him not to respond, or not communicate when he's supposed to?" I asked.

Sebastian's expression hardened. "Anton might not check in with me daily, but he's never ignored me before when I text him, and he calls when he's supposed to. I wish I knew more about what the deal was. All I know is it was in Inglewood, and that this Disciple named Tape is involved. Not much for you to go on, I know. Anton didn't offer too much info on exactly what he was doing. And it's not like I can waltz down to Inglewood and ask the Disciples what the fuck happened to my brother."

I completely understood that. Sebastian making inquiries about his brother would raise suspicions that the Gray Dogs were involved in whatever Anton had been doing. If the kid had been caught and executed, then the smartest thing for Sebastian to do would be to ignore the whole thing, pretend they were estranged and that both he and the Gray Dogs had nothing whatsoever to do with Anton's business. Losing a brother would be horrible. Having your gang suddenly in a war with the Disciples in addition to losing your brother would be worse.

I wasn't affiliated with any gangs. I was a Vulture and was licensed to salvage anywhere within New Hell. Sebastian trusted me. But I'd still be putting my neck on the line. Asking about Anton meant I might come under suspicion of being involved in his "business." I had no idea what Anton's fate had been, but I was pretty sure the kid was no longer among the living. I really didn't want that to be my fate as well.

"I know he's probably dead," Sebastian said. "But there's a part of me that thinks maybe he's not. What if they've got him stashed somewhere, beating on him to get information about whatever the fuck he was doing down there? If I knew that he was alive, knew where he was, then maybe I could get him out."

Getting him out would mean him putting the Gray Dogs at risk. I felt bad for Sebastian. This must be killing him, having to choose between protecting his brother, and safeguarding his other "brothers" in the Gray Dogs.

"So, you just want me to go find out what happened?" I asked. I needed him to outline exactly what he was asking me to do. Find out if Anton was dead or alive? Find out who was responsible? Discover what this business was that his brother had in Inglewood with some Disciple named Tape? Rescue his brother's sorry ass if he was still alive?

"Yeah. Just find out if he's dead or alive and, if you can, who's got him if he's still breathing." Sebastian reached across the table and grabbed my hand. "But I want you to be careful. If shit starts to go wrong, get out of there and don't look back. Don't go trying to rescue him, or go digging too deep into what he was doing with this Tape. Stay safe."

I curled my fingers in his. "What do you plan on doing if he's dead?"

Sebastian dragged in a ragged breath. "Nothing. Maybe find a way to bring back his body if I can. Just knowing he's gone is gonna have to be enough. Stirring up trouble isn't going to bring him back."

"And if he's alive?" I asked, still holding his hand.

Sebastian's mouth thinned into a tight line. "If he's alive, I'm going to get him. I have to, Eden. He's my little brother."

I didn't blame him. I would have done the same. Hell, I *had* done the same when Nevarra had been kidnapped. I appreciated a man who was loyal to those he loved. But Sebastian had more than one family, and rescuing Anton would put the Gray Dogs at risk.

Which meant I couldn't let him rescue Anton alone. If I were there, maybe I could keep him from being discovered by the Disciples—and keep peace between the gangs.

I didn't want to do this. I'd just gotten myself out of trouble and was trying to carve a life for myself and my own family. I didn't need to stir up anything with the Disciples. And I certainly didn't need to do anything that might make them connect me to the deaths their group had suffered two months ago. A man I still cared about was in a tough spot and needed my help, and I wasn't the sort of person who could refuse.

We had history. He'd been important to me and still was. I didn't forget that sort of thing.

Damn it, I was going to Inglewood, to Disciples territory, and I *already* had a bad feeling about it.

CHAPTER 9

The doorbell rang, and I just about had a heart attack. No one had rung the bell before besides that woman who'd come to borrow sugar. The first thing I did was check my phone, because my family or Telaney would have texted me before making the drive to my house. As I looked, the doorbell rang again, and I could have sworn the sweet notes sounded more impatient than they had the first time.

I jogged over and opened the door, expecting to see a neighbor pissed off about the pan of used oil in the drive from when I'd been working on my bike, or maybe the brown shrubberies in my front yard that I kept forgetting to water. My eyes focused on a broad chest, then traveled upward to the visage of a gorgeous surfer-god with sparks of gold in his ocean-blue eyes.

Bishop.

My breath caught, and I had to consciously inhale.

"Here." He held out a stack of money. "You overpaid your debt."

Where were you? I wanted to ask, still hurt that he hadn't been at Suerte this morning. But I didn't want to be a nagging, needy, not-girlfriend, so I kept my mouth shut and took the money, noticing that behind him a dozen neighbors were doing stupid things like tying their shoelaces, sweeping the road, pretending to text on their phone.

It was dark. It was almost eleven o'clock at night, and suddenly every neighbor had some reason to be milling about in view of my house.

"Is that…that's my shirt." Bishop pointed at my attire.

I *was* wearing his shirt. And I had absolutely nothing on under it either because I had nowhere to go and thought I'd go ahead and get ready for bed.

"I stole it," I informed him. "And I'm not giving it back."

His lips twitched. "Okay, then. Guess I should be glad you didn't carry off the furniture and the paintings as well. Anything else you stole while you were a guest in my house?"

"An apple and a bottle of water. But I assumed as a guest in your house, those were open for me to grab."

He nodded, his smile growing. "They were. So, how are you, Trouble?"

My whole body lit up at the nickname. I wanted to know where he'd been, why he wasn't there when I dropped off my final payment. But it really didn't matter. He was here now, and I suspected that the money he'd just handed over was a totally bogus excuse for visiting me.

He was here. At my house. And he'd called me Trouble.

"Why don't you come in, and I'll tell you all about my adventures." I opened the door wider, and without the slightest hesitation, Bishop walked through the door.

"Can I offer you a drink of…water? Or I can put on a pot of coffee." I went to the kitchen, stuck the money in a drawer, and opened the fridge, grimacing at the lack of contents. Telaney and I had drunk my bottle of cheap white wine, and I wasn't exactly prepared for entertaining.

There was a bottle of hot sauce, a bunch of ketchup and mustard packets I'd stolen from a fast-food restaurant, and my pesto from tonight. It felt wrong to offer him my leftovers from a dinner with another guy, so I just shut the fridge.

"Either one." He leaned against the counter. "That was a big sum of money you dropped off today. You rob a bank or something?"

I grinned over at him as I started the coffee. "Or something. An unexpectedly big score for Telaney and me down in the Palisades. I wish they were all like that. Cash everywhere and we didn't even get shot at."

He glanced down at my leg and the almost-healed cut.

"That was something else," I told him. "Some drugged-up woman that I think might have been a shifter had a psychotic break at a local market."

He frowned. "Shifters don't usually do drugs. They don't react to them the same way humans do."

I flipped the switch on the coffee pot and slid the little vial I'd picked up off the floor of the market over to him. "She had a bunch of syringes and a couple of these in her pocket. Was going off about how she needed to protect everyone against demons or something like that."

He picked up the bottle and rolled it between his fingers, then set it back down. "Did you kill her?"

I snorted. "No, the store owner did. He thought she was a demon because she was throwing stuff around and bending the produce racks like they were wire hangers. Her name was Lindsey Allen. ID said she lived on Sherman Way in Sun Valley. Do you have any idea who her pack might be? Someone I should notify?"

I had no idea why I cared so much, but the memory of that woman had haunted me all evening.

Bishop shook his head. "I've never heard of her, but it's

not like I know every shifter in the area. I'm guessing the police will notify next of kin."

I watched the coffee drip, my thoughts changing from the incident in the market to my meeting with Sebastian.

"I'm going to have to head down south to Inglewood tomorrow," I told Bishop. "The brother of an old friend is missing. He wanted me to ask around and find out if he's in trouble with the Disciples or dead. I should be back by tomorrow evening."

Bishop grunted. "You need my help tracking the guy down?"

"I don't think it will be that difficult of a job. If I end up with nothing but dead ends, then I might ask for your help." I wasn't eager to be in financial debt again to Bishop, but if I couldn't find Anton, Sebastian might agree to pay his fee.

"Don't get killed. And don't go promising yourself to any demons."

I laughed. "I'm hoping you'll swoop in to save the day if I'm in danger of either."

He rolled his eyes and shook his head. "I'll do my best, Trouble, but I'm not omnipresent."

"You promised me. You said if I was ever at death's door, that you'd be there to save me." I waved a finger at him, still smiling to show him I was teasing. Kind of teasing.

"That was before I knew how often you're at death's door," he retorted. "I'm realizing that keeping your ass out of the fire is a full-time job."

I wiggled my hips. "Good thing it's a fine ass."

His gaze roamed down my body, and I turned to get the mugs out of the cabinet, reaching high so he'd get a tantalizing glimpse of the body part in question.

"Milk? Sugar? Actually, I don't have milk, so your choices are black or with sugar."

"Black."

I turned to watch the coffee maker sputter the last bit of dark elixir into the pot while he walked into the living room.

"When did you get this?"

Poking my head around the corner of the kitchen, I saw him standing next to my angel-feather-in-a-vase. As he reached out to touch it, the thing quivered and came alive with a thousand sparkling lights.

I ducked back into the kitchen to pour the coffee. "I found it in my clothing after my dramatic fall from a down-town high-rise, and subsequent rescue by a winged being."

"Hmmm."

That was it. No confirmation of him as my winged rescuer, no comment about my keeping and displaying the feather. I wanted to tell him I thought it was the most beau-tiful thing I'd ever seen, that sometimes I sat on the sofa and just stroked it, thrilling to its softness, and the sensation that thrummed through me every time I touched it. I wanted to tell him a lot of things, but I still wasn't sure exactly where this thing was going between us, and HB's warnings still sat fresh in my mind. Bishop didn't get involved with women, and when he did, it seemed to never last beyond one night.

I'd take that one night, but I knew deep down it wouldn't be enough. What was worse? A night of passion, then noth-ing? Or not even having that one night?

When I brought the mugs into the living room, he was standing by the wall of windows, looking out at the incred-ible view of downtown LA. I went over to join him and handed him one of the mugs. We stood there, silent, the two of us, sipping coffee and staring at the sea of lights.

"It's your city."

His words were soft, full of some meaning I didn't quite understand. I'd grown up in the Valley. In general, I consid-ered LA to be my city, but he made it sound like all I surveyed was *mine,* as if I were Batman, standing on a rooftop overlooking Gotham City or something.

"It's a nice view." That was the most lame, unimaginative thing ever, but it was all I could think of.

He turned to face me. "It is."

Was that…was he…? For a grown-ass woman, I was suddenly very flustered and uncertain. The debt between us was paid. Did that mean we were now free to get it on, full steam ahead? I longed to climb all over this guy, right here, right now, but still I hesitated, not wanting to make a fool of myself because I misunderstood his intentions.

He reached out and gently took my chin between his thumb and forefinger. I tilted my head up, hoping this was going where I thought it was going. I expected him to kiss me, but instead an odd warmth brushed along my nerve endings, lighting up every cell. Something deep down inside me stirred, moved, swirled in a pattern of sound and color.

Screw it. I stepped in, gripped his shirt with one hand, and kissed him.

I'd spent too much time fantasizing about this moment to do some tentative peck. My lips met his, hot and hungry, my tongue taking possession of his mouth. He yanked me against him, and I snaked my arms around his waist, the hand not holding a coffee cup sliding up under his shirt to run my fingers across the warm muscular skin of his back.

His skin heated, as if he were on fire. He returned the kiss with the same burning intensity, his hand skating down my side to grip my ass. Shivery tendrils of longing snaked through me.

He hiked me up against him, and I wiggled against the clear proof that he wanted me just as much as I wanted him.

I felt him pressed impossibly closer without physically moving an inch, touching and stroking some part of me that wasn't flesh, blood, or bone. His tongue still tangled with mine, his hand still held my rear, but suddenly there was more. I ran my fingers across the muscles of his back, and he did the same to some secret part inside of me that I hadn't even been aware of before tonight.

I froze, not sure what the hell was going on. It was as if my very soul had lit up, as if he'd brought an incorporeal part of me to life. This other part of me stirred, vibrating and shifting, sliding along something that felt hot and cold, something that held all the colors of the sun setting across the water. This other energy pulled at me, and my soul broke free, as if it wanted to leave my body.

I squeaked out a breath and jerked away from him, suddenly frightened and confused.

"Sorry." Bishop lowered his hand, and that hot brushing-pulling sensation abruptly vanished, leaving me cold. His expression was unreadable, but I got the feeling he was hurt at my rejection.

"No, I just…" I shivered and folded my arms across my chest. "I didn't expect…I thought…. I've never—I mean, I *have*, but not that…stuff."

"You've never joined?" He tilted his head. "Oh. Of course. Because you're *human*."

My face was so hot that flames were probably coming off my cheeks. This was so embarrassing. That thing he'd done, was it a demon thing? An angel thing? Something I had no idea about because whoever had spawned me had dumped me in a church parking lot for humans to raise? Ugh, this was like being a virgin. Again.

"I've been raised and lived my life as a human. I'm just now figuring out that I'm more than human. I didn't know what you were doing, and…I didn't expect it." I bit my lip, trying to think of a way to explain what I meant. "It's like when you're getting it on with someone, and she whips out a set of handcuffs. And you think you *might* kind of like that sort of thing, but you weren't expecting it and it came out of nowhere. Yeah. It's like that."

His lips twitched. "So…no handcuffs?"

I ran a hand through my hair. "*Maybe* handcuffs, if that's the metaphor we're using for whatever you were doing there. Although, I might be okay with literal handcuffs. Especially if it's me cuffing you."

"So, literal and figurative handcuffs are okay, but only with appropriate warning and prior discussion?" He was clearly fighting hard not to laugh.

As much as I hated being laughed at, I didn't mind it when it was Bishop doing the laughing. And him thinking this was funny was a whole lot better than him being hurt or believing I was rejecting him sexually or whatever-ly.

I stepped forward, setting my coffee cup down so I could put both hands against his chest. "I want you. I do. I just expected it would be…*human* sex, not whatever that was."

He reached out and picked up a strand of my hair, sliding his fingers down a few inches before tucking it behind my ear. "I had a meeting today with someone I haven't seen in a long time. He wants me to return to a job I used to have."

I looked up at him, a little uncertain what this had to do with sex. "Are you going to take the job? Does that mean you'll have to move somewhere? What will happen to Suerte?"

"No. No. And nothing." He sighed, still playing with my hair. "In the beginning, that job had purpose. Now, it doesn't. It was a thankless job. I sacrificed everything and gained nothing, so eventually I just quit. I see no reason to do it ever again."

"Okay." I still wasn't sure what this had to do with me, or whatever was going on between us.

"Be careful what responsibilities you shoulder, Trouble." His fingers left my hair to trace a line across my jaw. "Sometimes your help isn't truly what people want. Sometimes good deeds only bring you scorn and envy."

"Luckily, good deeds aren't in my nature," I joked, wanting to get back to a lighter conversation, one where I understood what the fuck we were talking about.

He grinned. "No, they're not in your nature. But you seem compelled to do them anyway. It's one of the things that intrigues me about you."

"That and my fine ass," I informed him.

"That and your fine ass." He bent his head and kissed me. It was soft and far too brief. "I have to go. Two bears are about to break the vintage pinball machine that HB just spent way too much of my money for."

I wasn't going to question how he knew that. "Dinner sometime next week? Or coffee? Or drinks?"

"How about tomorrow? My place? Sevenish?"

I grimaced. "I don't know how long this thing in Inglewood is going to take. I hate for you to plan a big dinner, only to have me tied up south of the city until late."

He smiled. "Then how about drinks, if you're back in time and not too tired. Call me when you're done tracking down your friend's brother and let me know if you'll be by."

Before I could tell him I didn't have his number to call him, he vanished. Poof. Right out of my living room. I'd suspected he could teleport before, but he'd never done it in front of me. He'd never kissed me before, either. Or did that…thing he'd done. I'd felt him before, some weird non-physical connection between us, as if we could somehow touch without touching, but it had never been that intense, never that odd combination of euphoria and fear.

Sex with Bishop was going to be different. And I was increasingly sure it *was* going to happen.

My phone buzzed. I grabbed my coffee cup and went into the kitchen, realizing that Bishop had teleported with my other cup his in hand. I'd stolen his shirt, so I really couldn't complain about him taking my coffee cup. Picking up the phone, I saw a text from a phone number I didn't recognize.

Try to stay out of trouble, Trouble.

I grinned and saved the contact. Then I went downstairs to my bedroom and dug my vibrator out of the bedside table.

CHAPTER 10

The power and water were both out the next morning. I lingered for a bit, drinking cold coffee that had sat in the pot overnight and eating the leftover pesto. The fridge in this place was pretty good at keeping things chilled without power, but I didn't want to take the chance of coming home tonight to spoiled food—especially really good food that someone else had paid for. After a few hours, I realized we weren't going to have water or electricity anytime soon, so I took a quick bird bath using the clean water I'd left in the sink, got dressed, and left.

Bags was rearranging a display of tools in the front of the shop when I arrived. He had hot coffee, so in return I pitched in.

"I've got a job that's going to take me south of the city this afternoon, so I might not be in with much to pawn the next few days," I told him as I sorted drill bits. "Sebastian's brother Anton didn't check in when he was supposed to and isn't returning his calls. I'm going to ask around and see if anyone knows what happened to him."

"Mmmm." Bags shook his head. "What is this Anton into

that has his brother so worried? And if he's that worried, why isn't he out looking himself?"

I held up a bent five-eighths inch bit, then tossed it in a nearby trash can. "Sebastian is mid-level management with the Gray Dogs. Although Anton isn't officially a member, he was down south doing what appeared to be an arms deal on the side with a Disciple named Tape—maybe something to do with a guy named Aries."

I knew I could be completely honest with Bags. He might trade information as a side gig to pawnbrokering, but he was loyal. I'd trust the man with my life. I *had* trusted the man with my life, and he'd never let me down. And I liked someone knowing where and why I was away if things got messy.

Bags nodded knowingly. "*That* Sebastian. I know him. And I can see how he's got a problem with this. Gray Dogs and the Disciples have an uneasy peace. He wouldn't want his brother doing anything to jeopardize that."

"Right now, Sebastian just wants to know if his brother is still alive or not, and what the situation is."

If the Disciples had him, then Sebastian would have a hard decision to make regarding his brother. Knowing the man like I did, I expected he'd pay big to bail his brother out of trouble, kissing ass and apologizing the entire time. But if Anton had really screwed up, then Sebastian would need to choose between his family of blood and his family of choice. The Gray Dogs were everything to Sebastian. He loved them just as much as he loved his brother. I'd give odds either way on that one.

There was no doubt in my mind which way my choice would go. Bea and my sisters came first. Always.

Looking over at Bags, a tiny thread of doubt stirred. Would they? I had friends I loved. Who mattered more to me? What if thousands of innocent lives were at stake? The world? Two years ago, that choice would have been easy. Instant. But now? Life was so much easier when I could count the only people who mattered on one hand.

"Might be a short trip if the Disciples found out what Anton and his buddy Tape were up to," Bags commented. "They don't exactly hide the bodies anymore. If they killed him, people are gonna know."

People *would* know. Vultures would especially know, but those in my profession tended to be tight-lipped about their jobs. It had become incredibly competitive out there, and unless two Vultures were working together, like Telaney and me, information about jobs, both past and potential, was not shared.

"Do you know of anyone down around Inglewood that I can go to for intel?" I asked Bags. "Someone who won't charge a stranger a fortune for information. Someone who can keep their mouth shut, and who's not going to feed me a load of bull."

Bags tilted his head in thought. "Definitely talk to Shavonne down in Torrance," he said. "She has connections with the Disciples, although Inglewood is a bit north for her. Her business is mainly in Hawthorne, Compton, and Torrance, but she occasionally does some barter with folks from Inglewood."

I knew Shavonne. She'd been the pawnbroker who had helped with the sting on those cops who'd set me up last month. She and Bags were close. His name would be enough currency for her to tell me what she knew—probably for free.

"You should also contact this guy." Bags grabbed a notepad, wrote down a name, address, and phone number before ripping the sheet off the pad and handing it to me. "He owns a catering firm that supplies food to the casino. I'll vouch for him. He's good people."

"Erik Hook," I read from the paper. "Hook's Catering."

"It's not fancy stuff," Bags commented. "Pastries. Pre-made sauces. Soups. Frozen breaded chicken patties. That kind of thing. The Disciples own the casino now. He's got a few contracts with them. He hears stuff. If the Disciples killed or took this guy, then either Hook or Shavonne will know about it."

I pocketed the paper. "Anyone else?"

"I know a few other people, but I doubt they'd be in a position to hear about the Disciples' business." He blew the dust off a circular saw and put it on a shelf. "Check with Shavonne and Hook first. If nothing pans out there, I can give you a few more names. Do you want me to put the word out on this?"

"No. It would be best to keep it quiet for now."

Hopefully Anton was alive and just sleeping off a serious hangover with a broken or dead phone. Sebastian would be furious with him, but it would still be better than his brother being dead or in the hands of the Disciples.

"How about Tape or Aries?" I asked Bags. "Have you heard either of those names in connection with the Disciples? Or *any* gang?"

Bags shook his head. "I don't do a lot of business with the Disciples outside of the group that works the Valley. It's not surprising I've never heard of anyone named Tape or Aries, though. They're a huge gang."

I continued to help Bags until I'd finished my coffee, then I washed my mug, thanked him for the information, and headed out.

First stop was to put gas in my bike. Pulling into my usual spot, I swore to see that plain old unleaded was up to nearly eight bucks a gallon. Now that we were no longer part of the United States, most of the big gas stations had pulled out. The few that left found themselves paying double what they originally had for wholesale. Plus, they were charged extra for deliveries, due to the danger of hauling a fuel truck in an area where demons liked to blow shit up, and dragons routinely set things on fire. Gas station owners had to raise prices to make up for all that, as well as the cost of magical protection from demon vandals, and guards to protect against normal human thievery.

Thankfully, my bike got better miles to the gallon than a car or a truck. I stuck the nozzle in the tank, then went inside to pay, because everything was cash and you had to pay before you pumped. Inside, the cashier woman was chatting with a couple of guys. I overheard them say something about a neighbor who'd gone somewhere to fight. One guy said he wished he had the guts to do it. The other told him if he had enough money, he could pay someone to fight for him. I waited impatiently for them to finish their conversation up so I could pay, pump, and get the hell out of here.

The cashier shook her head. "I don't care what Jim does, I'm not fighting for Aries."

Aries. That was one of the names in Anton's texts. He'd mentioned something about getting Aries on their side. I'd focused more on his partner, Tape, but if these guys knew who Aries was and where to find him, it would be a good lead on what happened to Anton.

"Excuse me. Who is Aries?" I asked.

The three shut up faster than if I'd stapled their mouths shut.

I took a step closer. "Is he a member of the Disciples? I've heard the name before, and assumed it was one of the Disciples working down around Inglewood."

Was he one of their lieutenants? Were the Disciples planning some sort of attack on another gang or a militia? Based on their conversation, it sounded like this Aries was recruiting soldiers for the coming skirmishes. If that was the case, then if Anton was doing a weapons deal with Tape, the pair of them might also be working with Aries.

"I'll see you later, Shell," the one man said to the cashier.

Both men left, not answering my questions or even looking at me. I walked up to the cashier, handed her some money, and waited, hoping she'd elaborate on what the three of them had been discussing.

"Pump four is ready to go," she told me. "And don't go asking about Aries. Just stay away from that whole thing. It's a damned mess. People are desperate, and they're gonna get themselves killed doing stupid shit they shouldn't be doing."

"Like fighting for Aries?" I asked.

She nodded. "Isn't worth it. Pump your gas, and stay out of Inglewood. And stay away from Aries."

The woman turned away, closing the bulletproof, clear divider between us. I went outside and started pumping gas, thinking about what she'd said.

Inglewood. And fighting for someone named Aries. Once more, I wondered what the hell Anton had gotten himself into. Hopefully, it hadn't gotten him killed.

Hopefully, it wouldn't get *me* killed.

CHAPTER 11

I rode down the 110, then across the 405 toward Torrance. I figured I might be more likely to get information from someone I'd actually met before, so I headed for the pawnshop owned by Bags's friend Shavonne.

I hadn't been in Torrance since before the demons had come, and I was saddened to see how devastated the area was. I had to overshoot my exit since the ramp off the 405 had been destroyed, the lanes covered with yellow tape and signs warning drivers to stay on the freeway. I ended up on Hawthorne Boulevard. The road took me past a line of closed auto dealerships, the empty lots full of huge potholes. They looked like oversized, bombed-out parking lots. Cadillac. BMW. Volvo. Audi. The broken signs told a story of how profitable this area had once been, and how far Torrance had fallen in the last two years.

I wondered if the oil refinery was still in business? If the Honda and Toyota plants that had employed so many were still open, or if those companies had pulled up stakes and fled? A few big corporations had tried to stick it out in New Hell, but every day it seemed another one gave up and closed, leaving abandoned buildings that were quickly looted. Here, the empty shells that once housed Home Goods, Marshalls, Party City, and Trader Joes dotted the streets, alongside blackened, burned-out strip malls, and struggling fast-food franchises.

But people still needed to buy groceries, so at least the family-owned markets seemed to be hanging in there.

I doubled back to make my way east to Cabrillo Avenue, where Fast Cash Pawn had outlasted the two nearby pawnshops.

Parking a block away, I walked up a sidewalk that bore ominous scorch marks. The pawn shop was nestled between a cement-block building that had been painted an ugly beige-pink and another covered with gray stucco. The dirty Pepto-colored building was home to a sports bar; the swirly-font LED sign proclaimed it to be Lucky's. The gray building had once housed a sign-making company that, from the boarded-up windows and door, had long been out of business. The pawnshop between the two was plastered sidewalk-to-roof with signs proclaiming they provided payday loans and title loans as well as the usual buy/sell/pawn services.

It took me a second to find the door in between all the signs. Walking in, I noticed I didn't feel the wave of static I'd come to realize was my way of sensing magical security systems or other protective spells. Odd. Most pawnshops bought some sort of low-level magic to augment the security cameras, barred doors and windows, and shotgun behind the counter. Bags's place didn't, but almost every other pawn-shop I'd visited had some sort of magic. Maybe Shavonne was too poor to purchase magic. Maybe she hated magic and preferred to rely on the shotgun method of security. Maybe she paid for the protection of a powerful gang, and therefore, she didn't need the addition of a magical system.

I hadn't seen a tag outside indicating that the Disciples or any other gang watched over this place, but with all the damned signs I might not have noticed it. Locals would know, but the tags were important in warning outsiders to take their shit elsewhere if they were here to cause trouble.

A woman appeared from a back room. Shavonne was short and slight, her gray-streaked curls a tight cap on her head. Her broad smile faded as recognition flickered in her eyes.

"What can I do for you?"

The words were strained, as if she really didn't want to do anything for me. I got the impression if I hadn't been a friend of Bags, my ass would have been outside on the curb.

I really couldn't blame the woman. She'd told Bags about a couple of weirdos she'd had in the store who were trying to move a large supply of bullets, and within twenty-four hours she'd found herself part of a sting operation—one that hadn't exactly gone down as planned.

"I'm looking for a few people—two of them Disciples and the other a guy from the Valley who was supposedly doing business with them."

Shavonne glared at me. "I get along real well with the Disciples, and I'm not looking to screw that up. If you've got some beef with them, take your questions elsewhere."

I held up my hands. "I've got no issues with anyone in the Disciples." They had issues with me, but I wasn't about to tell this woman that particular story. "It's the guy from the Valley I'm really looking for. I'm hoping his business associates can help me contact him."

The glare lessened a fraction. "Don't you have cell phones up in the Valley?"

"He hasn't been answering his texts. It's kind of a welfare check." If a welfare check ended with me possibly dragging Anton's butt back to Van Nuys, where his older brother would lecture the skin right off his back, that is.

One of Shavonne's well-manicured eyebrows rose. "You're thinking the Disciples have him, that something bad went down in this business deal. And that means you'll start a fight. I get the feeling fights follow in your footsteps—deadly ones. I almost died in that stupid sting last month."

So had I.

"I don't know if the business deal took a hard left, or what. Things could have gone well and the three of them are too busy to answer texts. Maybe his phone broke or his car broke or he's stuck in the desert somewhere. Maybe he met some hot girl and they've been stoned, drunk, and banging for the last two days. Hell, for all I know the guy tried to steal a dragon hoard or fight a demon, and I'll be scraping his remains off the pavement."

Shavonne stared at me for a moment, then slowly nodded. "Who was the guy working with?"

"A Disciple named Tape, and someone named Aries. I'm not positive if this Aries is with the Disciples or not. I'm assuming he is."

She pulled a couple of bar stools over with price-tag stickers on them and sat, gesturing for me to do the same.

"Tape ain't shit with the Disciples. Normally I wouldn't even know who he is, except one of the guys I deal with regularly complains about him all the time. Tape's young, and he's a screwup. They took him off collection, took him off dealing, took him off guard work. He can't even manage the back-office stuff. Last I heard, he'd been in charge of scheduling deliveries, and failed out of that job, too. Six trucks ended up with spoiled produce because none of those drivers so much as sneeze without permission, and they were sitting for a week in Yorba Linda waiting for the okay to go."

Great. I had a bad feeling that this guy plus Anton were going to spell one giant disaster.

"Why is he still alive?" I wondered out loud, pretty much knowing the answer before Shavonne told me.

"He's someone's nephew." The woman wrinkled her nose. "Gangs. Corporations. Small business. There's always some idiot with connections in his family tree that ends up with a job they shouldn't have."

This put a kink in my plans. I couldn't find Tape and beat the truth out of him without pissing off whoever his uncle was. I'd just gotten one target off my back, and I wasn't eager to replace it with another. And if the guy was a screwup... well, there was a good chance he'd dragged Anton into some sort of mess. And while the Disciples might be willing to forgive one of their own who had a powerful uncle, they wouldn't be as forgiving of some dude from the Valley—especially if they figured out that Anton's brother was connected with the Gray Dogs.

"How about this Aries?" I asked Shavonne.

She pursed her lips, then slowly shook her head. "Never heard of him. Honestly, that's no surprise. The Disciples are a huge organization. I only know some of the ones who work in this area and a few of the big names. If this Aries is the same level as Tape, I'd have no reason to run across him."

Shit. That meant I was back to Tape. "Do you think I can meet with the guy you regularly deal with? The Disciple who complains about Tape?"

She snorted. "Uh, no. I'm not getting in the middle of your business. I told you what I know. You go find this Tape yourself."

I took some money out of a pocket of my cargo pants and handed Shavonne a twenty. It was a good thing I'd told Sebastian he was reimbursing me for expenses, because this was definitely not coming out of my own personal savings.

She took the money and just stared at me.

I peeled off another twenty. "Come on. I'm only asking for a meetup."

"That's what you said last time, and I nearly got shot," she replied, taking the second bill. "I'm not going to be there this time. I'm not vouching for you. I'm not giving you anything. I'll tell my contact that you want to meet with him about something to do with Tape. I'll give him your number, and the rest is up to him. I'm not doing anything more. Got it?"

I realized this was as much as I was going to get from Shavonne, so I gave her my contact information, thanked her, then left.

As I walked back to my bike, I thought about my options. There was a good chance her contact with the Disciples wouldn't bother to call me. Hell, there was a good chance Shavonne would just keep the money and not even keep her end of the bargain. But she was friends with Bags, and friendship came with certain obligations. She might not bend over backward to help me, but I did believe she'd pass my information along to her contact—especially since I'd paid her. I didn't know much about her, but I didn't think Bags counted dishonest people among his friends.

Her contact might despise Tape and think the guy was a screwup. He might want to just ignore the whole thing and let whatever bullshit Tape had gotten messed up in bite the guy in the ass. But he wouldn't. He wouldn't want to hang another Disciple out to dry, even if the guy was an ass. And he especially wouldn't want to abandon the nephew of a powerful member of the gang. No, he'd want to meet with me and hear what I had to say.

Getting on my bike, I headed north on Western Avenue, completely forgetting about the destroyed exit and on ramps until I reached the debris where vehicles used to be able to merge onto and off of the 405. I ended up driving west on the city streets, detouring around closed roads and hitting every single red light until I managed to get on the 110 heading north.

Three miles later, I found myself stopped dead in traffic. The slight breeze wafting from the shore a mile away did nothing to counteract the heat shimmering off the asphalt. I was about a mile from the El Segundo Boulevard exit and about five miles from where I'd wanted to get off the freeway, but none of that mattered. We were packed in so tight that I couldn't even find space to squeeze my bike between the cars and trucks. A Jersey wall served as the median, meaning I couldn't even pop over into the southbound traffic if I wanted to. The lack of options ultimately made my decision for me, so I sat, eventually shutting off my bike so it wouldn't overheat.

Slowly, we began to edge forward. We weren't moving fast enough for me to bother starting up my bike, so I pushed it along with my legs, sweat trickling down my back and soaking my shirt. I should have just kept going north up Western Avenue to Inglewood. At this rate, I'd get to the catering place just as they were closing.

At the El Segundo exit, I saw what the problem had been. I'd expected a wreck, or those damned lizard-demon things, but standing smack in the middle of the freeway was a troll. I recognized it from children's books, although none of those illustrators had truly captured the horror of a giant, gray-skinned, bulbous-nosed, yellow-eyed monster that smelled like a truckload of cod had overturned on the road and had been rotting in the heat for a few days.

No amount of honking or yelling budged the thing. Honestly, I was just grateful that the troll didn't react to the pissed-off humans trying to drive around it. It was big enough that with sufficient motivation, the thing could easily have rolled a few cars over and eaten the occupants in one bite. Worrying that the troll might suddenly spring into action and go on a killing spree, I started my bike.

Left or right? The troll was squatting in the center lane, his arms spread wide enough that we were all merging into the far lanes and the shoulder to get by. I stayed in the center lanes as long as I could, hoping to hold off making a decision until I had a better view of what lay beyond the troll.

Suddenly the thing grunted. A worse odor than decaying fish filled the air, and I worried I might actually puke. I heard the loud, wet noise even through my bike helmet. Chunky brown liquid squirted from the troll's ass onto the pavement and a few unfortunate vehicles to the left of it. The rotted cod smell was now mixed with fetid cabbage and, oddly enough, the odor of nail polish remover.

The angry yells turned to screams. I saw why as the pavement began to smoke and melt under whatever that troll was pooping out its ass. Paint blistered off the cars that had been splattered. Tires popped and liquified as they ran through the troll diarrhea.

I, along with everyone else on the freeway, decided it would be in our best interests to merge right to go around the troll, as the toxic brown stream slowly trickled into the left lanes.

The troll grunted again, this time depositing several large lumps onto the road along with an additional stream of brown. The smell intensified to the point where even with a helmet and a visor, my eyes watered. Drivers were gunning it through the stream of shit, no doubt hoping that if they went fast enough, their tires would hold out. The rest of us headed right around the troll, where the lanes were still acid-shit free.

I was three car lengths from the thing when it got up and walked into the right lanes, kicking a little Kia out of its way. At the shoulder, the troll vaulted over the edge of the highway, vanishing down below. A tremor shook the ground. The cars ahead of me sped up, and I followed.

Once I was past the acid-shit, traffic opened up and I managed sixty-five for the five miles until I merged onto 105, then fifty until I exited the freeway into Inglewood.

Hook's Catering was only a few blocks from the casino on South Prairie Avenue in a building that used to be a bakery. I knew it used to be a bakery, because the red letters on the side of the yellow building still advertised *Pasteles y Postres*.

Inside, two glass cases bisected the front area, remnants of the building's past purpose. Behind them, a glass door separated the room I stood in from a kitchen. I counted four people in the back, chopping, mixing, and kneading. After a few minutes of waiting, a man came through the kitchen door. He startled when he saw me.

"Sorry, I didn't know you were out here. We don't get many walk-ins. Are you placing an order?" He looked me over. "Or are you looking for the bakery? They closed up two years back. We're wholesale now, but we've got some day-olds I could sell you if you're interested."

My stomach growled, as if on cue. I hadn't had anything to eat since my leftover breakfast, and it was long past lunchtime.

"Actually I was hoping to speak to the owner—Erik Hook. But I'll absolutely buy half a dozen of the day-olds. Pastries or bagels or whatever." I wasn't picky, and I was starving.

"I'm Hook." He pointed a thumb toward the kitchen. "Let me grab your pastries, then we can talk."

He vanished through the door and reappeared a few minutes later with a white bag. I handed over five bucks and peeked inside. Two muffins that looked like they were blueberry, two pastries with lemon custard filling, and two bear claws. I put the bag in my backpack, then turned to face Hook.

He was younger than I'd expected—early thirties with short, dark, curly hair and a seventies era porn-stache. Red Converse sneakers peeked out from the hems of his boot-cut jeans, and his round-collared shirt was unbuttoned enough that I could see a gold chain around his neck and some curly chest hair.

Eclectic retro fashion aside, Hook seemed like a nice guy, and Bags had vouched for him, so I just got right to the point.

"I'm a friend of Bags. He gave me your name as someone who might be able to help me. I'm looking for a guy who came down here from the Valley for some business dealings with a Disciple named Tape, and possibly someone named Aries. I'm trying to track the Valley-guy down, and the only lead I have on him is this Tape. Do you know of him? Do you know how I can get in touch with him?"

Hook rolled his eyes. "Tape is a damned mess. He was in charge of coordinating orders and deliveries to the casino and the stadium for a few weeks. I was never happier than the day they replaced him. He'd forget to order stuff, then call at the last minute. You know how these guys are. We'd have to bust our asses and get it over there, because they're not going to blame one of their own for the screwup."

"Does he still work at the casino?" I really didn't want to walk into that place where security was most likely tight and Disciples were most likely lining the walls. But if that's where Tape was, that's where I'd go.

"I've got no idea. All I know is after a few weeks of me ready to pull my hair out, he got replaced by some dude named Luis, and my life got a hell of a lot easier."

Crap. "Would Luis know how I can get in touch with him? Or any other Disciple you might know?"

"I can text him, but he'll want to know who's looking for Tape and why."

"Mary Smith," I said, continuing my tradition of amazingly creative fake names. "And tell him Tape knocked me up."

Sebastian would have a fit to hear me say that, but too damned bad. Every time I was looking for a guy, people assumed it was because I was pregnant. Normally it pissed me off, but this time it made the perfect excuse. Tape might be some bigwig's nephew, but it sounded like most of the Disciples hated him. They'd cover for him on the big stuff, but getting a girl pregnant? They'd totally rat him out for that and enjoy watching him squirm.

Hook's gaze traveled to my midsection. Then he shrugged, got out his phone, and sent a quick text. He'd barely hit send before his phone buzzed a reply.

"Luis says he doesn't know where he is, but he'll find out. If I can get your number, I'll text it to you when he gets back to me."

I gave him the info, hoping that this Luis was intrigued enough by this potential soap opera to find Tape's whereabouts by nightfall. I'd hoped to get back home tonight, but I might need to check out what cheap hotels were in the area. Sebastian might be covering my expenses, but that didn't give me license to spend the night at the Hyatt.

Hook typed my number into his phone, then wrinkled his nose. "I don't want to be rude or anything, but what's that smell?"

I grimaced. "Troll. There was one on the 110 and I think the smell seeped into my clothes, my hair, probably my pores."

He laughed. "The one at the El Segundo exit? It lives under the overpass. Doesn't really bother the drivers until it needs to take a crap, then half the freeway is closed down until someone can get out there to repair the road. Thankfully it seems to only have a bowel movement once a week, and it occasionally decides to poop in Athens Park instead of smack dab in the middle of the northbound 110."

I shuddered. "If troll crap does that to asphalt, what has it done to Athens Park?"

"I live in that neighborhood, and it truly sucks." He grimaced. "It stays away from the playground, but it has really messed up the ballfields. The neighborhood pays some guy to go out in a hazmat suit, sprinkle some neutralizing stuff on it, then shovel it into the pool."

"The *pool?*" I was absolutely horrified at the thought of a pool filled with toxic troll shit.

"They drained it a few years back. There's no one to manage it and the kids kept sneaking in to swim unattended. A girl almost drowned, so the neighborhood decided it needed to go. Kids were still using it for skateboarding, but not after they started dumping troll shit in it."

The world just got weirder and weirder. "Doesn't it stink up the neighborhood?"

"Not after the Hazmat guy sprinkles that powdery stuff on it. It hardens, too. That way the pool isn't filled with liquid crap."

Solid crap wasn't much better, but I could see where the neighborhood didn't have many options. It took the demons coming for us to truly appreciate waste disposal's essential role in society. The county no longer provided the service, so independent businesses picked up the slack—and tripled their prices. The alternatives were to haul the trash out and shell out almost as much for the landfill fees, burn it in your backyard and piss off your neighbors, or find somewhere nearby that became the designated trash heap. At Bea's, we'd lived across the street from the transfer station, so whatever we weren't reusing or composting got heaved over the fence. Free and convenient. I'd never felt so lucky to live across the street from a literal dump.

Garbage. Troll shit. Hell, the county had even repurposed SoFi Stadium and hauled chunks of concrete and bent steel beams from the destroyed downtown buildings there.

"What does that thing eat?" I asked the question that had been on my mind since I'd smelled that horrible odor coming from the troll excrement.

"Rocks, wood, and metal, which means everyone needs to be really careful where they park their cars. It's chewed on some houses close to the overpass, and I can't tell you the number of people who have come out in the morning to find their cars missing. Nothing but gnawed-on rubber tires scattered around their front lawn."

"Damn!" And I thought having a Hellkitty living in the dump across the street was bad.

"Seriously. It won't eat rubber and plastic. It particularly likes chrome, of all things. Surprisingly, it doesn't seem to be eating humans—at least we don't think so. There has been a reduction in the number of homeless people in the area, but no one's seen any bones around where the troll lives." He shrugged. "Maybe it eats the bones, too, but I'd expect people would find clothing or personal effects left behind."

"Maybe it eats those too? I mean, if it eats stones and cars, then it shouldn't have any problems digesting clothing and shoes." I wasn't willing to give up my fears about the troll gobbling down human snacks. The ones in the fairy tales did, as I remembered.

"Maybe. But none of the neighbors or their kids, or even their pets, have disappeared. Other than the weekly crap and its generally bad odor, it's not that big of a deal—not considering we're now living with demons and far more dangerous stuff. The troll doesn't bother anyone unless they mess with it. Or unless they're driving some chromed-out restored '70s sedan down the street. Then it's game on. Other than that, don't poke it, and it won't pulverize you. That's the rule."

We had Hellkitty with his laser eyes, but West Athens had a troll. Yeah, I guess things could be worse.

I thanked Hook for his help, and for the pastries. He told me to say hi to Bags for him, and cheerfully suggested I come by some Thursday, when they made their sauces.

"We make a damned good Arrabbiata," he told me as I left.

It sounded good, but right now everything sounded good. Hopping on my bike, I drove to Athens Park, and parked as far away from the repurposed pool as possible. Then I sat on a park bench, waited for someone to call or text, and ate my pastries.

CHAPTER 12

Clearly Luis had it in for Tape, because I was just finishing the second bear claw when the text came in. Tape was working at a warehouse up by the stadium today. He was supposed to be there until five, but according to Hook's source, there was a good chance he'd bail early.

That meant I better hustle. Stuffing the remains of the bear claw in my mouth, I put the bag holding the rest of the pastries in my backpack, grabbed my helmet, and headed for my bike.

I must have parked downwind of the troll, because the faint odor of rotten fish and spoiled cabbage wafted in the light breeze. I glanced over toward the freeway. I was three blocks away from where the troll had set up shop, and I could still smell him. Must suck for those people who lived closer. They could never open their windows. Heck, the odor probably seeped right in through the walls.

Ugh. The thing might not eat people, but there were clearly a lot of disadvantages to living near a troll. I wondered how far he wandered when looking for food? The thing was huge. I half expected him to eventually be munching his way through the neighborhood cars, trees, and houses, but everything here looked intact. Outside of the occasional car and the houses he was gnawing on, as Hook had mentioned, the troll must go elsewhere for food. Too bad he didn't go elsewhere to shit.

Putting on my helmet, I left the park and the troll behind to head north, back into Inglewood. I drove right past Hook's Catering, past the bustling casino, and past the half-dozen empty parking lots once used for stadium patrons. Past the stadium was an old concert venue, and across the street from that stood what used to be an elementary school. I checked the address Hook had texted me, then looked back at the school. Normally I'd think Hook had made a typo, but public schools had been closed for the last two years, and an empty building with big open spaces for a cafeteria and a gym *would* be perfect to use as a warehouse.

I reluctantly left my helmet behind, thinking I might need both hands if things went bad, and headed up the walkway. Cameras were mounted over the door and at the corners of the building. I was a hundred feet from the door when a security guard came around the side. He didn't appear surprised, so I assumed he'd either seen me on the camera feed, or someone had let him know they had a visitor.

"This ain't a school no more." His hand moved to the butt of a pistol accessorizing his hip.

"I figured that. I'm looking for Tape." I tried to appear as harmless as possible. I didn't have blood all over my clothes, and the Glock in my shoulder harness was pretty much standard attire nowadays, so I probably had a fifty/fifty chance here.

He scowled. "What d'ya want with Tape?"

Let's hope this guy had the same sense of poetic justice that had led Luis to rat out his fellow Disciple.

"I'm pregnant."

It took a few seconds for that to sink in. A grin split the man's face, and he started laughing. "That's…that's fucking hysterical. Let me call him. No—let's just walk in and surprise him. I can't wait to see the look on his face."

He ushered me through the front door, not even bothering to take my very visible gun or pat me down for other weapons. I quickly realized that I hadn't thought this through completely. I had no idea what Tape looked like. Hopefully this guy would call him over, because if he just escorted me to a room full of men and expected me to take things from there, I was in trouble. If I'd screwed the guy, then I should at least be able to pick him out of a crowd. My mind raced, thinking of some plausible way of explaining why I didn't recognize the supposed father of my child. "It was dark" and "I was drunk" didn't seem like they would suffice.

We walked into what used to be the elementary school lunchroom, where men were breaking down cases of household products into smaller multi-product boxes. I stiffened, ready to draw my gun and get the hell out of here if things went bad.

"Tape! Get over here!" The guard chuckled, shaking his head and clearly anticipating some drama.

A tall guy who looked like he still should have been in high school jogged our way. He had floppy hair that had been dyed a deep purple, and a long scar on the left side of his thin face.

"Yeah?" He let his gaze roam over me, then returned it to the guard.

"Go ahead," the guard told me, gesturing toward Tape.

That was my scene cue.

"I'm pregnant," I snapped, folding my arms over my chest.

He looked back and forth between me and the guard, finally settling his gaze on me. "So?"

"You're the father." I said it loud and proud, and I can really project when I feel like it. All work stopped in the room as the other men left their worktables and came our way.

Tape's eyes bugged out. "Woman, I've never seen you before. Never. You got me confused with someone else."

"*That's* how you're gonna play this?" I shrieked. "You're gonna dump me, pregnant with your child, and act like you don't even know me?"

A bead of sweat rolled down his forehead. "I *don't* know you. Is this some sort of joke? Asher set you up to this, didn't he?"

"I am *pregnant* with your baby," I shouted, jabbing a finger at his chest.

A middle aged, balding, mixed-race man stepped forward. "You gotta do the right thing, man."

"Kids are a blessing," another man spoke up.

"Told you this was gonna happen if you didn't wrap that thing up," yet another intoned.

"I'm not...I didn't..." Tape looked around, his eyes wild. Then he straightened and turned to face me. "Okay, where did we meet? When and where did we fuck? I don't know you, so it was probably a one-and-done. For all I know, you screwed five other guys the same night and don't know *who* the father is."

"That ain't right, Tape," the kids-are-a-blessing guy warned. "Be a man and own up."

"Where?" Tape insisted. "When? How far along are you?"

I was back in dangerous waters. I didn't know where this guy hung out, or enough about him to even pick a date out of thin air. With my luck, I'd say the very week he'd been sent to NorCal for some job or another.

"You really want to get into this here?" I waved at the onlookers. "You want all these people up in your business?"

My bluff worked. Tape blanched, clearly wondering what sort of nasty thing I was about to reveal, and imagining weeks, if not months, of teasing from his co-workers.

"Let's step outside," he offered.

I'd been hoping we'd duck into one of the classrooms, but outside was actually better. Yes, everyone would probably be huddled in one room, watching us on the security cameras, but if I needed to rough Tape up a bit, it would take them a while to realize he was actually in danger, and arrive to defend him.

Tape led the way, glaring when the guard tried to come with us.

I followed him outside, down the walkway to the street, before he stopped.

"Who's fucking idea of a joke is this?" he snapped. "I might have had some drunken one-night stands in the past, but I at least know what they look like. I've never seen you before. And you're not my type."

"It's no joke." I stepped in closer, edging him back against a car parked at the curb. "I'm looking for Anton. He texted that he had some business with you down here three days ago, and he hasn't been seen or heard from since."

Tape bolted. I hadn't expected him to run quite this soon in our conversation, and the little bastard was quick. He slipped out between me and the car before I could manage to grab him, then was off down the sidewalk at an impressive speed. I took off after him. He had an inch or two on me as far as leg length went, and the distance between us grew. As long as he didn't duck into a building full of armed Disciples, I wasn't worried. The guy might be a tad bit faster than me, but I could run for days, while I got the feeling Tape spent most of his life in a gaming chair or behind the wheel of a car.

Three blocks and I started gaining on him. He made the mistake of looking behind him and panicking, veering off Prairie Avenue and weaving between buildings and through parking lots. I closed the distance as we were running through one of the parking lots for the stadium. Jumping him, I knocked him onto the pavement and added my weight to his skin-shredding slide forward. As soon as our forward momentum stopped, I flipped him over and sat back on him, pinning his legs with my feet and holding his hands out to the side. While I waited for him to catch his breath, I felt something twitch and harden right where I straddled him.

For fuck's sake, the guy had an erection. For all he knew I was going to put a bullet in his head, and his dick was ready to party.

I ignored what the guy had going on south of the border, and focused on his face.

"Where's Anton?" I kept my voice low and even-toned.

"I don't know," he gasped. "I met with him two days ago about some business we were tryin' to collaborate on and haven't seen him since."

"What business?" I asked.

His mouth thinned, his nostrils flaring now that they had to assume full duty for the guy's oxygen intake.

"What business?" I repeated.

"Drugs," he admitted. "We were talking about doing a deal off the books, just him and me, you know? I'm trying to make a little extra, strike out on my own a bit. He's got some connections in the Valley, and was looking to do the same."

Drugs? All this shit was over drugs? I'd seriously suspected military weaponry, given how Anton had been claiming this deal was going to put the Gray Dogs on the map as a major player. Years ago, drugs were a big money-maker. They still were a solid income stream for gangs and dealers, but they weren't going to bring any one gang into a high-powered position in the county or the state.

But I'd think about that later. Right now, I just needed to find out what was going on with Sebastian's brother.

"You saw Anton two days ago?" I asked Tape. "As in saw him alive? Or saw him dead? Has he texted or called you since?"

Sebastian hadn't heard from his brother in two days. If Anton was alive and was just ducking his brother's calls, *I* was going to be the one who killed him.

"He was alive," Tape squeaked. "And far as I know, he was still alive last night. Get off me, you're cutting off my air."

I wasn't, but I knew it was the hard-on pressing against my crotch that was making him uncomfortable.

"When are you supposed to see Anton again?" I shifted my weight, just to prolong the guy's agony.

"I don't know. He calls me; I don't call him."

Tape squirmed, and I clamped my legs tighter. This guy wasn't getting his rocks off while I was questioning him. Nope. Not going to happen. He could jack-off in some alleyway when I was done with him, but not before.

"Do you know where I can reach him? Somewhere he hangs out, or someone who can get in touch with him?

"He's staying at Loomis Motel over on 115th in Hawthorne. I don't know if he's still there, but he had me up to his room to grab something a few days back. Other than that, I don't know where he is. Like I said, he calls me. I don't call him."

I stared down at Tape, wishing I had some psychic truth detection, or Bishop's mind control abilities that he continued to deny he had.

"He's probably busy." Tape squirmed again. "Is he the one who got you pregnant? Is that why you're looking for him?"

"Yeah." I'd rather have him peg me as the angry pregnant girlfriend than dig too deep into who I really was, and potentially make connections between Anton and the Gray Dogs that might get Sebastian's brother killed.

"I'll tell him to call you if I hear from him again. Now get off me."

I scooted off the guy, standing far enough back that if he pulled anything, I'd have time to yank my gun from the holster. Tape just lay in the dirt for a moment, his pants tented out. Then he got up and dusted himself off. Nothing outside of a washing machine was going to clean the dirt off those pants, and the shirt had been torn. At least he didn't seem to have any bleeding road rash.

"Tell Anton…" I thought about how to word this, so I didn't get Sebastian's brother in any hot water. "Tell him he needs to get his ass home. If he doesn't call or show up in twenty-four hours, I'm coming back. And I'm bringing my brother."

There. Hopefully Anton had enough sense to know that message meant he needed to touch base with his own brother right fucking now.

"Okay. If I hear from him, I'll let him know." Tape kept trying to brush the dirt off, swearing under his breath about ruined clothes.

"If you hear from him?" I frowned. "What about the drug business you guys were planning? Is that on, or off?"

Because if Anton and Tape had parted ways after seeing each other two nights ago, there was no reason for Sebastian's brother to continue hanging around down here. He should have at least been back in the Valley by yesterday morning.

"It's up in the air." Tape scowled. "And it's none of your business. Go home. And I better not see you again."

I watched him walk off, unbothered by the threat. I'd

been the one who'd chased him down and tackled him. I wasn't afraid of Tape. But I *was* afraid of that school-turned-warehouse full of armed Disciples, and I wasn't sure what they'd do when Tape returned dirty and scuffed up. So I jogged to my bike and got the hell out of Inglewood.

115

I headed south on Prairie Avenue to the 105, only a few miles from the casino and Hook's Catering. In one day, I'd gotten to know more about Inglewood, Torrance, and Hawthorne than I had in the past twenty-two years of my life.

The motel was actually called the Loomis Inn. It was one of those two-story, two-star hotels that airport travelers used when they couldn't afford the hotels actually close to the airport. At one time it might have been a Comfort Inn or some other big chain, but it had clearly been sold long before the demons came, and now it was barely hanging on.

The pool out front, screened from a view of the 105 exit ramp by a chipped concrete wall, was not filled with neutral-ized troll crap. Neither was it filled with water beyond a greenish-brown puddle still hanging out in the deep end from the last rain. I parked under the marquee, hoping the sagging roof didn't collapse on my bike, and went in.

The lobby area had a tile floor broken up by two large sections of worn carpeting. Some ratty chairs and junkyard-worthy tables were on the carpeted sections. The woman behind the front desk reading a book didn't even look up at my entrance. I walked up to the desk, pulling a brochure off the table stand. It was a color tri-fold advertising the casino.

"Can I help you?" The woman finally looked up from her book, clearly irritated that I'd disturbed her.

"I'm looking for one of your guests. Anton Kovalenko?" I stuck the brochure in one of my pockets.

The desk clerk set her book aside with a sigh and tapped on a keyboard. "Room 209."

So much for guest privacy. "Can you tell me when he checked in, and when he's due to check out?"

She eyed the computer screen. "Checked in four nights ago. He's supposed to check out tomorrow."

"Thanks." I went to leave, then hesitated. "Can you give me the room key?"

She pulled her book back toward her. "Nope."

Couldn't blame a girl for trying. I might be able to bribe her to give it over, but there was no sense in wasting good money. I left the woman reading her book and walked through the lobby, following the signs to room 209. After a brief knock on the door, just in case Anton was actually in there, I picked the lock. Normally I would have had to use my electronic thingy instead of physical lock picks, but the hotel had replaced all the card swipes with old fashioned keyed locks.

I closed the door behind me, attached the privacy chain to buy me a little time in case Anton or someone else came by, then surveyed the room. Two queen beds, one with the sheets and blankets tossed. A few random clothes balled up on a chair by a window that overlooked the freeway. Sample sized toiletries in the bathroom that looked as if they'd come from a hotel vending machine. There wasn't any sort of suitcase, or clothes in the drawers to indicate Anton had planned a weeklong stay. But he'd checked in a day before he'd last texted Sebastian, and he'd paid up front for a six-night stay.

I sat on the unused bed and thought. Anton came down here to set up a drug business with one of the Disciples, realized after that first meeting that this might take a few days to a week, so he got a hotel room. He wanted to be nearby so he could quickly meet with his potential business partners as they set up their side gig. He figured a little less than a week, then he could head back home to the Valley. The second night in, he texts Sebastian, clearly optimistic about the deal and its potential. Then he stops responding to texts or calls, but according to Tape, he's still down here, working to close the deal.

Was he? Or had Tape lied and Anton was dead, this room unused and untouched until he was due to check out? Clearly there was no maid service here to let me know if he'd been in the room the last few nights, and I doubted the front desk clerk even noticed when guests came and left.

I got up and went into the bathroom, sticking my finger in the toothpaste blobs in the sink basin, and feeling up the towels discarded on the floor. A couple of them were stained pink. Sliding the shower curtain aside, I grabbed the washcloth hanging on the spigot. Damp. Also pink. Going back to the sink, I looked with greater thoroughness and found a streak of blood at the edge of the drain.

The toothpaste and the washcloth hadn't completely dried like they would have had Anton not been here in three days. I was guessing he'd showered early this morning or late last night. Or someone had. There were no signs that anyone else had occupied this room, so I was guessing the person cleaning up this morning had been Anton—and he'd been washing off blood in addition to the usual daily grime.

Going back to the clothes on the chair, I picked each one up and examined them. Ripped. Bloodstained. Filthy.

Tape hadn't lied, but he'd not completely told me the truth about what was going on with him and Anton. Alive? Yes. Beaten to crap? Also yes. I was willing to bet Tape'd had second thoughts about their deal and ratted Anton out.

I was starting to get really irritated at Sebastian's little brother. Guy comes down here into a rival gang's territory to establish a side job with a member of that rival gang, and neglects to check in with his brother for days? He deserved every bit of ass whipping Sebastian was going to deal out when he got home—in addition to the one he most likely had received from the Disciples.

Ripping a piece of paper off the pad by the television, I wrote a note telling Anton to call his brother. Putting the note on the pillow of the used bed, I left, locking the door behind me.

* * *

"HE'S AN IDIOT," I pronounced.

Wanting to put a few miles between me and Inglewood, I drove to East LA and called Sebastian from a chicken shack off Fraser, where I could eat something besides day-old pastries.

"Because Anton was trying to run some drug business behind the Disciples back? More like he's a fucking moron," Sebastian growled.

"He's just being enterprising in a world where you gotta take risks to get ahead," I disagreed. "He's an idiot for not leaving when he got the crap beat out of him for it. There's times when you have to just take your losses and go, and this is one of them."

But instead, Anton had cleaned up, changed into some clothes he'd either bought or stolen, and gone out...somewhere. That's what made me uneasy. The deal was clearly off

119

the table. There was no reason for him to stay—unless he had some thought of revenge in his head.

Idiot.

"Think they know he's my brother? That he's got Gray Dog connections?" Sebastian asked.

"If they knew that, they wouldn't have just beat him up and let him go," I told him.

They would have either killed him and dumped his body somewhere in the Valley where it would be quickly found, or held him and asked the Gray Dogs to pay a humiliating ransom to get their boy back.

"I left a message in his hotel room to call you. I'm not sure there's anything else I can do other than plant myself there and wait for him to come back."

I really didn't want to do that, but I would if Sebastian asked me to. I could be sitting in that tiny hotel room for the next two days, staring at the freeway or trying to watch whatever shows that cheap-ass hotel managed to get on their televisions. If Anton didn't show up by check-out time, then I'd know something had happened to him. If he did, then I'd beat the crap out of him myself and haul him home hog-tied on the back of my bike.

Sebastian sighed. "Let me think on it. Maybe he'll call tonight or tomorrow morning, or show up at home."

Or maybe not.

I had an uneasy feeling about this whole thing. It had been four years since I'd seen Anton. He'd been a hothead then, and I was pretty sure he still was. His potential partner had ratted him out, got him roughed up and probably dumped in some alley. He'd be angry, embarrassed, and probably longing to put a bullet in Tape's head. I just knew the guy was going to pull something—and that something would probably get him killed.

"I'm heading home," I told Sebastian. "Call me if you

change your mind and want me to go camp out in his hotel room. And definitely call me if he shows up or gets in contact with you."

"Will do." His voice softened. "I appreciate this, Eden. I owe you—and not just what we agreed upon either. Once this is all settled, I'll buy you dinner. Lobster, steak, you choose."

I recognized that tone in Sebastian's voice. He wanted to give me more than dinner and money, and in a sudden fit of nostalgia, I was tempted. But it wouldn't just be us reminiscing in the sheets. Sebastian would want more, and I didn't want more. Not with him, anyway. And there was that girlfriend of his that I really didn't want to have jumping me in a dark alley some night.

"Sure," I replied, not wanting to have this discussion right now. No, I'd wait to set Sebastian straight about the nature of our relationship—at least wait until after I'd eaten my lobster and gotten paid.

Disconnecting the call, I packed up the rest of my chicken, then got back on the road.

I wanted to go straight to Bishop's, but I forced myself toward Los Feliz and the house I needed to get used to calling home so I could clean up a bit first. Maybe even put on some makeup and do something with my hair.

It was close to seven o'clock when I pulled in my driveway and shut off my bike. The sun was still up, and it seemed like every single neighbor was outside. A few of them made a pretense of doing lawn work or fiddling with their vehicles, but most just stood on their lawns and stared at me. A woman from two doors down jogged over, speeding up to intercept me as I neared my front door. I recognized her from the fight with Dennis when I'd tried to claim squatter's rights on this place. She'd whispered something to Kevin, and I think she was probably the first one who'd recognized me from the times I'd been in Bishop's bar.

"I'm Lila." She held up a bottle of wine. "And this is a late 'welcome to the neighborhood.'"

"Thanks." I took the bottle of wine, then realized the offer probably included her helping me drink it. Crap. I wanted to get a shower and head to Bishop's, but this was a rare opportunity to actually socialize with one of my new neighbors. Maybe if I made friends with this woman, she'd spread the word that I wasn't some weird stranger. Besides, she'd brought me a bottle of wine. Gifts of food and booze earned points in my friendship book.

But…Bishop.

Maybe we could drink the wine super-fast, and I could get her out the door in half an hour.

"Do you want to come in?" I asked reluctantly. "I'm Eden, by the way."

"Yes, I know. And I'd love to come in."

She waited patiently while I unlocked the door, then followed me inside. I dropped my keys on the counter, then put the leftover chicken and four remaining day-old pastries in the fridge that was humming away and nicely cold. Then I grabbed the two wine glasses I had drying in the dish drainer from when Telaney had been here and poured us each a glass as Lila wandered around the house.

"You haven't changed much here," she commented as I handed her a glass.

"I haven't been home much," I countered. Not that I was big on home décor. There was furniture. That sufficed for me. Telaney was the one picking up lamps from our salvage jobs for her home, not me.

"Is the woman you had over the other night your girlfriend?"

Pry much? Sheesh.

"A friend from work," I told her, although it was none of her business. I'd share a little with these people if it stopped them from treating me like an unwelcome cockroach that had moved into their home.

She frowned, sniffed her wine, sniffed the air, then sniffed in my direction. "Were you at the wharf or something? You smell kind of like rotted cod."

Drat. I'd hoped a few hours of doing sixty-five on the freeway would have blown that odor away.

"Troll. I was down south of the city today. There's a troll under the 110 overpass at El Segundo in Hawthorne. He took a crap on the freeway, and everyone within a mile probably has the smell baked into their clothes."

"Ugh." She shuddered. "At least we don't have trolls in Los Feliz."

No, we just had big cat shifters, the occasional demon, and a nice view of a dragon flying over downtown.

She took a sip of her wine and regarded me with curiosity before asking, "What were you doing in Hawthorne?"

I bit my tongue. Nosy neighbors weren't my thing. Nosy anybody wasn't my thing. But I'd need to learn to be polite and play along, or I'd find myself having to fight Dennis again—or someone who might *really* kick my ass.

Make friends, Eden. Be nice to the lady who brought you a bottle of wine.

"I'm a Vulture." It didn't answer her question, but I thought it was a good redirect.

"Isn't your territory the Valley? Why drive all the way to Hawthorne? Is there some big thing going on down there?"

"We don't really have set territories, but it's easier to work in a familiar place. Some times we'll make the drive if the job is worth it." I forced a smile onto my face. "What about you? What do *you* do for a living?"

I was sorry I asked. For the next fifteen minutes Lila regaled me with tales of her job as an arborist, trimming trees and treating sick ones throughout LA and the Valley, while I urged her to drink her wine as fast as possible. In all honesty, it *did* seem like an interesting profession, but I couldn't tell a Canary Island date palm from a Moreton Bay fig, so I did a lot of nodding and uh-huhing.

"Bishop came to your house last night," she suddenly said.

I blinked at the lightspeed change in conversation topics. "Yeah."

She grabbed the wine bottle and refilled both our glasses with what was left. "Does he do that a lot? Visit you?"

"Occasionally." I wasn't about to get into Bishop's and my professional history and hopefully personal future.

She glanced over at the feather. "Did he give that to you?"

Clearly my clipped, one-word responses were not conveying the message I'd intended.

"Not exactly."

Lila took a deep breath, then drank down the rest of her wine. I watched her, wondering if she had somewhere she needed to be right now, and didn't want to leave her drink unfinished.

"I need to ask you a favor," she said as she put her empty glass on the coffee table.

"Um, okay?" I wasn't about to agree to this favor when I had no idea what she was going to want from me.

"We've got this problem." She clasped her hands together, twisting them back and forth. "The last three weeks, shifters have been disappearing. They've gone missing. Most of them from packs south and east of LA."

I frowned, wondering if Desiree had started up her human trafficking business again and decided to specialize in shifters this time. "Kids?"

"No, adults. They're all between the ages of twenty-five and fifty. Strong. Fit. Able to take care of themselves if they came across trouble."

"Has anyone tried to track them down? Found their bodies?" That sounded harsh, but in this new world we all lived in, no one bothered to hide the bodies. The murder rate was through the roof, the police were overwhelmed, and justice moved at the speed of molasses in Alaska in January.

"No bodies have been found. Their packs tried to track

them down through conventional means, looking where they'd last said they were going to be and asking around the neighborhood. Nothing. They tried tracking through smell and quickly lost the scent. We're tight with our packs, even us here in this neighborhood. If we were going to move or join another group or something, we'd at least tell the alpha. One or two shifters missing…well, it's not usual, but I could see that maybe happening. This is *thirty*. Thirty shifters missing in three weeks, all from within an easy commuting distance of LA."

I was intrigued, but I didn't see what any of this had to do with me.

"Two nights ago, an old friend of mine went missing. I haven't seen or heard from her in almost a year, but someone in her pack called last night to see if maybe she'd come up to visit me after a job interview she was doing down around Torrance."

My eyebrows shot up. I was just down there, and it didn't exactly look like the area was booming with employment opportunities.

"She just vanished." Lila's eyes sparkled with tears. "I'm so worried."

"I'm sorry about your friend, but I'm not sure what you want me to do." I held out my hands. "I'm a Vulture. I hang around violent crimes-in-progress and basically rob the dead. I don't track down missing people."

But I knew who did, and I was surprised she hadn't showed up at *his* house with a bottle of wine, wanting help.

"You're the Ksatrei," Lila said.

Suddenly, all this made sense.

"I'm begging you to intervene. I need Bishop's help. *We* need Bishop's help. Thirty missing shifters in three weeks. We're being targeted. We're being attacked. Our people are missing, and we can't find them. We can't even find their bodies. We need Bishop to pick up the mantle of protector, to find our brethren, to keep us safe from those who would do us harm, just as he vowed to do ten thousand years ago."

"Whoa. Wait. What?" I was so lost right now. "Bishop runs a bar catering to you guys. What's this 'mantle of protector' shit? And what does me being a chihuahua have to do with this?"

She blinked at the chihuahua thing. "Can you ask him to help us? You're the Ksatrei. He'll listen to you."

"Why don't you ask him yourself?" I wondered. Why was I suddenly the messenger? Was that part of the chihuahua job duties or something?

Lila recoiled from my suggestion. "Me? I can't speak to him! I can't even look at him."

Okay. That was a little weird, but I wasn't in a position to start throwing shade at someone else's culture. "How about Kevin then? Kevin Wong? Isn't he your leader or alpha or something? Surely, he can speak to or even look at Bishop. Why doesn't he go to him about this?"

"He did. Bishop declined to intervene."

I frowned. "Declined? Was it because you all wanted a freebie or something? I mean, I get that Bishop is expensive, but maybe if you all chipped in, you could afford his fee."

She scowled. "We're not supposed to have to *pay*. Bishop is the protector."

Maybe that was the problem. The guy did have a right to make a living—Bob too. If there was some expectation of his help, some former commitment he'd made to them, then perhaps he should have offered them a discount, but I couldn't imagine why the guy should have to do this for free.

"He's the *protector*," she repeated. "We don't ask for anything ever. We haven't asked for his help in over a dozen generations. He intervened a few months ago with the Big

River Pack when their alpha was being a total dick. This is just as important as that. It's *more* important."

"What did he do for the Big River Pack?" I had a bad feeling I knew what this was about, but I needed confirmation.

"King." She spat the name out. "He was abusing his position as alpha. Rape. Murder. Beating the crap out of anyone in the pack who looked at him funny. And they couldn't defend themselves or he'd kill them. They just had to take it. Two years ago, three of the pack members appealed to Bishop for help. He refused. King killed the three of them. Then suddenly two months ago Bishop goes to talk to King. People said there was a whole lot of yelling, then silence. Then Bishop walks out carrying King's head. It hung on the wall at Suerte until HB convinced him to get rid of it."

King. The racist guy who'd initiated the attack on me when I'd first walked into Suerte two months ago. I'd given Bishop a whole lot of shit about that afterward. And I'd been a bit disturbed to walk into Suerte the next time and see that head on the wall.

"We're not idiots," Lila told me. "We know Bishop didn't suddenly decide to intervene in this one case after a thousand years of inaction on everything else. He took out King because of you. King attacked you. And he paid for that."

I held up my hands. "Others attacked me as well. They're still alive."

At least I thought they were.

"King was their alpha. Alphas are responsible for actions pack members take under their direction. And every alpha defends their own. Bishop retaliated for the attack on you that occurred in his territory, on his property. If Kevin had recognized you, he never would have made you fight to live here. He would have welcomed you, told you that your presence in our neighborhood honored us all. I tried to tell him, but he didn't believe me, and when he found out, he just about wet his pants trying to track you down and apologize."

Suddenly this Ksatrei thing was sounding better and better. HB had warned me not to get attached, but these didn't sound like the actions of a guy who just wanted one roll in the sheets with me before waving goodbye.

"I'm begging you to help us," Lila continued. "Please ask Bishop to help find the missing shifters, and to stop whoever is taking them. Please."

I understood her concern, her fear. Sebastian's brother had gone missing, and he'd been worried sick. When Nevarra had been taken, I'd been frantic. Even though these weren't children, their families still must be missing them and frightened about what might have happened to them.

"I'll talk to him, but I can't promise anything," I warned her. "I don't have the kind of influence with Bishop that you seem to think I have, but I'll ask him to help."

"Thank you, Ksatrei. Thank you so much," she gushed.

"Eden," I told her. "Please call me Eden." Because Ksatrei would forever be linked in my mind with a yappy chihuahua.

"Ooo, look at the time!" Lila glanced out the window at the darkening sky. "Jake is probably wondering where I've gone off to."

I escorted her to the door, and opened it to find a familiar gray kitten sitting on the welcome mat, looking up at me with shining green eyes.

Lila gasped. By the time I'd turned my head to look at her, she was clear across the room, her back plastered against the windows that overlooked the city. Her eyes were huge. I was pretty sure every hair on her head and body was raised. I shrugged and turned back to the kitten.

"Mittens!" Reaching down, I scooped the gray ball of fluff into my arms. "I'm glad you're here and not bothering Bea and the neighbors. How have you been? Have you laser-eyed any mercenaries lately? Set fire to another pile of scrap lumber? You shouldn't have burned that shrub at the corner of Bea's lawn, you naughty thing you."

The kitten nudged me with his little head and purred.

For some reason, this temperamental and absolutely lethal creature liked me. Actually, he tolerated me. The Hellkitty had wandered down our street one day, slicing through vehicles with his laser eyes and hissing at everyone. Then he'd gone into the dump across the street—the transfer station for the county landfill. There he'd lived, occasionally appearing to terrorize the neighborhood. Twice he'd sought me out—once coming into my bedroom through the window screen to sleep at the foot of my bed, and once walking up to me as I sat outside Bea's home and rubbing against my leg for petting. That's when I decided he needed a proper name, and that I would henceforth call him Mittens. I hadn't seen him since, and I was surprised he was here, outside of my new home all the way in Los Feliz.

"How did you find me?" I asked the cat. "Do you want a can of tuna? Or I've got some leftover chicken from dinner tonight."

Lila whimpered from across the room. "That's not a cat."

"I know. It's a Hellkitty. And his name is Mittens."

Mittens swiveled his head at Lila's voice and hissed. Red sparks came to life in the glowing green eyes.

"Oh no," I warned him. "Not in the house. If you're going to start burning shit down with your laser eyes, you're gonna need to do that somewhere else."

"That can't...Kevin isn't going to let that thing stay here," Lila said.

"What's he going to do about it?" I shrugged, putting Mittens down and getting out my only can of tuna. I'd clearly need to buy more if the Hellkitty was going to be a frequent guest.

Lila didn't have a reply to that. She edged around the perimeter of the room, wide eyes on the kitten the entire time. Once she got to the front door, she practically bolted outside.

"Thanks for the wine," I called after her, remembering at the last minute that I should be polite to my new neighbors. "It was nice meeting you."

I fed Mittens, who curled up to sleep on my sofa after eating his tuna. While he was snoozing, I ran downstairs and grabbed a shower, putting on some clean clothing and thinking I might want to set aside some money for a dress or two. Slapping a coat of mascara on my lashes, I ran out the door, texting Bishop that I was on my way.

The neighbors were still outside, still watching me as I fired up the bike and pulled out of the drive. But their scrutiny felt different this time. It felt more respectful.

Lila had clearly told them about our conversation, or maybe they'd managed to hear us talking through the walls. Either way, I liked the change. And I hoped their new respect continued.

CHAPTER 15

"Hey," I said, feeling ridiculously self-conscious. I'd texted Bishop that I was on my way and headed straight over, but now that I stood at his front door, I felt awkward. Should I have brought something? Wine? Cheese? Some gourmet snacks, although I had no idea who even sold gourmet snacks.

"Hey yourself."

He stood aside with the door open, and his warm, lazy smile zinged through me, heating my blood. As I walked in his gaze slowly traveled down my body. My breath hitched. Screw the wine and gourmet snacks. I wanted to go straight back to the bedroom.

I turned and his eyes met mine, his smile widening. I wanted him. And clearly that was written all over my face and my body.

"Hungry?" he asked.

"Yeah," I replied, walking right into his arms.

This time it was he who dipped his head, molding his lips to mine. I met his tongue with equal passion, shivering as I felt him once again stroking the part of me that wasn't human.

"No handcuffs," he murmured against my mouth. "Not until you're ready. But I can't keep from touching you—the real you. Is that okay?"

It was more than okay. I moaned some incoherent affirmative, then got busy with my hands, yanking at the buttons on his shirt in my hurry to get him naked as quickly as possible. He kissed me again, then paused to pull my tank top up and over my head while I finally managed to get his shirt unbuttoned and off of him.

"Damn." He sucked in a breath as he eyed my chest.

I didn't own any sexy lingerie. Hoping we'd end up in bed, I'd gone braless, figuring the discomfort was better than trying to wrestle off my usual sports bra when I was trying to be sexy.

Clearly I'd made the right choice. Bishop had always struck me as an ass man, but right now he looked like he was rethinking his preferences.

"Beautiful."

It was all he said before his mouth was on my breast, tongue hot and wet on my nipple. I gasped, clinging to him and losing myself in the sensation. A bright light temporarily blinded me, and when I blinked my vision back, I realized he'd teleported us to his bedroom.

My hands went to his hair, and his went to my jeans, removing them with a practiced ease. Scooting backward, I felt the back of my knees hit the edge of the bed and toppled onto it.

He never paused, his mouth exploring every inch of me while the non-corporeal part of him continued to touch and stroke my equivalent. I lost myself in the sensation, giving up on any attempt at reciprocal action on my part. My bones felt as if they'd dissolved. Every nerve in my body vibrated.

My very soul sang, reaching for that sunset-on-the-water, eager and no longer afraid.

The angel in him held back, but the physical Bishop did not. His mouth made its way down my body until he was between my legs. His tongue teased, his fingers entering me, pressing all the right spots. He built me up, then brought me down, edging me closer and closer to the precipice until there was no coming back. Everything inside me tightened, then released in a crashing wave of orgasm.

Bishop eased me down slowly, stroking and kissing the inside of my thighs and up my stomach. Just when I was beginning to think I might be ready for round two, he stood up.

"No!" I reached out for him. "I want you. I need you. Inside."

I felt like I was babbling nonsense, but he must have understood, because he stripped out of his jeans and stepped between my legs, positioning himself. He loomed over me, his blue eyes eerily alight with gold. I breathed in, suddenly seeing the angel behind the gorgeous physical form. He was all heat and bright light and power. He was breathtaking and terrifying all at once.

And he was mine—even if only for tonight.

"Eden."

The word was a guttural rasp. He bent his head to claim my lips, and pushed himself inside, moving slowly, rhythmically. I shuddered, my arms wrapping around his waist, my short nails digging into the skin of his lower back as I urged him on.

"Harder," I said, my hands moving up and pulling until his mouth was on mine again.

He complied, his pace increasing and growing erratic as I felt everything inside me coil up once more.

"Come with me," I pleaded. Just as the orgasm rolled

through me, he tossed his head back, every muscle taut as he came. I watched him, enjoying the feel of him inside me. Letting out a long breath, he shook his head and opened his eyes.

They were still glowing golden, the blue almost extinguished by that light that shown from within.

"You are very bad for my vibration pattern, Trouble," he said as he gathered me up and rolled so we were facing each other on our sides.

I snuggled close, no idea what he was talking about. "Don't blame me for that. I have a feeling your vibration pattern, whatever that is, was shot to hell long before you met me."

He snorted. "Probably. You're not helping, though."

We lay there together for a few moments, slowly coming back to reality. Then Bishop got up and went to his dresser. He opened a drawer and grinned as he tossed me a shirt before digging out a pair of sweatpants and stepping into them. I slid on the shirt, buttoning the two top buttons, then slipping into the bathroom to freshen up. When I came out, Bishop was already downstairs.

I found him in the living room, pouring wine. He handed me a glass, and I plopped down on his couch as he poured one for himself.

"Did you find your friend's brother?" he asked, coming to sit beside me.

I grimaced. "Sort of." I told him about my day, about finally tracking Anton down to the hotel room where all I'd found were torn and bloody clothes. "Hopefully he'll be home tonight with his tail between his legs," I finished.

Bishop's eyebrows shot up. "You believe that?"

I took a sip of the wine before answering. "No. Anton's a hothead with an over-inflated ego. Maybe he's learned something in the last four years. Maybe he'll realize he can't win this fight and just come home. Unfortunately, I have a bad feeling he'll want revenge."

Revenge that would get him killed.

Bishop shook his head. "Idiot."

"I agree." I scooted closer to him, and he put a hand on my thigh, stirring me up once more.

Maybe we could do it on the couch. And in the kitchen. And in his truck. The shower. Back in the bed again. I was seeing a long night filled with lots of sex ahead of me, and Bishop's hand edging its way up my thigh told me he was thinking the same.

But I'd promised Lila I'd talk to him about the missing shifters. It was probably a good idea to do that now, before I got too wrapped up in mind-blowing, nonstop sex and forgot all about it.

"A shifter came over tonight to ask me a favor," I told him.

His hand stopped on my thigh. "And?"

I took a breath before saying, "She said you were supposed to be the guardian angel of the shifters, here to look over them and keep them safe, or something like that. She said that thirty shifters have gone missing in the last three weeks, and she wanted me to ask you to find them, to protect them from whatever is preying on them."

Bishop looked at me, his expression inscrutable. "Guardian angels watch over the gates to Hel—at least they're supposed to. It's more of a class of angel than a job description, but over the ages, they've come to have a specific task. I'm not a guardian angel."

"That's not what I'm asking." I scowled at his ability to sidestep. "Are you here to protect the shifters?"

"No."

I stared at him, willing him to elaborate.

Bishop sighed and focused his gaze out the window as he leaned back on the couch. "In the beginning...kind of. It wasn't just me. There was a powerful archangel in Aaru who felt as I did when it came to Nephilim and their descendants —the shifters. We believed that the sins of the father should not be visited upon the son, but this angel couldn't openly support such a radical view. He did the work behind the scenes, and I stayed here as the boots-on-the-ground."

I watched him for a moment, waiting to see if he'd continue without prodding. I should have known by now that Bishop was far more skilled when it came to patience and waiting than I was.

"In the beginning?" I asked. "So that was the plan ages ago, but then something happened? You're no longer dedicated to protecting the shifters?"

"A lot changed since then. I've changed. The shifters have changed. Humans have changed. Angels…well, some of them have changed. Time feels different here than it does in Aaru, and taking on corporeal form alters an angel in many ways. It changes a being of spirit—in far more than just in their vibration pattern."

I sipped my wine, continuing to watch him. The sparks of gold in his blue eyes settled and extinguished. He relaxed against the cushions, and suddenly he seemed very human.

He *felt* human. It made me realize that he'd never truly felt human to me before. There had always been a zing of other to Bishop. Seeing him like this was disturbing. Reaching out with some sense I didn't quite understand, I searched for that non-human part of him and found it deep down, buried in layers of flesh and bone.

With a start, I yanked back whatever freaky extrasensory thing I'd just done and gulped some wine.

"Around ten thousand years ago, a major project went to crap," he went on, as if he hadn't noticed my psychically feeling him up. "Aaru panicked and reacted with the usual extreme actions. Some of us disagreed, but we kept quiet.

The war that millions of years ago split the angelic host in two was still a raw wound, and none of us wanted to see further violent division, so we just did what we needed to do. I stayed behind, and the last ten thousand years here among the humans has truly felt like the equal of five hundred million in Aaru."

"You went native," I said, finally understanding what he'd been trying to say.

"I went native." He turned to face me, the sparks of gold returning to his eyes. "And the longer I've been here, the more I've realized the shifters really didn't need our help, nor do the humans. They just needed us to leave them the fuck alone. So after a few thousand years, that's what I decided to do."

"But they need your help now," I told him.

"No, they don't. They need to help themselves."

I eyed him in astonishment. "Really? Here, surrounded by demons and humans? Yes, they're stronger than humans, but this is a human world, and the shifters are very much aware that they're a minority. There's only so much super strength and speed can do when you're surrounded by billions of humans."

He shrugged. "They need to fit in. Me solving their problems isn't going to really help anything."

"This isn't them wanting you to hold their hand filling out a job application at Target, or figuring out how to renew their drivers' licenses," I argued. "They *tried* to find their missing packmates. They looked for them, tried to track their scent, asked around where they were last seen. Thirty, Bishop. Thirty shifters in three weeks. Gone."

"Humans go missing too."

"Yeah, but they don't have an angel who'd sworn to look after them," I retorted, putting the wine glass down and jumping to my feet. "You have a responsibility here. You made a promise."

"And when does that responsibility end, Eden?" he snapped. "It's been ten thousand years. If they can't handle their shit after that long, then it's not my fault. I made that promise to a generation that is long dead. *Long* dead. Am I forever to be cleaning up the messes of other people?"

I sucked in a breath at his words. "I'm not asking you to help them with basic everyday tasks. I'm asking you to find out what is happening to these people that are disappearing—people *you* once looked after. You have the power and ability to do something, to make a difference. You can't just refuse to help them."

"Yes, I can, and I will. That used to be my responsibility, but it's not anymore. Now I own a bar and track down durfts and stolen shit if people pay me enough money. That's it. I've given enough of my life making up for others' stupid decisions. I'm done. I don't owe the shifters anything. I don't owe the angels anything either."

Bishop spun around and stomped out, slamming the door closed behind him. It took me a second to realize how ludicrous it was that he'd stormed out of his own home wearing only a pair of sweatpants.

I was so angry at him, so furious that he'd refused to even help. These weren't strangers; they were shifters. They were his people. They were the very people he'd once vowed to protect.

And now he'd abandoned them, just like the angels had abandoned us.

I put my clothes on and tossed the shirt I'd been wearing in the laundry. Then I left, but not before I stole two of his paintings right off the walls, because I was pissed and because Bishop and I seemed to have this stealing-stuff thing going on. I took two of the smaller ones since I was riding my bike and couldn't exactly drive down the street with two three-foot pieces of art strapped to my back. I picked one of the ocean scenes and an abstract, thinking I'd give them to Sadie and Nevarra to hang in their rooms.

Right before I left, I grabbed my coffee cup off his kitchen counter, and stole that back as well. If he wanted the paintings back, his shirt back, my coffee cup back, then let him come to my house and get them.

CHAPTER 16

It was far too late to drive over to visit Bea and the girls, so I went home, and took a chance that they'd still be up, and called them instead. Bea was thrilled to announce that she'd gotten a raise at work. It would allow them to expand their food budget, and she was planning on upping their savings. Nevarra had evidently changed her mind about the community garden and had spent the day organizing one in the vacant lot down the block. She already had six neighbors signed on to the co-op. Sadie had found a book about raising poultry and was learning all she could so she could take over their budding backyard-chicken enterprise.

Both girls asked again if they could come over to spend the night this week, or maybe even an entire weekend. They wanted to go hiking in Griffith Park, visit the observatory, have a picnic. Both wanted to meet kids their age in my neighborhood. I thought about Lila and the woman who'd come to borrow sugar, and wished my encounters with the neighbors had gone better. Maybe when Nevarra and Sadie came over, I could have a small party to introduce them around. Hopefully, two friendly teens would break the tension between me and the shifters.

I told the girls I'd have them over again soon—maybe this weekend. Now that I didn't have a price on my head and Bishop was paid off, I felt like I could actually take a few days off if I wanted. And maybe the neighbors would relax a little to see me out doing normal things with two human girls. Maybe they'd finally view me as less of a threat if their children played stickball in the streets with my sisters.

It would be fun. I'd love for the girls to come over and spend Saturday night and Sunday here with me. A normal weekend, just like it was before the demons came. I smiled, thinking about how mundane, how normal, how *perfect* that all sounded.

I wished the girls and Bea a goodnight, and then stared at my phone a while, wondering if Bishop would call or text me. It was a stupid argument. If we couldn't move past one argument, then there wouldn't be much hope for this relationship. Hopefully he'd cool off and text. If not, then I'd be the one to make the first move. But not tonight. I was still irked at him. Maybe I needed to cool off as well.

Putting my phone aside, I went into the kitchen to wash the wine glasses and the bowl I'd served Mittens his tuna in. It was a good thing I hadn't kept that Instant Pot. I rarely got home until late, if at all. What would happen if I was detained with work, and by some miracle the electricity stayed on and the thing ran all night long? Would it catch fire? Would the food burn? Would my neighbors smell the disaster and intervene before my house and the neighborhood burned down?

There would be no Instant Pot in my future. No reason to antagonize my neighbors any more than necessary. No, Mittens would probably be doing enough antagonizing for the pair of us.

* * *

WHEN I WOKE up Mittens was gone, although the kitten had left me with a little present on the bathroom floor. I'd have to pick up a litter box just in case the Hellkitty decided to make visiting me a regular thing. I ate the leftover pastries, had some coffee, then prayed the electricity would stay on and my leftover chicken would still be good when I got home tonight. Then I headed over to Bags's to get the scoop on any potential goings-on that might make for good scavenging. I was deciding between a potential scuffle in Sunland and a hit in the West Hills when I got a text from Telaney.

"Gotta go," I told Bags as I slid off my stool. "Pasadena. I'm meeting Telaney there."

It should have taken me no more than half an hour tops to make the relatively short drive, but traffic on the 132 had been a fucking nightmare. The exit ramp I should have taken to head into Pasadena was blocked by a ten-foot mountain of what looked like giant-sized bones, so I'd needed to go down to the next off ramp and circle back. When I finally arrived at the no-tell motel, the only things still alive were the crows circling overhead and Telaney standing next to her car, eyeing the whole scene with disgust.

I pulled up next to her and yanked the helmet off my head. "Sorry. I swear if it's not troll shit, it's dinosaur-sized bones. Maybe I need to stay off the freeways and just put up with all the traffic lights."

"Wouldn't have mattered. This all went down before I got here." She nodded toward the carnage.

I got off my bike and the pair of us walked over to see if there was anything left to pick through. I'd expected to find bodies and evidence of a shoot-out. I hadn't expected to find that the dead also included the dismembered corpses that I somehow recognized to be two Vultures.

"Shit," Telaney commented.

"Yeah," I agreed.

Being late meant you arrived after all the good stuff had been taken. Being early meant you got caught in the cross-fire. These guys weren't just shot by a stray bullet though; they'd been killed on purpose.

And not with a gun. The Vulture's bodies were broken, both arms actually torn off one of them. It was as if someone had snapped them like twigs—and their manner of death was eerily reminiscent of what Telaney and I had seen go down at the Palisades Militia.

"Are you thinking what I'm thinking?" Telaney pointed to where three men had suffered a similar death. One had his head punched through the windshield of a car.

"Why would Big Studio Guy have an issue with these guys, whoever the hell they are, and two Vultures?" I asked.

Telaney shrugged and shook her head. "Beats me. I got a tip that some indies were planning to rob the motel. As far as I knew, three punks out of Glendale were going to do a smash-and-grab. Rumor is the hotel doesn't like banks, so they keep all their cash in a safe onsite."

No one liked banks anymore. Outside of one or two holdouts, they'd all closed up shop and fled. When the demons came, looting and robbery were the norm. Every-thing nowadays was cash or barter.

I glanced over to the motel office. "Do you think maybe the desk manager is a shifter, and he defended himself when the robbery went down?"

"Then why kill the Vultures?" Telaney nudged one with her toe. "And why are the bodies out here in the parking lot? I would have expected to find them closer to the office, or even *inside* the office."

I shrugged. "The shifter manager sprouted claws and fangs, these guys took off, and he chased them down?

Although you're right, I can't see why he'd stick around and kill the Vultures."

A loud bang rang across the parking lot, making me grab for my gun. A second bang sounded, and I realized the noise was coming from the office.

"Maybe we should just get out of here," Telaney whispered.

We should, but I was curious. It was a failing of mine. Clearly any guests staying here knew better because no one opened any of the room doors, or even pushed curtains aside to look out the window. I, on the other hand, pulled my pistol and made my way to the office.

Two more bang noises rang out, along with a stream of curse words. I hugged the wall and peered through the window. There was another body, crumpled up like a wad of used Kleenex, and on the floor next to a display stand with brochures of local tourist sites. The old-fashioned cash register was open and lying on the floor next to the body, the metal dented and twisted. More banging and cursing enabled me to pinpoint that the noises were coming from a small room behind the desk—one I assumed would have been for storing guests' luggage as well as the hotel safe.

Bang. Bang.

Telaney moved up beside me, ducked down low, then took a peek inside before ducking down once more.

"Anyone who had the strength to break five men in half isn't someone I want to meet," she muttered.

"I think he's trying to break into the safe. With his fists, from the sound of it." I edged a few steps closer to the open door.

"More power to him." Telaney reached up and tugged on my shirt. "Let's go, before he decides to come out here and kill us."

An enormous crash sounded from the back room. I began to see the wisdom of Telaney's words.

She got in her car and left, saying she'd call me if she caught word of another job. I started my bike, but instead of going home, I drove around the back of one of the million closed and abandoned bank buildings next door, hid my bike, and snuck around the side to watch the trashed motel. I wasn't there long before a figure emerged from the office. I couldn't see the man clearly enough to recognize him if I saw him again, but I was surprised that someone so short and slight had managed to kill six people with his bare hands.

He stuffed two bags into the backseat of a car, then fumbled around in his pockets for a moment before pulling out his keys. The guy seemed really agitated. A normal robber probably *would* be anxious, trying to grab and go before the cops came or he got caught. But no cops would be responding for a while, and only then because there were bodies on the ground. And any man who'd snapped six people's bones like toothpicks shouldn't be acting like he was nervous about someone catching him.

I squinted, watching the guy carefully as he got into his car and left. Shifter? Demon? Or something else? The broken bodies were making me think shifter, but I couldn't overlook the similarity between this scene and the one between Big Studio Guy and the Palisades Militia. Bullets had freaking bounced off his skin, and although shifters healed quickly, they didn't have bulletproof skin. I'd ended up thinking he was some sort of demon. Was this guy the same?

No one else appeared, so I left my bike hidden behind the old bank and went to check things out. First stop was the office, where the manager still lay dead next to the rack of brochures, the twisted cash register beside him. The room in the back was trashed, drywall and splintered framing lumber everywhere. There was a giant hole in the wall where the safe had once been, the pieces of metal tossed on the floor.

So…robbery was the motive? And the man had just taken out the competition, Vultures and all? Killing the manager seemed kind of extra, but maybe the guy had tried to shoot the robber. From what Telaney had said, the contents of that safe were probably worth the body count.

I grabbed the master-key from the lanyard around the manager's broken neck and went to check out the rest of the motel. Popping my head into each of the twenty rooms, I saw nothing besides cheap fiberboard furniture and ratty bedspreads. No guests. That explained the complete lack of response to all the noise of the fight and coming from the office during the robbery.

I returned the pass card to the dead manager, figuring whoever came in for the next shift would need it. Crime scene clean up had become a booming business in LA after the demons had arrived. They'd just call in a guy with a truck, throw a couple of Benjamins his way, then be back in business in a couple of hours.

Wiping the sweat from my forehead, I went to head back to my bike, only to make a quick detour through the lot to where the robber's car had been parked. Fresh oil glistened on the blacktop, making me think that guy was going to need to spend some of his stash on auto repair. A crumpled chip bag and an empty soda can lay near where he'd shoved the bags of money into the back seat. I nudged the bag with my foot and saw the glint of brown glass. Bending down, I picked up the object.

It was an empty vial—a small, unlabeled drug vial with a rubber-stopper cap.

I rolled it between my fingers, immediately recognizing it as the exact same sort of vial the woman in the market had dropped.

CHAPTER 17

I slid the vial I'd picked up from outside the motel across to Detective Juke.

She stuffed another spoonful of grits in her mouth, then picked the bottle up using a napkin. "Yeah, this looks like the same bottles in evidence from the woman who got killed at the market yesterday."

I'd told Juke I'd been there. I hadn't told her I lifted the full bottle of drugs before the cops had arrived, leaving the empty ones that were now in evidence on the floor. For some reason, I was reluctant to hand that bottle over.

"I looked into that case," she continued. "There was no rush on anything. Hell, we didn't even assign a detective to it other than to sign off on the paperwork. But if the stuff we found with her is the same as this from the motel massacre this morning? I'm absolutely fast-tracking the labs, just in case."

"Was she a shifter?" I asked. "Lindsey Allen?"

Juke shrugged. "We don't really have any way of telling unless they change form right in front of us. I glanced over the notes. The responding officer notified the family and went ahead and took their statements. When I talked to him right before I left, he said the family seemed sad, but a bit resigned. They were proud of her. They made some comment about Lindsey sacrificing herself for the family and the neighborhood."

"She drew the short straw," I mused, thinking of the woman's words.

"It's a shitty world. People step up. Drug addict or not, her family *should* be proud if she was doing something to help them all." Juke added another pat of butter to her grits. "I recognize the neighborhood, though. They had a real demon problem a few months back. Shit getting stolen. People getting nabbed or killed. Right in broad daylight."

"It would explain why she was so paranoid about demons," I commented.

"And maybe why she turned to this stuff." Juke pointed at the vial. "Either way, the neighborhood somehow managed to resolve their demon problem. There haven't been any reported attacks in the last three weeks."

Lindsey Allen and the motel robber/murderer. I was beginning to doubt my initial thought that they were shifters. Two humans. Two people on drugs. Two very different people, doing very different things with the super-strength that I was beginning to think this drug gave them.

And then there was one more person I suspected fell into this category.

"Don't forget about Big Studio Guy," I reminded her.

Juke frowned. "The detective on that Palisades Militia case questioned Joshua Van Marten, but didn't get far. There were no survivors in that incident, outside of you and your Vulture friend, who I'm sure aren't going to testify."

I snorted. "Uh, no. We're not."

She nodded. "Doesn't matter. The guy's on camera killing

everyone, but his lawyer claims it's a demon that copied his form."

I wouldn't put it past a demon to waltz up and kill a bunch of people just for grins, but BSG had motive. "He had his wife murdered for cheating on him. This was retaliation for the Palisades Militia bombing his limo."

Juke sighed. "He denies he was involved in his wife's death, and he's got an alibi. He also has an alibi for the Militia slaughter, but it's bogus. The final nail in our case's coffin is that the camera footage is clearly someone with super strength, whose skin is seemingly bulletproof. The guy has never been able to pick up anything heavier than a bag of rice in his life, and had a minor bullet wound two years ago, so clearly, he's not bulletproof."

I pointed to the vial. "The other two cases have this in common. I'm betting Big Studio Guy was on the same stuff. It's a drug. It's in your system, then it's out. I'll bet if you catch the motel killer, he'll be just a normal human. It's the drug that's making them superhuman."

Juke scooped the vial into an evidence bag along with the napkin and sealed it up. "Maybe. I'll admit it does seem more than a coincidence. I'll get this to the lab, see what they say about Lindsey Allen's tox screens, and go from there. But Van Marten…that's not gonna happen. The guy's got a good lawyer and money enough to buy his way through the system. As long as this feud between him and the Palisades Militia doesn't escalate, then the whole thing will get swept under the rug. I don't like it, but I've got so many cases on my desk that I can't spend too much time being pissed off about this one."

I continued to eat my grits. I'd done my civic duty—for once in my life, anyway. I'd turned in the one vial, and I'd told Juke my suspicions. Maybe it would help her find the guy who'd killed all those people at the motel. Maybe it would help whatever detective was on the Palisades Militia case. I didn't see where it would help Lindsey Allen, though. Poor woman. Paranoid. Violent. Were they side effects of the drug, or what made her turn to the drug? She'd said she'd drawn the short straw. The neighborhood had been plagued by demons. Her family was proud of her sacrifice.

Maybe she hadn't turned to drugs to cope, but to help. She volunteers to take this drug and go after the demons that plagued her neighborhood. And then she's a hero.

A dead hero.

Still, I could understand her motivations and her sacrifice. Take a drug, and suddenly be able to face down and even kill demons. Take a drug and single-handedly kill competing robbers, two Vultures, and a motel manager, then rip a safe out of the wall and get away with a ton of money. Take a drug and slaughter a dozen militia armed to the teeth. That was a mighty powerful drug, side effects aside. One person on this drug was formidable.

An entire gang on this drug could rule the city, the county, probably all of New Hell.

Fuck.

Anton and Tape had been working on a drug deal, one that Anton claimed would change everything, that would put humans back in charge—specifically the Gray Dogs.

The people at the gas station were talking about fighting for Aries.

What if Aries wasn't a *person*? What if Aries was the name of this drug?

CHAPTER 18

I stared at my ringing phone, not recognizing the number. Normally I would have just let it go to voicemail, since most of these calls were someone with dire warnings about my vehicle's expiring warranty, or a message telling me I needed to return an important call from the IRS.

For some reason, I decided to answer this one.

"We've got your boy, Anton," a deep, masculine voice said. "Meet us at the platinum parking lot at the stadium in two hours. Drive all the way to the back of the lot and wait there. We'll hand him over to you, but only you. Bring anyone else, and we'll kill him. Do not bring his brother. Don't send his brother instead of you. Only you, or he's dead."

The call disconnected.

First, how the hell had this guy gotten *my* number? The only one I'd given it to was Shavonne to give to her contact, and she was supposed to tell him that I was looking for Tape.

Fuck. Her contact must have spoken to Tape and put two and two together. Did the Disciples really have Anton? Or was this just a ploy to get me down there so Tape could enact some revenge? They clearly knew about Sebastian, knew Anton's connection with the Gray Dogs. The first time they'd grabbed him, they'd just beaten him up and let him go. Had Anton gone back for revenge, gotten caught, and inadvertently revealed who his brother was? But if that were the case, then I would have expected they'd want *Sebastian* down there and not me.

My finger hovered over Sebastian's number, but I hesitated.

Hoping Anton was home safe, and this was Tape just being a dick, I sent Sebastian a quick text. He replied immediately that he still hadn't heard from his brother, and that he was going to wring his neck once he showed up.

If he showed up, I thought.

Sebastian knew as well as I did that if his brother had gone back to the Disciples with some idea of revenge, then this time he probably would wind up dead.

The only thing that made sense was that Tape and some of his buddies had Anton, and the screwup nephew of a high-level Disciple wanted a payback against me more than he wanted to stir up shit with the Gray Dogs. Tape probably figured he and a few friends could manage to kidnap me, and teach me a lesson. He wouldn't fare so well if Sebastian came down there with a few of his heavy hitters. He'd get some revenge on me, send me and Anton—if he was still alive— back to the Valley battered and bruised, and not be the guy who started a gang war.

My finger hovered over Sebastian's number for a second, but then I put the phone down. If I told him what was going on, he'd insist on handling it himself, and then there really *would* be a gang war. He'd had me go down to Inglewood and ask around for his brother, but there is no way he'd sit back and let me meet with the Disciples and negotiate for his release.

So, the smartest course was just not to tell him until after I'd done it.

I still wanted someone to know what I was about to do, though. I picked up my phone again, and this time scrolled to Bishop's number. Would I ask him for help? Just give him a heads-up that I was going to probably get my ass kicked by some gang members? Shit, I really didn't want Bishop to know that. And I didn't want him thinking I couldn't handle my own business. I'd needed his help to find Nevarra. I'd needed his help to track down the cop who'd set me up. He'd rescued my ass when Fixers had drugged me outside Suerte, rescued my ass when I went off the side of a high-rise downtown.

He said he'd be there if I truly needed him, if it were a life-or-death situation. I needed to have faith in that, and stop running to him to fix my problems. If I was ever going to have a relationship of equals with this guy, I couldn't be some fucking damsel.

A relationship of equals. With a millions-of-years-old angel. Right. Even so, I wasn't going to call Bishop.

So I called someone else.

"Hey," Telaney picked up on the first ring. "You got wind of a job?"

"If only," I said—and then I told her about the phone call I'd received.

"Think it's a hoax?" she asked.

I shrugged, even though she couldn't see the gesture. "It could be. Tape strikes me as the kind of guy who'd want to get back at me. In spite of his uncle, he's near the bottom of the food chain with the Disciples, but he must have a friend or two he could rope into participating in an ambush."

"Sounds plausible," she commented. "What do you think the odds are that they actually have him?"

"Fifty-fifty? Tape flipped on Anton, and the Disciples beat

him up. He hasn't come home yet, or called his brother. I'm guessing he's still down there. Either he made a move and they grabbed him, or Tape is lying."

"Shit." Telaney went silent for a few seconds. "You go down there, you're gonna get your ass beat or worse, whether or not they have this Anton guy. And if they know he's connected to the Gray Dogs, he's probably dead whether you show up or not. I'd blow it off. Screw that kid. He got himself into this mess. No sense in you getting any more caught up in it than you already are. No ex is worth that crap, even if he was the best lay you ever had."

"He wasn't," I assured her.

And she wasn't wrong, either. I'd done a favor for Sebastian, but even he wouldn't want me doing this. I had no obligation to go to Inglewood and pull Anton's ass out of the fire. Hell, they probably didn't even have him.

But what if they did?

What if this was Nevarra or Sadie?

I didn't want Sebastian to lose his brother. I didn't want his mother to have to bury her son. Life was precarious, and death an all too familiar visitor, but that didn't mean I could sit back and do nothing about it. Sebastian and I had history. We may not have a present or a future, but that history meant he mattered—he'd always matter. And those he loved mattered, too.

And more to the point, there was the drug Aries that was now showing up on the streets. Aries connected the massacre at the hotel, the woman at the market, Big Studio Guy. And Anton. He and Tape had worked on a business deal about Aries, and I had a bad feeling that drug was going to make things worse, not just for Anton, but for all of us.

I sighed, really wanting to say "no" to this whole thing. If it was Tape, I could take him. I was pretty sure I could take him and his friends as well. I would just have to do it in some way that didn't end with the Disciples tracking me down to avenge their boy—which meant I couldn't kill him or his friends.

That would be the hard part. My electrical magic was kind of uncontrolled as far as voltage or wattage or whatever. And although I was a good shot, there was no guarantee someone wouldn't bleed out before they got medical attention.

But I had to help Sebastian's brother. And I had to find out what was really going on with this drug.

"You're gonna do it, aren't you?" Telaney's voice was accusing, and at the same time, resigned.

"Yeah." And when I was done and returned to the Valley, I'd tell Sebastian everything and put it all back in his lap. This was it. One last time to put my neck out for him and his idiot brother.

One last time.

Even I didn't believe that.

"You need back-up?" Telaney asked. "I know the caller said come alone, but they always say that. I'm pretty good at hiding. And I've got a decent rifle for sniper work."

I was tempted, but the caller had known Anton was part of the Gray Dogs. Sniping Tape and his boys would start that gang war I was really trying to prevent.

"No, I'll be fine," I told her.

She snorted.

"No, really." I was a little offended at Telaney's lack of faith in my abilities. "Come on. I've handled a lot of shit in the last few months. Gangs. Militia. Bounty hunters. Demons. If Tape really has Anton, I'll get him out of there. If it's a trap, I'll get out."

She sighed. "So, who do you want me to call if you don't show up by midnight?"

I thought for a second. Not Sebastian. Bags wouldn't be

able to help. Neither would Juke. And I was trying not to run to Bishop for every little thing. That left one other person.

"A shifter friend of mine named HB. I'll send you her contact info as well as the phone number that the guy called from. If I don't text or call you before eight tomorrow morning, then get in touch with her and tell her everything."

"Midnight," Telaney countered. "I'm not waiting until morning. You could be dead by then."

I could be dead by midnight, but I wasn't going to remind her of that. "Okay, midnight it is. Thanks, Telaney."

"You're welcome," she grumbled. "Be careful, Eden. Don't make me and this shifter woman have to come down there and rescue you."

CHAPTER 19

By the time I made it down to Inglewood, the setting sun had painted the sky a gorgeous mixture of orange and gold. To the east, the colors faded to violet and gray. I paused at the side of the road to take it all in, thinking how much the colors reminded me of the angel's feather I had at home.

I wanted to get to the meeting spot early, so I didn't linger. Turning into the lot, I rode slowly to the back. The stadium loomed two lots over, shading the parking areas to the east with its bulk. I'd never been to any of the football games back when the stadium was actually used as a stadium. Actually, I hadn't been here afterward either. I'd certainly seen the five-billion-dollar venue on TV, but the small screen didn't truly convey the sheer size of this thing. The actual football field was a postage stamp when compared to the nearly one-hundred-thousand-person seating capacity of the stands.

Originally, it was earthquake resistant, heated, cooled, with internet, with a giant, double-sided video scoreboard. It was surrounded by plazas and retail stores, and enough parking that every one of those hundred-thousand attendees could drive separately.

And now it was a giant, domed dump used to house building rubble from downtown.

In the lot were a few cars scattered here and there, some of which looked like they might have been here for a while. The closer lot was packed. If I had to guess, it looked like hundreds of vehicles parked near the entrance, or maybe more. I wasn't sure what that many people were doing here. The retail shops had closed years ago, and there shouldn't be anything left to loot in the stadium. I couldn't imagine why that many people would want to go and stare at bent, rusty rebar sticking out the sides of huge concrete chunks.

At the back of the platinum lot—where I was supposed to meet the anonymous caller—was a white panel van. It was the sort of thing serial killers were supposed to drive, so I circled around it, tensed and ready any moment to hit the throttle and get the hell out of here if anyone jumped out.

I couldn't see anyone in the driver's or passenger's seat of the van, so I parked fifty feet away and took in my surroundings.

Outside of the van and the few scattered vehicles, there was nowhere to hide. I felt terribly exposed and not particularly reassured that the somewhat empty parking lot meant I'd see any attackers coming long before they reached me. There was that damned van, and I was well aware that a sniper could take me out from any of these cars, or even from the stadium itself.

I'd super-healed from a gunshot wound before, but that took time, and if someone was trying to fill me full of bullets, I wouldn't have hours or even a day to recover. I wished I had instant super-healing. I wished I was bulletproof like that crazy Big Studio Guy had been. But even super-healing wouldn't help me if someone hit me with a head shot.

I shook out my arms and breathed deep, not wanting to think about that right now. Once more I checked the Glock in the shoulder holster as well as the Smith and Wesson 1911 in another holster on my left hip. If that wasn't enough, there was my little 43 in an ankle holster. I didn't have any weapons in hand, because I was still hoping this would just be a parlay, a negotiation for Anton's ransom. But I was a quick draw, and I wasn't taking any chances.

The time for the meeting came and went. The shadows from the stadium had stretched long and were slowly edging closer through the parking lots like a living beast. I eyed the van once more, thinking I'd give these guys another half an hour, then I was getting the hell out of here.

Maybe this had been a hoax, a set up by Tape to enact some retribution for my running him down yesterday. Maybe he'd solicited a few other Disciples for help, and they'd talked him out of it. Maybe he'd cooled down and decided ambushing and beating the crap out of a woman wasn't a good look for him. Maybe the call had been legit, but Anton had escaped and there was nothing for them to bargain.

Or he'd died, and there was nothing left to bargain.

I started my bike, deciding to drive around a bit before leaving, just in case the idiots were waiting in a different part of the lot from what they'd told me. As I drove past the white van, I saw a movement out of the corner of my eye. Before I could gun the bike, I heard a pop noise, and two electrodes hit my thigh, barbs sinking clean through my jeans and into flesh.

The electricity surged through me. Instead of falling off the bike in a convulsing mess like any other human would have done, I spun the motorcycle around to a stop perpendicular to my attacker, grabbed the Taser wires, and shot a stream of electricity backward into the gun.

It exploded in a shower of sparks. I yanked the electrodes from my leg, kicked the stand, and jumped off. Pulling the Glock out of my shoulder holster, I shot the guy beside the one with the Taser. Two others returned fire from elsewhere, and I crouched behind what little shelter my bike provided.

I realized immediately that bullets would go right through this thing, and that one penetrating the gas tank wouldn't be good. Deciding to risk myself over my bike, I jumped up and ran, diving behind a dusty Mustang convertible. Bullets pinged off the metal, one ripping through the soft top, and another shattering the glass. I pulled the 1911 and cowered behind the car, trying to gauge how many shooters there were. I was pretty sure Taser guy and his buddy were down if not dead, and I'd only seen two others jump out of the van, but that didn't mean there weren't more.

The gunfire ended, my ears ringing in the silence. Silence wasn't good. It meant I didn't know where these guys were. It also meant they were probably regrouping and figuring out how to flush me out from behind this car.

I didn't have any options. In the wide-open space of the parking lot, they could shoot me or run me down with the van before I managed to get out of here. I was going to need to shoot my way out of this Wild West style.

Just before the van started up, I heard the sound of another vehicle approaching. It might just be some rando driving through the stadium parking lot to meet a dealer or find a spot for some car sex, but I doubted it. These guys were going to use the vehicles to surround me, to herd me where they wanted me to go, then to take me out.

They'd initially hit me with a stun gun, which gave me hope that at least they seemed to want to take me in alive. Not that being grabbed alive would be all that wonderful.

Knowing I needed to make a decision and do something, I sprang up from behind the Mustang and opened fire. I managed to hit the one guy sneaking up on me from the side, but I missed the second one, and his return fire made me dive back down behind the car. The tires on the van squealed. I jumped up again, but a bullet slammed into my left shoulder. I spun sideways, dropping the 1911 from numb fingers, and continuing to shoot with the Glock in my right hand.

I'd expected the van to come around behind the Mustang and trap me, but instead it rammed the convertible. I tried to jump out of the way, but I wasn't fast enough. The car slammed into me, and I flew backward, smacking hard into the pavement as I landed. The pistol clattered from my hand and slid across the ground.

I jumped up, pain nearly dropping me back to the ground. I dove for the gun, only to have it kicked away from me.

Someone tackled me, and I saw white as pain shot through me.

I'd had the courtesy of flipping Tape over when I'd pulled this move, but my assailant clearly wasn't taking any chances. They also had to have weighed over two hundred pounds—at least that's what it felt like having them sitting on my back.

I tried to twist and buck the guy off, but he was too damned heavy—or I was too injured.

"Hold still," a voice growled.

A hand shoved my face against the pavement, then I felt my arms twisted behind my back and secured. The agony in my shoulder and chest took my breath away, and I nearly passed out. The weight came off my back, replaced by a foot as I tried to scramble up to make a run for it.

Once my captor had tied my ankles, the foot came off my back and a hood went over my head.

I felt myself yanked to my feet.

I blacked out for a few seconds, coming around to feel myself being tossed into what I assumed was the back of the van. I didn't think my body could hurt any more than it did right now.

The van started up again. I felt it move and begin to pick up speed. The thing hit every pothole, and I bounced around the van, finally passing out again as my injured shoulder smashed into something hard.

CHAPTER 20

I woke up to darkness. It took me a few seconds to realize the hood was still over my head. I could see some light from under the bottom edge of the dark fabric. I was seated, tied to a wooden chair in addition to the restraints on my hands and feet. Someone had slapped duct tape over my mouth while I'd been unconscious.

I wiggled my fingers and toes, testing the limits of the restraints and trying to figure out if my super-healing had kicked in yet. I definitely felt like I'd been hit by a car, but that was an improvement over how I'd felt when I was bouncing around inside the back of that van. My right shoulder and right hip ached from where I'd hit the pavement. My ribs and hip on the left ached from where the Mustang had slammed into me. My left shoulder where I'd been shot felt…fine?

How the hell could I heal gunshot wounds easier than bruises? Not that I was complaining. I'd take bruises over a gunshot wound any day.

The hood came off my head, and I blinked as my eyes adjusted to the sudden light. I was in a room with three men.

One guy stood to the right of me, holding the hood in one hand and a bat in the other. Another guy was to my left, also holding a bat. Across from me sat a musclebound bald guy with tattoos who I immediately recognized. He had a pistol in his hand, finger hovering over the trigger.

Piers.

A trickle of fear ran through me. Had he recognized me as well? How much did he know? Could I manage to get out of this with just a smackdown and a warning not to mess with the Disciples, or was I going to pay for the deaths of the gang members in the customs warehouse that I'd killed two months ago?

Or was he going to hand me over to Desiree? Detective Juke had said the demon had stopped her human trafficking operation with the Disciples, but that didn't mean Desiree didn't have other business with the gang.

But Desiree was the one who had claimed responsibility for the dead in the customs warehouse. Maybe the Disciples had stopped doing business with *her*. Maybe they believed she'd been the one killing their people two months ago, and they hadn't connected me at all to that incident.

"I got a call yesterday from a pawnbroker down in Torrance," Piers said, his voice frighteningly calm. "She told me some woman was looking for Tape. Wanted to know where she could find him."

Piers stood up, still facing me, finger still hovering over the trigger of his pistol.

I had a feeling about where this was going, and it wasn't to a good place.

"Tape is a fuckup, but he's a Disciple and his uncle is an important guy, so I ignored her call. I figured a woman looking for Tape was some personal shit I didn't want to be involved in. Then that evening I hear a story going around about some woman showing up at the school claiming Tape knocked her up. The other guys claim they went outside, that she chased him down the street, and when Tape came back in, he was pissed as hell and looking like someone had dragged him six blocks behind a car. The guys teased him about it all, and he claimed it wasn't him that got this woman preggers, but some asshole from the Valley who he'd had dealings with."

He walked up to me, grabbed the edge of the duct tape, and yanked it off my mouth. It hurt almost as much as getting shot.

Piers recognized me. I could tell from the way he was looking at me that he knew I was the same woman as "Andrea"—whom he'd sent to the customs warehouse for an interview the night every guard in the warehouse died a violent death.

"None of this shit is my business," Piers continued. "So, I kept my nose out of it until I got a call early this morning. Tape and eight guys are all dead, killed at the school where they were unloading and re-boxing a shipment late last night."

I licked my lips, sticky and raw from the tape, thinking that Anton had gotten himself into a whole lot of trouble. Killing nine guys? Nine Disciples? What the hell was he thinking?

Anton was either dead, and they wanted to know what I had to do with him, or they somehow thought I was the one involved in this massacre. It was more likely that Anton was alive, and they were going to use me to bring him in.

Little did they know that having me wouldn't bring Anton in.

"I didn't kill them," I told Piers. "I just wanted information from Tape on where this other guy was. I got my information and went home. It wasn't me who killed him and the others."

I had neighbors that would be my alibi, because they seemed to know every time I so much as sneezed when I was home. But would Piers give a rat's ass if I had an alibi or not?

"We know who killed them because there was a witness that got away." Piers loomed over me. "So I sat there, thinking that although I might not be able to find Anton, I do have the number of his knocked-up girlfriend that was trying to track him down through Tape. I figure if I get her, I can get Anton. Either the guy's gonna come rescue his girl, or she'll help me find him, with a little encouragement, that is."

I squirmed, because being tortured for information on Anton wasn't much better than being tortured because Piers thought I might have something to do with the dead guys in the customs warehouse.

Piers stepped closer and put the muzzle of the gun against my head. "But then something interesting happened. I don't like going into things without all the information, so I looked at the security tape from the school, trying to get an idea of what this pregnant girl-friend of Anton's looked like. Then low and behold, I saw *you*. Andrea Delgado. But your name isn't really Andrea Delgado, is it?"

He paused, staring at me as if he was expecting an answer. And because he had a gun at my head, I answered, "No. It's not."

He nodded. "I called Shavonne back, started asking some questions about you all polite-like. And she didn't figure anything was wrong, so she answered those questions. Eden Alvaro. Licensed Vulture. From the Valley. You've had an interesting few months, Eden Alvaro."

I took a careful breath, very aware of the gun pressed against my temple.

"I started thinking there was more to what happened last night than just some hothead wanting revenge for a beating, and you're not just some pregnant girlfriend trying to track down the father of her kid."

Shit. I needed to figure out a way to talk my way out of this situation before they killed me.

"I didn't have anything to do with what went down last night between Anton and Tape and those other guys," I told Piers. "I swear to God, I was not involved in that at all. Anton is the little brother of an ex-boyfriend. He went dark a few days ago, wouldn't answer texts or calls. My ex was worried he'd gotten himself into trouble, and he asked me to help."

The guy to my right snorted. "Damn right he got himself into trouble."

"What kind of pansy goes crying to his ex-girlfriend for help when his brother goes missing?" the guy on the left said.

I ignored them, focusing on Piers instead. "I swear to you all I did was come down here and ask around. I ran Tape down and got some info on where Anton might be. Then I went to his hotel room, left him a note to call his brother, and went home."

Piers scowled. "Right. I wouldn't go to all this trouble to find an ex's brother."

"Wouldn't you?" I met his eyes. "Someone you'd dated when you were in high school? Someone you think about now and then and wonder if things would have been different if you'd not broken up with them and keyed up their car?"

"You keyed the guy's car?" Right-Guy shook his head. "Damn. That's brutal."

"I'm guessing this ex is an accountant or something," Left-Guy sneered. "So yeah, your life would have been different. Three kids. A Prius in the driveway. Really shitty sex life."

Whatever. I'd rather they think Sebastian was some pencil pusher than realize Anton was connected to the Gray Dogs.

"Yeah. I'd probably help my high school sweetheart if she asked," Piers admitted. "But we've still got a problem here, honey. Your ex's little brother killed nine of my guys and is in the wind. And that sounds eerily like what happened at the customs warehouse that night I sent you down there for an interview, *Eden*."

I shut my mouth, my brain working double-time trying to think of an explanation for what went down at the warehouse. Desiree had claimed responsibility for the deaths, but it was clear Piers had his doubts.

"Leave," Piers commanded.

For a second, I thought he meant me. The two other guys must have been equally confused because they exchanged puzzled looks.

"Out." This time Piers faced one, then the other, scowling.

They shrugged and left, closing the door behind them and leaving me alone with Piers. He still had that gun pointed to my head, and I was on the edge of panic, thinking I was about to die.

Come on Bishop. You better show up before he pulls the trigger.

Then the gun left my temple. Piers took a step back, lowering the pistol to his side. "What happened that night? What really happened that night at the customs warehouse?"

"I got there, and no one answered the door," I lied. "So, I left and drove home."

"And you didn't call me back to double check the appointment and location?" Piers's eyebrows rose. "Or to bitch at me about wasting your time, making you haul all the way to the airport from the Valley? That doesn't sound like the badass I met, Eden."

I took a breath, keeping an eye on his pistol. "Okay, okay. The place was unlocked when I got there, so I went in. I found everyone dead and a cougar running loose around the place."

"Interesting how a cougar both mauled the guards and shot them." Piers walked over to a table and picked up my 1911. "I recognize this gun. And I'm pretty sure the bullets that killed at least two of those guards came from this weapon."

Fuck. I'd kept Soprano's gun and been stupid enough to bring it here to a meeting where I knew there was a chance I'd been jumped by the Disciples. I was such an idiot.

"I found it on the floor," I said. "I'm a licensed Vulture. I take what I find. The guards were all dead when I got there. A cougar was running around the place. I heard some yelling, and opened a door and found a bunch of kids in there, so I let them out."

Something flickered in Piers's dark brown eyes. Sympathy, colored with a hint of disgust, maybe? He walked back over to me and stood.

"Desiree said the kids were gone when she got there, and that's why she killed the guards." Piers holstered his pistol. "That's the opposite of what you're saying."

"Demons lie," I reminded him.

He pointed to a corner of the room. I spotted my motorcycle helmet—his motorcycle helmet—and I nearly growled in frustration. Could this situation go any more to shit?

"That's my helmet. You stole my fucking bike helmet right after you met with me at the In-N-Out. Stole. My. Helmet." He snarled. "You steal. That means you also lie. You've got one last chance to tell me the truth. One. Lie again, and I'll have my guys beat the truth out of you."

I took a deep breath and met his eyes once more. The truth. The truth might get me killed, but clearly lies were going to as well.

"I've got two little sisters—foster sisters," I told him. "One of them got grabbed by the Fixers, and they sold her to the Disciples to traffic. I knew what was going to happen if I didn't get to her in time, so I lied to you. And when I got to the customs warehouse for my interview, I killed those guys, and set all the kids free. I lied. I killed. I did everything I could to get my sister back."

This time I was pretty sure it was respect that flickered across Piers's face.

"There *was* a cougar loose in the place," I continued. "I took that gun. I set the kids free. I did what I needed to do to find my sister and bring her home."

"And my helmet?" Piers asked.

"Someone stole mine," I admitted. "I didn't know it was yours when I took it. I just saw a helmet sitting on a bike, and I needed one."

"It was a brand-new helmet," he growled. "I like that helmet. And it was sitting there on the bike because *no one* has the balls to steal from me, from a Disciple."

Evidently, I did.

"Sorry," I squeaked out, a little nonplussed that he seemed more pissed off about his helmet being stolen than about the killings at the customs warehouse or last night.

He glared at me for a few minutes, as if he wasn't sure whether he was going to shoot me or not.

"I did what I had to do," I repeated softly. "And I hoped I'd never see any of you again. But when my ex came to me for help… Anton is an idiot. I came down here, found Tape and encouraged him to get a message to Anton. Tape told me where he was staying, so I went to his hotel room and left a message for him to call his brother. Then I went home. I figured his side deal went bad, and that you all had taught him a lesson. I'd hoped he would have packed up and come home after that. I didn't know he was going to take a bunch of your guys out. I left the kid a message and went home. Next thing I know, I'm getting a phone call that you've got Anton and you want me to come down here and meet you by myself." I shrugged as best as I could, hogtied to a chair. "I figured you were going to discuss a ransom, not shoot me with a Taser, then try to fill me full of bullet holes."

"Fucking Taser malfunctioned." Piers rolled his eyes. "Piece of junk laid Bear out. Guy's probably got heart damage now."

I winced. I shouldn't feel guilty for zapping the guy, but I kind of did. They'd had nine of their own murdered the night before, and for all they knew, I was in on it.

"We need to find Anton." Piers's voice was stern. "The guy was poaching. We gave him a warning, and I considered the matter closed, but when he came back and killed nine of ours, then he as good as declared war."

I swallowed hard, knowing that they wouldn't rest until Anton had paid the price for what he'd done. And if he ran to the Valley to hide behind his brother, the Gray Dogs would find themselves in a war with the Disciples.

And I knew full well how that war was going to end.

"I don't know where he is, or how to contact him," I admitted. "I checked with his brother before I came down here to meet you, and he hasn't heard or seen from Anton. I'm assuming you already tossed his hotel room. I honestly don't know where else to look."

Piers scowled at me, his hand moving toward the pistol once more.

"Honest to God," I told him. "I haven't seen Anton in four years. Hell, I haven't seen my ex but twice in the last four years. I don't know who Anton's friends are, where he hangs out, or any of that. I'm not your ticket to finding him."

"See, I think differently. I think you *are* my ticket to finding Anton."

Piers pulled his phone out of his pocket, then turned it to show me a picture. One by one, he scrolled through grainy pics that must have been from the security cameras at the school. Then he showed me a video. A man I recognized from his resemblance to Sebastian was picking up tables and even a forklift, like they weighed all of ten pounds, tossing them through the air. Bullets bounced off the man. I watched as he scooped people up, snapped their limbs like twigs, then smashed them into the concrete walls with inhuman force.

Inhuman. And oddly reminiscent of what I'd seen Big Studio Guy do. And that crime scene at the motel in Pasadena.

"I'm doubting the guy is a shifter, because he wasn't fighting like this when we gave him that beatdown two nights ago," Piers informed me.

"That's got to be a recently acquired thing," I agreed. "Otherwise, he wouldn't have lost so many fights in middle school."

Piers stuck his phone back inside his pocket. "There's only one thing I know of that gives humans those kinds of abilities, and it doesn't come from a sorcerer."

Aries. The same drug Lindsey Allen was on, as well as the motel robber and Big Studio Guy. Aries.

Piers walked back over to the table and picked up a small vial. "I found this in your backpack. Is this what you used when you killed those guys at the customs warehouse? How many times have you fought in the arena?"

I stared at him, no idea what he was talking about. "There was a woman at the local market. She was strung out, bending metal racks and ranting about protecting us from demons and shit. The shopkeeper shot her. She had two empty vials on her, and that one as well. I picked it up."

"Because you're a licensed Vulture," he mocked. "You're telling me that you're not taking Aries? That you've never taken Aries?" He walked over and yanked the neck of my shirt to the side, poking my left shoulder. "You were shot. Bleeding. And now there's nothing but smooth, unblemished skin. You're either a shifter or on Aries. Which one is it, Eden?"

"Neither," I protested. "Up until a few days ago, I'd never heard of Aries. I'm a human. I'm not a shifter. And I'm not on that drug."

His eyebrows went up. "So, explain your healed gunshot wound."

"I…I'll admit I have some magic." No way I was going to get into the details of my possible parentage and abandonment with this guy.

He poked my shoulder once more, then walked back over to the table and put the vial back down. "I want the name of your mage. I'd pay some serious coin for a charm that does this."

I made some non-committal noise, hoping Mathias actually made healing spells since he was the only mage I knew.

Piers walked over to the door. "I'm going to give you some time to think about all this. When I come back in, we're going to talk further."

He left, letting the other two guys with the baseball bats back inside with me before closing the door hard behind him.

Talk further? I had no idea what else we had to talk about, but I was all for conversation if it would stall them further.

Midnight couldn't come soon enough. I needed Telaney and HB, and maybe even Bishop and Bob to get me out of this mess before I ended up with a bullet in my head.

had no idea how much time had passed while I sat there, bound to a chair, with two guys staring hard at me while they bounced one end of their baseball bats off their other palm. I knew they were itching to beat the crap out of me. I also knew they wouldn't touch me without Piers okaying it first.

It had to be getting close to midnight by now. How long would it take HB and Telaney to get together and drive down here? Once they got down here, how long would it take them to find me? Hopefully HB would bring Bob, and he could sniff my trail from the stadium parking lot to wherever the hell I currently was. Or maybe HB had the same tracking skills as Bob did. I didn't doubt a Cougar's super smelling abilities, but I didn't know if she'd be at the Bob level or not.

The door opened, but it wasn't my friends coming to rescue me. It was Piers. He held the door, ushering the two guys out. Then he walked forward to stand in front of me. He still had his pistol, but it remained in his holster, and I took some solace in that.

"Tell me what you know about Aries," he demanded.

I shrugged, thinking what I knew about the drug most likely wouldn't fill a thimble. "I don't know where to get it, who sells it, or anything. I've seen three people I believe were on the drug. They were violent, paranoid, manic. I'm not sure if that's from repeated use of the drug, if those are side effects or not. I don't know how long those behaviors last after the drug is out of their system, or if they become permanent with repeated use. I'd assumed Tape and Anton were putting together some kind of weapons deal. I didn't suspect that their business involved Aries until today."

Piers stared at me for a second, then pulled over a chair and sat facing me. "The demons supply it. I don't know if they make it themselves or have someone who does it for them. That's a tightly kept secret. The only reason I know about it is because those fucking demons are running some gladiator shit at the SoFi stadium and are using Aries as the prizes. Three weeks ago, I'd never heard of the stuff. Now there's a hundred or so people either selling their vial to the highest bidder, or taking it themselves."

"Gladiator shit?" I blinked in surprise. Suddenly the conversation I'd overheard at the gas station made sense. I'd thought when they said people were fighting for Aries that they were getting paid as mercenaries for a Disciple named Aries. In actuality, they were participating in a fight to win a vial of the drug.

"Yeah. Right in our own damned backyard." A muscle twitched in Piers's jaw. "They have humans fight shifters or demons in the stadium. If they survive, they walk out with a vial of Aries. There's an audience—a big paying audience. And the Disciples don't get a dime."

No wonder he was pissed. And no wonder Tape and Anton had put together some scheme on their own. How were they planning on getting their hands on enough Aries to either sell, or to juice up the entirety of the Gray Dogs?

Were they going to steal it? From the *demons*? Or were they planning on fighting in the arena for bottles one at a time? It didn't seem like the payoff would be worth the effort. And while I could imagine Anton fighting to win something of value, Tape didn't look like he could fight his way out of a paper bag.

"I don't know anything about fights in the stadium," I told Piers, just in case he was trying to pin that on me as well. "I'm from the Valley. I haven't been down here in years. Well, outside of the customs warehouse thing."

"Didn't figure you *did* know anything about it," he grumbled. "They've only been at it for three weeks. That's how we knew about Aries. None of us like that drug. None of us like the demons running gladiator games in our neighborhood either. We want them gone—especially if they're not going to give us our cut."

Their "cut" was seventy percent. I was pretty sure the demons wouldn't agree to that, but the Disciples didn't have the muscle to kick them out.

"I had to make a couple of calls, but I've got approval to offer you a deal," Piers told me.

"What kind of deal?" I eyed him. Any deal where I ended up walking out of here alive and relative unharmed was a deal I wanted to hear more about.

"You get in there, find out what the fuck is going on with the fight games and the Aries, and get information back to me on their setup, their strengths, and their weaknesses. Then you work with me to run the demons out of there. Out of the stadium, and out of Inglewood. In return, you get to walk out of here with your stuff."

I had committed to work for the tax demons, and to Desiree, and now this. Wasn't like I had much choice, though.

"One more thing," Piers added. "We're willing to not pursue Anton if you agree to this. If he steps foot in Inglewood again, or raises a hand against any Disciple, he's dead. But if he goes back to the Valley and stays off of our radar, we won't hunt him down."

I sucked in a breath. Now *that* was a deal. Anton had screwed up big-time. This was his one chance to get out of this mess alive. And all it costed was…me.

Me. Just like Sebastian, Piers wanted me sneaking in and doing reconnaissance. He didn't want to send in any of the Disciples and risk pissing off a bunch of demons who might decide to wipe his gang off the face of the earth.

Nope, me. I was, apparently, disposable to all of them.

"I'll get you information, but I don't know how I'm going to help you get rid of the demons and their gladiator contest," I cautioned him.

He smirked. "You single-handedly killed all those guys in the customs warehouse. And Shavonne told me about that fight at the rooftop bar of the hotel last month."

"I had a cougar helping me at the warehouse," I countered. "And as for that fight at the rooftop bar, I nearly died."

I didn't tell him that I'd been thrown off the building, because that would open up all sorts of inquiry about how I'd survived that kind of fall.

"Doesn't matter. Find out the info, and at the very least, I expect you to fight by our side if we have to drive the demons out by force."

I sighed. "Okay. I'm in."

He let the other two guards back in and watched as they untied me. My arms and legs were numb and stiff, and it took me a while to loosen them up enough to stand. I went to gather my stuff together, noticing that Piers had texted me his phone number.

"You've got forty-eight hours to check in," he warned me. "We know how to find you, and we will."

"I know."

I reached down to grab the helmet. His hand shot out and grabbed my wrist.

"That's *my* helmet," he informed me.

I wanted to tell him where he could stick the helmet. Instead, I jerked my arm away from him, strapped on my holsters, and grabbed my backpack. He and the other two guys walked me out the door. My bike was sitting outside in the parking lot. I looked around, recognizing that they'd taken me to the old school turned warehouse where I'd caught up with Tape—where Anton had killed nine people.

"Forty-eight hours," Piers reminded me.

"Forty-eight hours," I agreed.

Then I got on my bike, kicked it to life, and drove.

I wanted to put some miles between myself and the Disciples. And I needed to think about what I was going to do next.

CHAPTER 22

I pulled over before I got on the freeway and texted Telaney with minutes to spare. I wasn't surprised when I pulled into my driveway to find her car there, and my friend sitting on the porch steps waiting for me. She had a shopping tote next to her. I hoped it contained food.

"Your neighbors have been watching me," she said as I climbed the steps and got my keys out of my backpack. "I tried to look harmless, but I'm pretty sure they believed I was going to break in and steal stuff."

"You're lucky they didn't make you fight Dennis." I opened the door and Telaney followed me in.

She put the tote on the kitchen counter and shoo'd her hands at me. "Go shower and put on something clean. You want breakfast comfort food, or dinner comfort food?"

"You pick." I was tired and sore and wanted to just crawl into bed. But I wasn't getting in my clean sheets this filthy, and I knew that as exhausted as I was, all the stuff running through my brain wouldn't let me sleep, anyway.

I let Telaney take charge, trying to wash the horrible evening down the drain with the dirt and dried mud. I hadn't expected roses and wine, going down to Inglewood in response to that summons of a phone call, but I definitely hadn't expected to be shot, nearly crushed by a car, tied to a chair, and almost killed.

Clean and back in Bishop's shirt—I should probably wash the thing sometime soon—I followed my nose upstairs to see Telaney sliding an omelet onto a plate. She waved me over to the dinner table, and I sat.

I eyed my omelet, which looked like it had been cooked in a pound of butter. It was stuffed with pepper jack cheese, onions, diced tomatoes, and bacon. Telaney plopped down another plate of bacon, then went back into the kitchen. She returned with two mugs of coffee.

"Decaf," she informed me. "With a little something-something to help you get to sleep once you've eaten."

Whisky, from what I could smell. I took the mug and saw she'd added a big helping of whipped cream to the top, along with some chocolate shavings.

"We're celebrating," she told me. "Because you're not dead."

"I'll drink to that." I toasted her and took a long pull from the mug, licking the whipped cream off my top lip when I was done.

"You eat and drink, then you can update me about what went down afterward." She took a sip of her own coffee as I dug in. "Confession time. I know I wasn't supposed to call your shifter friend until midnight, but I was really worried, so I called her around ten."

I shoveled down a few bites of omelet before responding. "It's okay. Really. For a few moments there, I would have given anything for you guys to come crashing through the door. I was worried too."

She held up a hand. "You eat. Tell me later. Your friend HB is very nice, by the way. She said she didn't want to jump the gun, that you'd said midnight and she felt we should respect that. Didn't want to run in and screw up something you had going on. Gotta say, the woman really talked me off the ledge."

I was glad, although I honestly would have appreciated a rescue, sitting there with Piers's pistol jammed against my head.

"Still, she said she'd be ready. Said she'd have some tracking dog on standby, and be on the freeway within seconds if I texted her. She also reassured me that if shit really went bad, she could get there faster than driving."

Really? Could HB teleport as well as Bishop? Or had she meant that she'd prevail upon Bishop to teleport her to my location. Could he even do that?

I finished eating, then I got up to help Telaney with the dishes in spite of her protest. While we washed up, I told her about my night. Everything. Because I trusted Telaney just as much as I trusted Bags, Bea, and the girls, HB, and even Bishop.

"What's your next move?" Telaney turned around and leaned against the counter.

"Haul my sorry ass back down to SoFi stadium. Enroll to fight in their games. Find out everything I can. Hopefully survive. Leave with another vial of that Aries shit, and maybe a plan to help Piers get the demons out of the stadium and Inglewood."

Telaney snorted. "That Piers guy is the one on drugs if he thinks he can get the demons to do anything they don't wanna do."

I nodded in agreement, then reached over to my backpack and took out the vial of Aries that I'd picked up at the market where Lindsey Allen had died.

"You could sell it," Telaney commented. "And assuming

you make it out of the gladiator contest alive, then you'll have two. That stuff probably fetches a high price."

"Yeah," I mused. "It can't be impossible to win at those games, even fighting against shifters and demons. I mean, people are clearly getting out with prizes in hand. Big Studio Guy probably paid someone to fight for him, but they clearly won. Lindsey Allen had two empty vials and this one, so she'd either fought and won three times, or people in her neighborhood fought so they could give it to her. And the guy at the motel. And Anton. Hell, if Anton can survive fighting in an arena and walk out with a vial of this stuff, I should be able to do it without breaking a nail."

She arched an eyebrow at me.

"Okay, maybe I'd break a nail." I laughed.

Telaney chuckled and grabbed her tote. "I'm outa here. You get some sleep, and text me when you go down to do your battle arena stuff, okay? Let me know when I should call in the cavalry to come rescue you."

"I will." I walked her to the door. "And you can cook for me anytime."

She opened the door and turned to face me.

"This is not a regular thing." Telaney shook a finger at me. "It's only because I was afraid you were dead."

"I almost die a lot," I teased her. "Get ready to be making me meals a few times a week at a minimum."

"Right. Get some sleep. Clean your guns. And don't you die on me, Eden Alvaro. You're the best friend I've had in years. Don't you go dying on me."

"I won't," I promised. "I won't die."

CHAPTER 23

The demon at the ticket booth stared at me with solid black eyes. Her arms were covered in midnight blue scales and ended in something that looked more like raptor talons than fingers. Her lipless mouth pursed out, as if it were a tiny beak.

"You here to watch, or to fight?" she asked.

I tried not to stare at her mouth. Or her eyes. Or her talons. "Fight, I guess. I want to get some Aries. I was told this is the only place that distributes it?"

She nodded. "Only us, and we don't sell it. Fighters get a dose for their fight, depending on what sort of opponent they're facing. If they win, they get one more for the road. If they want any more than the one dose, they have to sign up to fight again."

"One vial? So, is this like a boxing match? An MMA fight?"

She shrugged. "Whatever. You don't get to pick. You get assigned a fight, and you either do it or you don't. But there's no Aries unless you fight."

"I can refuse?" I clarified. *That* didn't sound right. "If I agree, but change my mind, I can leave?"

The demon glared at me. "Uh, yeah. There's dozens of people lined up to fight for a dose as a prize. You don't wanna do it, then we don't care."

I frowned at her. "So what do you guys get out of this?"

She rolled her eyes. "Money. And entertainment. We're demons. We get bored, and *that's* no fun."

"Entertainment." I shouldn't have been surprised. Humans shelled out to watch exclusive pay-per-view boxing matches. They gathered for cock fights, and nothing drew a crowd like two guys duking it out on a street corner.

"That's why I'm here, genius." The demon sighed. "I sell tickets for the fights, and I send prospective fighters to the back to be interviewed, and either accepted or tossed out on their asses. We don't give two shits if you die. Actually, that sort of thing draws more of a crowd. But we only want people who are going to be entertaining when they win or die. Boring humans get tossed out."

If they weren't demons, they never would have gotten away with this. The Disciples ruled their territory with an iron fist. Shit, they ruled everyone else's territory with an iron fist as well. But the demons were running this show— demons that the Disciples fumed about, but that they didn't dare move on.

I was a little nervous that a certain demon who I was trying with all my might to avoid might be the brains behind this operation.

"I'll fight," I told her. "What do I need to sign or do to get in on this? Like tonight, if I can. I don't want to wait."

She snorted. "Like I have any input on who gets it. I'll sign you in. You'll interview. You'll fight. If you walk out of here alive, you'll get the drug. We don't care about anything else, just provide entertainment for our patrons, and you'll get your prize."

Anton had survived this. He'd fought and walked away with his Aries prize. Then he'd gone and killed a bunch of Disciples.

He had to have known that would put a price on his head. He would have wanted to get another dose to hold, just in case the Disciples tracked him down and he needed to be superpowered and bulletproof once more. I was betting he'd come back here to fight once more. But was he still here, waiting to fight, or had he done his bit and left this morning with his payment?

"Can I just walk in now, fight tonight, then leave directly afterward with a dose of Aries? Or do I need to get a date and a time to come back for my match."

She shrugged. "If you interview and they take you, you stay here. There's barracks the fighters stay in while they're waiting for the matches. Usually, your fight is scheduled for the same day, but sometimes it's the next day. Depends on how many we've got and what time the fighter gets here."

"Can I check the barracks? Walk around and see what's going on before I sign on?" I knew what her answer would be, but figured I'd try anyway.

"Nope. Only fighters and staff in the barracks." She stared at me with those unreadable black eyes. "So…you in? Or are you out?"

I was so not taking this drug, but it wouldn't be the first time I'd been in a fight, and it probably wouldn't be the last. I'd agreed to find out all I could for Piers, formulate a plan to dismantle this shit and get the demons out of Inglewood. I'd danced around this all I could, but it seemed there was no way for me to avoid fighting in this stupid game.

It would save Anton. And I'd made a deal with Piers. Yeah, he was a dangerous guy who was, unfortunately, one hundred percent the kind of man I usually went for. He'd also shoved a pistol at my head and maneuvered me into this mess. He didn't seem to give two shits whether I survived this or not. But I'd made a deal, and I had a really hard time reneging on that sort of promise.

I'd fight. I'd gather all the information I could. I'd fight beside Piers if I needed to. And if I survived, I'd walk out of here with a second vial of what was clearly a drug with a seriously large street value.

I could sell the Aries they gave me and add the profit to my savings. Win/win.

If I survived, that is.

Anton survived. If that arrogant, reckless shithead made it through this, then I could as well.

"I'm in," I told her.

I was, but there was no way I was taking that drug. I'd have to fight without it, which was going to suck. My super healing had kicked in and not only was the gunshot wound from last night completely gone, and my aches and pains from getting whacked with the car and bounced along the asphalt were as well, but that didn't mean I was up to fighting a shifter or even a demon. Dennis had kicked my ass when we fought, so I was pretty sure any other shifter was going to do the same.

The bird-demon pushed a button in the ticket booth. There was a loud buzz, and the gates to my right slid open. A bear with leathery wings and an insect head came around a concrete divider and stood by the gate.

I went in and followed him as we wordlessly wove our way through the closed concession area and down the steps past the stadium seats to where the football team locker room used to be. The demon opened a door to some sort of office and ushered me in. The door closed behind me, leaving me alone in what must have once been the manager's or coach's office. Huge action shots of guys in football gear decorated the walls. The desk had long claw marks across the top and a stack of folders on the left. I'm nosy, so I went over and looked through the folders. Some held lists of numbers. Others had old football schedules and play diagrams. I plopped them back on the desk and was just about to go through the drawers when the door opened and a man walked in—a man with curved ram's horns and vertical-slitted pupils in golden yellow irises.

The ram's horns were fitting, given that we were standing in a stadium where the LA Rams football team used to play.

The demon looked me up and down, a sulfurous curl of smoke coming from his nostrils. "You here to fight?"

My resolve wavered. "Maybe. I'd like some more information before I decide."

He rolled his weird goat eyes. "You're either here to fight, or you're not. If you're not, then get the hell out of here and stop wasting my time."

My last attempt to wiggle out of actually doing combat had failed. Guess it was time to buck up and get this over with.

"I'm here to fight," I told him. "Absolutely going to fight. But I just have a few questions first."

He sighed, the sound full of exasperation. "Of course, you do. I've got questions as well. I'll go first. Are you a shifter?"

"No, I'm a human. Am I fighting a shifter? Another human? How many am I supposed to fight?"

He waved my question away. "We don't know that until right before the fight begins. Are you sure you're not a shifter? You smell kinda funny."

I'd showered, and no one else had ever commented on me smelling weird, so I gave him the only explanation I could think of. "I'm pretty sure a bunch of my neighbors are shifters. Would it be a problem if I were a shifter? Are shifters not allowed to fight?"

"Shifters aren't allowed to fight for Aries. They aren't allowed to have Aries at all."

I frowned, wondering why. Would it kill them? Or would a juiced-up shifter be someone even a high-level demon would be afraid of?

"I only care that you're not a shifter," the demon continued, "and that you can put on a show. Have you ever been in a fight before? Like a fistfight, not some slappy-slappy on the playground bullshit."

I held my shirt away from my body, pointing to the holes, the caked-on dirt, and bloodstains that no amount of washing seemed to get out. I'd worn this beaten-to-crap outfit, thinking if I was going to ruin an outfit fighting in this arena, it might as well be the one that was on its way to the rag bin.

"This isn't exactly a fashion trend," I told him. "Yes, I've been in a fight before. Lots of times. I was just in one last night, to be exact."

He grunted. "We'll try to fit you in tonight, but if we don't, then you'll be the first fight tomorrow night. You fight until your opponent is knocked out or dead. You might get a dose of Aries before the fight, depending on what's on the agenda. Either way, you'll get a prize dose to take with you once you leave."

"Wait, wait." I held up a hand, as if I were back in grade school. "What if *I'm* the one that gets knocked out?"

He chuckled. "Then you fight a second time, and a third. You only get to leave with the drug if you've won. It won't be too hard if you're one of the ones who gets a shot of Aries before you go in. If you don't get the shot," he shrugged, "well, that's the risk you take signing up for this."

I frowned. "Will my opponent have a shot too?"

"Nope. I told you that shifters and Lows don't get Aries. That's who you're fighting, although sometimes the humans fight each other too. Idiots."

Anyone who signed up to do this was an idiot—which said a lot about me right now.

"What determines whether I get a shot going into the fight or not?" I asked. "Is it based on the skill level of who I'm up against? Or a flip of the coin?"

He shrugged. "Either. Whatever provides the best entertainment. Humans dying quick at the hands of some shifter is pretty damned funny, but it's better if the fight lasts longer and they've got a chance of winning, so lots of humans get the shot."

"That seems kind of unfair." And besides that, I was in real trouble, because I had no desire to take this drug.

"We're in the entertainment business, not in the fairness business," he informed me.

"What if I die?" I wondered. "What if my opponent dies?"

He shrugged. "Shit happens."

That was not the answer I wanted to hear.

"We'll need to keep all of your belongings while you're in the barracks awaiting your fight," he continued. "They'll be put in a locker, and you'll get the combination. You can collect them once you're done with your fight and ready to leave. Same with clothes. We'll provide you with clothing and any weapons necessary for the fight. You can keep the clothes you fight in, although they'll be pretty trashed once you're done. When your fight's over, you can get your extra dose of Aries at the betting booth."

I'd had my guns taken away last night and wasn't eager to be parted from them again, but I really didn't have much choice here. My clothes were already trashed, so I wasn't particularly concerned about their fate, but if they were going to outfit me for this fight, I'd go with it.

"You in?" he asked me.

I took a deep breath and nodded. "Are there women's barracks and men's barracks?" I really should have asked that before agreeing to this, because if we were housed separately, my chances of finding Anton were probably zero.

The demon snorted. "Right. There are human barracks, then non-human barracks. We're not putting you in different places because of your reproductive parts."

The one time I'd fought a shifter, I'd had my ass handed to me. Unless I counted that time in Suerte when I'd needed to defend myself. I'd barely held my own in that incident. If HB hadn't intervened, I would have lost that fight as well.

The only demon I'd ever fought was Navy Seal Guy. And I wasn't positive he actually was a full demon. This would be far more difficult to survive, let alone win, especially without taking the drug. Too bad I couldn't count on Mittens to waltz in and laser-eye my opponent in half.

I followed the demon out of the office and down to where the players' locker rooms used to be. We paused in an outer room, and he handed me a pair of unisex gray sweatpants and a matching T-shirt. I looked around for a changing area. Upon realizing that there wasn't one, I went ahead and stripped down to my underwear and bra, handing my clothes to the demon before putting on the ones he'd given me.

My clothes, weapons, and backpack all went into a locker. The demon filled out a form on a clipboard cataloging my belongings, then tore off the bottom stub with a series of numbers for the combination and gave it to me. I felt around my sweatpants, annoyed to find that they had no pockets. Luckily, I was wearing a sports bra, and that's where the stub went.

The demon walked me to a metal door, opened it, ushered me through the opening, then closed it behind me. I looked around, feeling a bit uncomfortable that I might be locked in here with a bunch of strangers.

I'd never been in a stadium locker room before, but I had certain expectations. The rows of lockers weren't in place. Instead, the room was one giant open area with beds lining the left and right walls. In the back was the entryway to what looked to be showers and bathroom facilities. A rough estimate had me guessing there were thirty cots in here, although there were only eight people that I could see. Two guys snoozed on cots. Four sat on the ground, playing poker with a beat-up deck of cards, using almonds and walnuts as betting chips. One guy was reading a very worn paperback. One stood off to the side, watching the poker game. He lifted his head when I came in, and I recognized him.

Anton.

CHAPTER 24

 nton hadn't changed all that much in four years. He was taller. His face had thinned out into that of a man, and the beard he sported certainly hadn't been there when he was fourteen. In spite of all that, this man in front of me was clearly Anton. He looked just like Sebastian had at that age, and my heart twisted a bit at the memories that surfaced when his eyes met mine.

Memories weren't the only thing that flooded me. Anger did as well. What the fuck was he doing here? I'd assumed he'd fought the night after getting the crap beaten out of him by the Disciples, then gone straight out to enact his Aries-fueled revenge on Tape and his buddies, but why was he here *again*?

"Anton!" I walked over to him.

He blinked a few times. "Eden? What the hell are you doing here?"

"What are *you* doing here, you stupid idiot?" I snapped.

His eyes narrowed. "Probably the same as you—fighting to win a dose of Aries."

"You fool," I hissed. "First you stupidly get involved in a deal right in Disciple territory with one of their own guys."

"It was worth the risk. If we woulda pulled it off, we would have been rich." He scowled. "And how do you know about that, anyway?"

I ignored him and kept going. "Then, when you get caught and taught a lesson, you don't just lick your wounds and go back to the Valley like any smart person would, thankful that they didn't kill you, that they never made the connection between you and your brother. No. Instead you risk your ass in this ridiculous fight, take a drug with unknown side effects, and go back for revenge. There was a witness who saw what you did, Anton. There was fucking video footage of it. How the hell did you ever think you were going to get away with something like that?"

His mouth set in a mulish line. "I wasn't going to crawl back home like some coward they beat down. Teach me a lesson, huh? Well, I taught them a lesson."

I waved my hand around the room. "So, what's your long-term plan, genius? Fight here every other night and stay hopped up on Aries twenty-four/seven, just so you can fight off the guys that are going to be coming for you every single night of your soon-to-be very short life?"

He glared. "That's none of your fucking business. And how do you know all this, anyway? I haven't seen you in four years, and suddenly you show up knowing every move I've made in the last two days."

I tried to calm down a bit, but all I kept thinking about was that I'd put myself on the line for this dickhead. I was here, about to fight someone who was going to probably kick my ass and might kill me, just to keep this idiot out of a fire he seemed happy to return to again and again.

I was the idiot, not Anton.

"Your brother came and ask me to check on you," I finally admitted.

His eyebrows shot up. "Are you two back together or something?"

I recoiled. "No! It's just…he can't exactly come down here himself looking for you or send someone that he works with. I'm a Vulture. It's not a big deal for me to be down here, and I could come up with plausible reasons to be looking for you and the guy you were meeting with without raising suspicion."

Anton grunted, clearly not buying my story. "Right. My brother hasn't seen you in four years. Every now and then he talks about you and gets this look on his face that makes his current girlfriend explode, but that's it. And why send a woman down here into Disciple territory, asking for me or Tape? It's dangerous. What asshole puts a woman in danger like that?"

I bristled at his assumption that I couldn't take care of myself. Anton hadn't seen me in four years, and I'd certainly become more capable in those years, but even in high school few were willing to take me on. I'd had a reputation as a fighter—a reputation that either hadn't reached Anton's ears, or one that he hadn't wanted to believe.

"That doesn't matter," I told him. "What does matter is that your brother is worried about you. I found out what you were doing and told him. I wouldn't be here now except I got a call that the Disciples had you. When I got back down here, I found out that you'd gone on a killing spree and were now their most wanted guy."

Anton shrugged. "Tape and I had a deal, and he turned me in. They beat the shit out of me, and they had no reason to. Aries isn't their drug. Hell, the demons don't even pay them a tax for dealing right here in their own backyard. Tape and I were trying to figure out a way to find out where they store the stuff and run a smash-and-grab. Until then, we were working out a deal where we paid people to come in to fight and get the drug, then sell it for double. It didn't have nothing to do with the Disciples."

I couldn't believe I had to explain this to him. "You're in their *territory*. You were trying to run a drug business in their territory with one of their members. The Disciples might leave the demons alone, because they're not fools, but they're not going to let a human leech onto what they consider to be theirs. Your brother…well, you should fucking know this, Anton."

His expression hardened. "If they're too stupid to take a piece of this pie, then it's mine for the taking. Those guys deserved to die. And when I'm rich enough and powerful enough to make every one of the Disciples kneel, they'll regret they ever messed with me."

That didn't sound like the Anton I once knew. Yeah, he'd always been an arrogant, annoying teenager, but this rich, powerful, kneeling-before-me bullshit was new. And weird.

"Well, you don't need to be here," I informed him. "I made a deal with the Disciples. Pulled some strings. They're willing to forget what you did last night."

He laughed. "Right. Like I believe that."

"Believe it," I told him. "As long as you stay out of Inglewood and stay away from them, they won't come after you. So, leave. Go home. And don't come back."

"That's not gonna happen." He sneered. "I need more Aries. I don't care if they come after me or not, because I'm going after them. I'm paying two of these guys for their doses after their fights. That'll give me three doses. If I plan things right, it should last me a week."

Plan things right? What the hell was he planning? He wasn't just getting the drug to defend himself against the

Disciples, he was getting it to launch some sort of preemptive strike against the gang.

"And what if those two guys decide to keep the doses for themselves?" I shook my head, wondering again how this guy could be so stupid. "I don't care how amazing this Aries is, it's not enough for you to take on the Disciples. A dose lasts what? Twenty-four hours? Twelve? How long? What happens if they ambush you when you're not on it? What happens if instead of nine guys, you find yourself facing fifty?"

Anton shrugged. "I'll have guys working for me by then. Starting my own gang, all of us with a steady supply of Aries. The Disciples won't mess with us. The shifters won't mess with us. The demons won't mess with us, either. We'll run this city."

Whatever. This guy was beyond saving, and I was seriously regretting that I'd stuck my neck out for him. I'd get the fuck out of here, tell Piers what was going on. Then I'd head back to the Valley, meet up with Sebastian and dump the whole thing in his lap. His brother, his problem. Not mine.

Did I have to actually fight, though? Maybe I could gather intel, tell that ram-horned demon that I'd changed my mind, then hide so I could stick around and watch the fight. Maybe I could get information for Piers without having to actually set foot in the boxing ring, or whatever they were using. Nothing about the demons I'd met with had indicated we were prisoners here. If I wanted to back out of this, could I?

That was something I needed to ask Anton, who had been through this song and dance once before and had a lot more knowledge about this operation than I did. Actually, there were a lot of things I wanted to ask Anton.

I motioned for him to follow me to a few cots that looked clean and unused, then we sat.

"So tell me everything you know about Aries," I said. "How does it work? How does it feel? How long does it take to kick in and how long does it last?"

Anton grinned, and I really didn't like that expression on his face. I'd seen junkies look like that, talking about their next fix, so I guess I shouldn't have been surprised.

"You inject it into your muscle, not vein. You'd think that would delay the onset, but it doesn't. I swear you *feel* it. Push the plunger down, and it's instant."

Which was probably why the woman in the market was fumbling for the syringe and the full vial. She knew it was wearing off, and knew that as soon as she jabbed herself, she'd be powerful once again.

Anton's gaze focused into the distance. "You feel strong, invincible, like you can take on the world and win. Bullets, knife blades…they all just bounce off of you. It's not like wearing a vest where every bullet feels like someone hit you with a bat. You don't feel anything at all. Your skin becomes sort of like tank armor. And you're strong enough to pick up cars, to rip poles out of the concrete, to snap a man's neck like it was a toothpick."

"How long does it last?" I asked.

He shrugged, his focus returning to me. "I think it depends on how crazy you go on it. Fight one guy, it might last twelve hours. Fight fifty, it might only last two or three. I felt it wearing off after eight hours."

That seemed like a lot to pay for a drug that didn't even last a full day, but then again, I'd seen heroin addicts go nuts for a high that lasted not much longer than that.

"Any side effects?" I couldn't help but glance down at Anton's trembling hands. That was clearly one side effect. What else? I suddenly imagined Anton with shrunken genitals. Ugh. I really didn't want to think about my ex-boyfriend's brother's dick and balls, shrunken or not.

"Headache. Thirsty." He shrugged again. "A little tired, but that's it. Nothing worse than a mild hangover, in my experience. But you want more. Shit, Eden, you feel like a damned god on the stuff. Is this what shifters feel like all the time? What demons feel like?"

I certainly hadn't felt like a god at any time in my life and —despite what I claimed—I knew I was more than human.

"No cravings? No shakes? No feeling like you're gonna puke?" I prodded.

"Nah, but I heard if you take a double dose, that can happen. A double dose though…I could probably take down a dragon with that. I could probably kill every demon in this arena with that."

That I seriously doubted. Okay, so one of the side effects was clearly delusions of grandeur.

He grinned at me, looking once more just like a younger version of his brother. "I wanna be top of the heap for once in my life. No one can hurt or kill me. I can do what I want, whenever I want. The Gray Dogs, the Disciples, all the militias? They'll all fall in line to follow where I lead."

Yeah. Famous last words.

I didn't like the idea of this drug at all, but I couldn't blame Anton for taking it. I couldn't blame any of these people for wanting it. We humans had gone from top of the food chain to quite a few rungs down. The shifters seemed to keep to themselves, but I'm sure having them in the neighborhood and knowing about their enhanced abilities made humans feel vulnerable. I know demons made everyone feel vulnerable. A drug that could equalize things, give humans less of a disadvantage, didn't seem to be a bad thing—except for the paranoia, violent tendencies, and sudden urge to become a dictator.

"How does this whole thing work?" I gestured around at the locker room. "Is it some sort of boxing match? The demon who interviewed me said you have one fight, then you get to leave with your drug."

"If you win." Anton grimaced. "Most win. Some don't. If you don't win, you have to keep fighting until you do. Sometimes they don't give someone the drug, they get sugar water in a syringe instead. Those poor saps know right away something's wrong. They're the ones who die and die fast."

Lovely. I wasn't about to take the drug, and I really didn't want to die and die fast, so my only option would be to not fight at all.

"Tell me about your last fight," I urged. "Who were you up against and what sort of weapons did they use?"

"I had to fight a demon," he said. "The one I faced had these long claws instead of fingers on one hand, and he had sharp teeth and a tail, but his main way of fighting was with some sort of electrical attack."

Just like me. Well, except for the claws, sharp teeth, and tail.

"The electrocution hurts," Anton continued. "Which is weird. Bullets and knives, claws and teeth don't do nothing, but electrocution feels like you're getting zapped. Nothing that knocks you out or disables you, but you definitely notice. If you don't let it slow you down, you'll be okay."

I nodded and let him go on.

"If you have to fight a shifter, then you've got more of a problem," he said. "One of the guys who had to fight a shifter didn't make it out alive, but I've heard that doesn't happen much. On Aries, you're stronger than most of them, and their skin isn't as armor-like as yours will be. They're faster though, so you'll probably need to take a few punches until you can manage to get a good grip on them."

"Why are you all fighting shifters?" I asked.

But the real question was why were shifters fighting them? Few of them were even out of the supernatural closet.

The demon who'd let me in said they weren't awarding Aries as prizes to shifters, so that wouldn't be their motivation. Were they getting paid for this? The shifters I'd met didn't seem like the type that would be willing to expose who they were for monetary gain, but maybe I was wrong. My sole experience with them was through Bishop's bar, my new neighbors, and Javier and his family, who I hadn't even realized were shifters until this past month.

"We fight whoever they put in the ring with us," Anton explained with an exasperated sigh. "I told you that. Usually it's these Low demons, but sometimes it's a shifter. Sometimes it's both, but if they pit us against more than three, they usually put two humans in as well."

"They *want* to be there? The shifters, that is?" I couldn't let this go, wondering why in the world a shifter would sign up for something like this. "Do they get paid?"

He held up his hands. "Fuck if I know. They look kinda nervous. I don't think they like the audience thing. They fight well. Maybe they're paid. Maybe they're captured and made to fight. I've got no idea."

And he really didn't care, was the part he hadn't said. Had Anton ever met a shifter outside of this arena? He probably went to school with some and hadn't even realized it. He'd probably even chatted with them on occasion. They were just like us, for fuck's sake.

I wasn't just like us. And if Anton knew that, I doubted he'd be sitting on a cot next to me, talking. I'd be an "other". I'd probably deserve killing, just like the Low demons and shifters did.

"So, do you overpower the shifters? Or outlast them?" Or outsmart them, which was my usual first line of defense since it wasn't easy for me to overpower or outlast anyone— at least without revealing my non-human abilities.

Anton eyed me, clearly doubting I had any fighting abilities at all. "You should probably try to outlast them. The drug will help if you can actually manage to land a punch."

I bit back a sharp retort and focused on getting as much information as I could about what was going on here. It didn't matter what he thought about me or my skills.

"How are the fights structured? Boxing ring? Cage match? Are you all allowed weapons, or is it just bare hands? Are the shifters permitted to fight in their animal form, or human?"

"Sometimes it's a cage match, and sometimes they just turn us loose in the arena and let us run around, like a maze. It's all televised through the monitors so everyone in the stands can get a close-up look at what's going on. Bare fists, although there's a ton of demolition debris out there. If you can grab something, you can use it. Opponents are in human form, although some of the shifters manage to sprout fangs or claws as they fight."

It made sense. From what I'd heard, it took shifters a while to morph into their animal form, and they were vulnerable during that change. They'd enter the ring as humans, and pretty much just need to fight with whatever advanced abilities they had in that form.

"The demons who run the show like to mix things up a bit to keep it from being the same boring old shit every night," Anton continued. "So, you don't really know what you'll get."

I looked around the locker room. "So what do you all do in the meantime? Just sit around and nap?"

He shrugged. "Pretty much. They bring in sandwiches and stuff for us, and there's cards and some books."

"Are we locked in here?" I glanced toward the door. "Stuck here forever until we win a fight? No backing out?"

He gave me an odd look. "The door's not locked. You can leave at any time. But why would you? This is the only way to get Aries."

"I don't want the drug, and I'm not going to fight," I told him.

"Suit yourself." He shrugged.

Getting up, I decided to test the door and nearly fell over when it swung open. It wasn't locked. There were no guards anywhere that I could see. I was free to go. So that's exactly what I did.

CHAPTER 25

I was free, but I had no idea how to get out of this stadium. Actually, I didn't truly want to get out of the stadium, I wanted to find a good place to hide where I could watch all the action and not be detected. Which meant I couldn't exactly retrace my steps and risk running into the ram-horned demon or any of the others.

Walking out of the locker room, I stepped into an adjoining one with huge whiteboards spanning one wall and chairs lined up in rows facing it. I'd come in through some sort of manager's office, but I assumed this room also led to the outside. Deciding I had nothing to lose, I tried the first door and found it to be a closet with cleaning supplies.

So I tried the second door. It opened into a hallway spanning to my left and right. The left branch went on forever, ending in darkness. The one on the right went about two hundred feet and opened up into what had to have been the stadium field. I headed that way, not seeing any of the guards who'd escorted me earlier.

I walked right out into the center side of the football field, blinking at the sudden light. The building debris was mostly at the left end of the field, with a few scattered six and eight foot diameter chunks of concrete here and there, and a mountain of pulverized asphalt near the twenty yard line. To the right of the field were piles of twisted metal and smashed furnishings. Smack in the middle, directly in front of me, was a huge metal cage. It reminded me of some MMA cages, except this one was four times the size and it didn't have mats lining the floor.

Surrounding the cage was turf for twenty yards either way, with something that looked like an announcer's booth off to the side. I scuffed my foot over the artificial grass, noting that the vibrant green didn't look or feel like I'd expected it to. In my mind, artificial turf consisted of sharp, thin strips of plastic shaped to look vaguely grasslike. That or the horrible green indoor-outdoor carpeting so many people had slapped on the floors of their enclosed porches when I was a kid.

Glancing around, I saw the cameras that Anton had talked about. They were mounted on the cage, on the announcer booth, on poles that had been stuck in the ground here and there, and even on top of some of the debris piles. Looking out to the audience areas surrounding the field, I saw boxes mounted along the aisles. Speakers. People could watch the action on the huge jumbotron monitor, and these speakers would allow an announcer to let them know what was going on.

I didn't think it would be a good idea to hide in the stands, since I didn't know exactly where the spectators tended to congregate and didn't want to risk running across any of them. Nor was it a good idea to hide down here in the arena where the fights would occur. I glanced at the announcer's booth, but the door was locked. I didn't have my lock picks, and although I could probably manage to force the door open, it would really suck if there was actually an announcer tonight who would waltz in and find me there.

Searching for a place where I'd be relatively safe but still have a decent view, I walked across the field and down the tunnel to what would have been the opposing team's locker room. This area was completely different from the one I'd just come from. The strategy room with the whiteboards had a huge metal gate instead of a door, and no chairs. It hummed with electricity, and I assumed, magic. Cots were lined against the walls. Sitting on them were three of the ugliest humans I'd ever seen. One of them turned to look at me, and I took a step backward.

Not humans, demons.

The guy who was looking at me got up and waddled toward the gate. He was short and stout, with a pockmarked face, a pointy nose, and bulging eyes with a jaundice yellow tinge to the whites. He grinned, revealing a mouth full of crooked teeth.

"Hey, they finally sent us lunch. You're a little under-cooked for my liking, but you'll do."

The other two got up and wandered over to stare at me as well. One had tufts of red hair sprouting from his nose and ears, as well as from several large moles on his face and neck. The other's mouth hung open, as if he lacked the ability to close it all the way. A long-forked tongue rolled out to hang a few inches past his chin.

"Why are you three locked in here?" I would have thought demons would be thrilled to have the opportunity to brawl with a group of humans, even those on a fight-enhancing drug.

"Duh. It's so we don't escape." Jaundice turned to the one with the open mouth. "Put your tongue away, Drool. I was joking about lunch."

"Hungry," Drool slurred, rolling the tongue back into his mouth and remaining slack jawed.

"They're not feeding you?" I don't know why I cared. They were demons, for fuck's sake. If our positions were reversed, they wouldn't give two shits about me. Hell, without the electrified magic gate in between us, they'd probably try to eat me, as Jaundice had said.

"We haven't eaten in two days," Hair Tufts complained. "Not since that rat I caught. It ran out of where they're keeping the shifters, and I snatched it right up."

"You didn't share either," Drool whined.

"They grabbed us off the street and brought us here," Jaundice told me. "Two days of fighting with no food. They've been doing this for three weeks now—grabbing us and making us fight, so I'm sure there were Lows here before us. They're probably all dead. We'll probably be dead soon, too. Either starving to death, or killed by the humans."

Tufts shrugged. "They'll just grab more of us when we're dead."

That was wrong. Yes, they were demons, but it was still wrong to go kidnapping them, forcing them to fight until they were dead, then just tossing their bodies aside and kidnapping more.

I took a step forward, trying to peer through the room into what, based on the layout on the opposite side of the field, was probably the locker room.

"I did die," Drool reminded Tufts. "Well, almost died. I've still got a dent in my head from last night that I can't fix."

"So, you gonna let us out?" Jaundice motioned toward the gate. "If you're here to rescue the shifters, you're gonna have to let us go as well. They're back in the locker room and the only way out is through here."

I'd planned on hiding and watching the fight, swinging by to tell Piers what I knew before leaving and heading back to the Valley to put all this shit behind me. I'd done what I could for Anton.

The plan was that I'd let Sebastian know what was going on down here and drop the whole thing in his lap. If he wanted to haul his little brother kicking and screaming out of this mess, then he could have at it. Anton didn't want my help. I certainly didn't want to get hooked on Aries or die at the hands of the Disciples.

It was Anton's choice if he wanted to dope up so he could get revenge against the gang, or settle a score with a shifter, or stand his ground against a demon. Not my problem. I'd barely managed to get out of the situation with Piers and his goons alive. The longer I stayed in the open, the higher the chance I'd get caught, and I wasn't sure what the demons would do if they found me nosing around. I needed to find a spot to hide over in the concession areas or behind the lower bleachers or something.

But these demons were being held against their will, and evidently so were shifters.

"I should be able to get to the locker room through the office," I mused, assuming the layout this side of the field would be the mirror image of the other. That way I wouldn't have to go through this room where the Lows were being kept.

"Might not want to do that." Jaundice looked down at his hands and picked something out from under his nails. "Besides, if you rescue the shifters through that door, we still can't get out. You're not going to just leave us here, are you? Let us get killed by humans high on some drug? Leave us to eat nothing but rats—if we can manage to even catch them."

I frowned, thinking this guy suddenly had a larger vocabulary than he'd had ten seconds ago.

"Don't leave us here," Drool slurred, his tongue starting to poke out again. "I've never done anything wrong in my whole life, like ever. Just stole food and peed on the carpet that one time. That was it."

"And drew on the statues and paintings," Tufts added. "And bit that warmonger."

Drool shrugged. "I couldn't help it. I'm a biter."

"We're Lows," Jaundice told me. "No one gives a shit whether we live or die. The other demons kill us for fun, just like they do the humans. You can't just leave us here."

I hesitated. These Lows were the kind of demons that ran around LA and the Valley, stealing stuff, setting things on fire, defoliating people's lawns with their toxic jizz. They'd most likely assaulted people. Hell, they most likely had killed people. They weren't as terrifying as the other demons, and they weren't as hard to kill. I'd heard stories of people running them over on the freeway and squashing them dead. I'd also heard that if you pumped enough bullets into them, they would die from that as well.

I suddenly wondered if we'd killed more of them than they'd killed of us. I didn't know. I hadn't had the best experiences with demons so far. Yeah, the ones at the tax office hadn't harmed me, but they'd basically extorted money from me that I didn't owe them, even by their own convoluted rules. They'd put out a hit on me, sent mercenaries after my family. I didn't owe demons anything. I probably didn't owe the shifters anything either.

But I lived next to shifters. HB was my friend, and she was a shifter. Nevarra's maybe-boyfriend was a shifter. And as for demons…I didn't want to think too much about what I was, but maybe I shouldn't be tarring all demons with the same brush.

People who live in glass houses…

"How do I disarm the door magic?" I asked the Lows.

"Just flip that switch over there." Jaundice pointed to a lever on the wall.

"You're joking." I walked over and saw it was just a plain kill switch. "That's it?"

He shrugged. "It's not like they worry about anyone wanting to set us free. We're demons."

I stepped closer, looking across the room at the door that led to the locker room. "How do I get through that one?"

"Oh, you just open it." Tuft blinked innocent eyes at me.

Right. If it were that easy, the demons would already be in there with the shifters. Did the door lock from the other side, allowing the shifters to bar themselves from the demons? I looked back and forth from the three Lows to the door, wondering who would be the larger threat. Shifters or demons? Who would need protection from whom?

One group at a time. If I let the demons out, they might cause enough of a distraction to buy me time to free the shifters. Although I hadn't seen a guard since I'd come out of the human locker room, so I might be able to free everyone and find somewhere to hide without anyone noticing. Maybe it could be that easy.

Nothing was ever that easy.

I walked over and flipped the switch. Before I could head back to open the gate, the demons had already flung it wide and were racing through the opening to freedom. I waited for them to get out, then jogged through the meeting room to the wooden door. There had to be some kind of notice or alarm that went off when I flipped that switch, which meant I needed to get these shifters out of here as soon as possible.

As expected, the door was locked from the other side. I didn't have my lock picks or any way to get it open, so instead I banged on it, yelling out that this was a jail break and they needed to run for it. No one answered. Worried that time was running out, I dashed back through the meeting room and around to the office, hoping to get in that way.

Throwing open the office door, I slid to a stop. There was a gate to the locker room similar to the one that had been in the meeting room. But to get to that, I'd need to go all the way across the room and past the...thing that stood in my way.

It was a snake-rooster. Or a rooster-snake. Either way, the thing was huge with a long slithery body that stood on two stumpy chicken-feet legs. It had a rooster head, but with jaws instead of a beak. As it turned to face me, a hood expanded from its neck, like a feathered cobra. It opened its mouth to reveal front fangs as well as a mouth full of sharp teeth.

I took one look at that thing and ran. It ran as well, and for something with stubby chicken legs, it was damned fast. As I headed back toward the tunnel, I noticed a man cautiously peering out.

Fuckers couldn't open the door when I was banging on it, could they? Noooo, they waited for me to go and nearly get bitten by this monster, *then* decided to come out.

"Run," I shouted to the man. "Chicken-snake on the loose."

The guy looked behind me. His eyes widened. "You let the basilisk loose?"

"I meant to let *you* all loose." As I passed the tunnel, the man dashed out followed by about a dozen other people. They were behind me for all of half a second, before they ran past as if they were Olympic sprinters and I was a sloth.

Great. The Lows were probably halfway to San Diego by now. The shifters would be out of the parking lot before I managed to cross the football field, and I'd be left behind with a pissed-off basilisk.

Basilisk. Weren't they incredibly venomous? So much so that whatever they spat on remained toxic for centuries afterward? Clearly their gaze wasn't petrifying, or I would be a statue standing in the doorway of that office. That part of the legend might be a lie, but I didn't want to test whether the venom thing was or not. And either way, I really didn't want that thing to bite me.

Not all the shifters were super-speedy. Halfway across the field, I managed to catch up to one.

"How do we get out of here?" she shouted at me, making me realize that she'd purposely slowed down to ask me for directions.

"Fuck if I know," I panted, trying to keep as much distance between me and the thing chasing me as possible.

I didn't want to lead the basilisk to the other tunnel and the humans who absolutely weren't equipped to handle something like this. Maybe we could jump the fence, climb the bleachers, and they could exit through one of the gazillion fire escape doors this place must have had in order to have met code when it was built. Glancing up as I ran, I realized a few of the shifters were doing exactly that. And that Low, Tufts, was trying to do the same, except he'd fallen off the fence into a pile of scrap lumber.

Fire shot past me and I dove to the side, nearly knocking the shifter woman into one of the concrete blocks.

"There," she shouted, pointing at the tunnel that led to where the humans were quartered.

"No, not there," I yelled back. "Up through the stands and out, or some other door, but not there."

She turned to speak to me, then abruptly stopped, staring with horror at something behind me. "Lenny!"

I spun around and saw the basilisk bearing down on one of the shifters. The creature shot out a stream of fire. Lenny dodged it, tripping over some rubble in the process. He stumbled, fell, and slid across the ground, coming to a stop next to a steel beam.

"Lenny!" The woman next to me covered her eyes as the basilisk took a breath, its hood expanding.

Except for that one time I was being shot at outside of Bags's pawnshop, I didn't have super speed. I didn't have super strength. I couldn't compel people or animals. I didn't have my guns or my knives or anything.

There was one thing I did have.

"Hey!" I shot a bolt of electricity from my hands right into the basilisk.

It squawked. Smoked. Turned its head slightly my way as if it were trying to decide whether it wanted the bird in the hand, or the one attacking it from the side. In an effort to help the basilisk make better choices, I strode toward it, slamming two more bolts of electricity into it as the shifter guy crawled out of range, got up, and ran.

"Fuck you, you fucking snake-chicken," I shouted, waving my arms as if I were trying to shoo some squirrels away from a bird feeder. "Pick on someone your own experience level, asshole. That's me. Yeah, that's *me*! Come on. Let's dance, motherfucker."

As soon as the shifter was in the free and clear and I was sure I had the basilisk's attention, I ran. All that bravado was talk. I had no desire to fight this thing and end up with third degree venomous burns all over my body.

The electrical attack hadn't seemed to do anything to the creature but piss it off—which was highly unfortunate, since that was my only weapon at the moment. I ran further in to where the building debris was stored, weaving in and out of concrete chunks and piles of metal as fire blasted behind me. Thank God the thing was stupid. If it had stopped running and tracked me, ambushing me at a turn, I would have been in trouble. But no, it squawked and hissed, stomping after me and announcing how far away it was with frequent mini fireballs.

How much fire did that thing have? Magazines ran out of ammo, and I was pretty sure this thing would as well. Just as I was trying to figure out how long I'd need to keep running to wear the thing down, it spat a gob of green slime that hit a pile of rebar to my left and immediately melted it into a steaming, liquid-metal puddle.

Oh shit.

I put on the speed, starting to feel the strain of my efforts. I was in great shape. My Vulture job meant I had the cardio of a high school track sprinter, and the strength of a gym rat, but I still wasn't used to doing laps at top speed around a football field.

What killed a basilisk? Staring at itself in a mirror? No, that was Medusa. Drowning? Well, I was out of luck there. I needed a supernatural mongoose right now. Or Mittens. But the Hellkitty had no reason to be down in Inglewood. Yes, he'd followed me from the dump to my new house, but he wasn't a dog, he was a cat. And cats roamed around doing whatever the hell they wanted—even ones without laser eyes.

I glanced up at the bleachers, seeing the shifters pouring through one of the fire escape doors. Tuft was running up the stairs in that direction. Someone must have helped the Low get over the fence. I hoped the two others had managed to get out.

More acid spit dissolved a pile of scrap lumber into greenish-brown goo. I put on the speed and whipped around a corner, plowing straight into someone.

We crashed to the ground. I got a whiff of hyacinth and campfire smoke, and for a split second, thought the combination was some strange new perfume.

"Sorry." I scrambled up and reached down to grab what I thought was a shifter who'd been left behind. My gaze met eyes with orange irises and lizard-shaped pupils. Blonde hair. A grin that revealed razor-sharp teeth. My entire body went cold, and I almost peed my pants.

Desiree.

I dropped my hand and turned to run, but she grabbed one of my ankles in an iron grip and brought me down. The basilisk rounded the corner and sucked in a breath, its hood expanding.

"Bellatrix! Down!" Desiree snapped.

The basilisk dropped flat, chicken feet splayed out to the side. The hood snapped tight against its neck, and it stared at the demon with absolute attention.

Desiree had a pet basilisk. I guess I couldn't throw stones, since I sort of had a pet Hellkitty. Sort of. As much of a pet as Hellkitty would ever be to anyone, I guess.

The hand on my ankle tightened, the demon's blood-red nails digging into my skin.

"You know, I've been looking everywhere for you. Surprisingly, your name isn't really Andrea Delgado, and you're not from Crenshaw. I figured you'd eventually come across my radar, but I hardly expected you to show up here, in my arena."

I couldn't speak. I couldn't do anything but try to pull my ankle out of her grasp. Electricity sparked from my fingertips, but I couldn't seem to manage more than that. In desperation, I reached out to one of the piles of rebar, trying to telekinetically pull a rod toward me, or launch it at the demon. Either one. I wasn't picky.

Nothing happened.

"You just let loose all my prey *and* tried to electrocute my sweet Bellatrix. I'd approve if there had been a paying audience here to witness the show, but all this was wasted on empty stands." Desiree made a *tsk* noise. "A few guards are going to lose their jobs and quite possibly their heads over this. As for you...well, if we can't manage to round up our escapees, then you'll just have to fight the humans yourself tonight. Every single one of them."

She yanked me toward her, then stood, pulling me upright with a hand around my neck. My self-preservation instincts overcame my fear, and I punched her in the stomach, kicking at her legs with my feet. She laughed, as if I wasn't doing any more than tapping her with a feather. Then she dragged me all the way over to where the shifters had been housed and tossed me in. Bars shot across the doorway. Even without the physical barrier, I knew that Bellatrix would be guarding me as well as other demons.

Desiree had me. And she knew what I was, even if I wasn't ready to admit that myself. She knew. And now she was going to make me fight humans hopped up on Aries—humans who were very motivated to win that fight so they could walk out of here with their extra doses.

How was I going to survive?

More than that, how was I going to get out of here, even if I did survive?

CHAPTER 26

I didn't have anything else to do in my new prison, so I went ahead and cleaned up in the shower area, having to put my dirty clothes back on since there didn't appear to be any extras lying around to change into. When I walked back into the locker area, I saw I wasn't the only one who'd been caught. All three demons were back, as well as the female shifter. The demons were busy exploring the space. The shifter sat on a cot, staring down at her entwined fingers. I walked over and sat across from her, noting that her clothing was in worse shape than mine, and she had dried blood caked in her dark hair and on her right temple.

"I'm Eden."

She glanced up at me. "Isha."

"I'm sorry you didn't make it out." I glanced over at the demons, feeling equally bad that none of them had managed to escape either.

She sighed. "At least the others got away. And I'm sorry you're stuck in here with us. I'm guessing that's punishment for setting us free? And they probably took your Taser from you, too. That took some serious balls shooting a stun-gun at a basilisk."

I blinked for a second, surprised that she'd thought the electricity had come from a stun gun and not me. She believed me to be human. And I wasn't all that eager to correct her, either.

"Yeah, they took my weapons," I told her.

She sighed. "They're not going to give you any Aries when you fight. You know that, right? You're going to go out there with only your bare hands and whatever you can grab off the ground to fight with."

I nodded, knowing she didn't expect me to live through the night. Heck, I wasn't sure *I* expected me to live through the night either.

She reached out and patted my shoulder. "You don't have anything to fear from me. I promise I'll do all I can to protect you from those demons."

"I'm not afraid of you or them," I said, which kind of surprised me. It was true, though. Over the last few months, I'd come to have a respect for shifters. And as for demons… well, I decided I needed to judge each of them individually, well aware that I too would be facing others' judgement someday soon.

I couldn't hide forever. Every day I faced situations where there was a strong possibility that I'd need to use my magic to survive. People knew about me—people outside of Bea and the girls. And one of these days enough people would know to have me branded not-human.

Maybe that was why I felt for these shifters. They'd hidden their secrets, living next to humans for generations. They just wanted to be left alone to live their lives. But the moment they were discovered, the whole world looked at them differently.

"There's not going to be much I can do for either of us

out there tonight," she warned me. "I've survived this long, but I get the feeling this is going to be my last fight."

"Thanks," I told her. "I'll try to protect you as well."

She'd have strength and speed on her side, and I'd have whatever of my abilities I could get to cooperate. I glanced over at the Lows, wondering if they'd work with us as a team, or if that sort of thing was beyond them. Shifters seemed to be good at team fighting, but demons? Lows?

"What kind of shifter are you?" I asked Isha. "Where are you from?"

She stiffened at the first question, then relaxed with a laugh. "No sense in lying, I guess. I'm a wolf with the Arcilla pack. We live east of the mountains, near Temescal Valley."

Sixty miles, give or take. Anywhere from an hour to a three-hour drive depending on traffic.

"What are you doing in Inglewood?" I wondered.

"Evidently sitting in a cage, fighting humans in some exhibition until I either die or escape," she drawled.

Desiree had called them prey, but for some reason I still figured they were here to serve out a sentence or pay a debt they owed to her. I never thought that debt would be paid with their lives, even though the intake demon had hinted at the occasional death.

"It was supposed to be an interview for a data entry job." She looked back down at her hands. "There's no work where I live. All the companies have closed up and pulled out. My pack...we've got skills, but we're not survivalists. We need money to buy things. *I* need money to buy things. I figured the job would be working for one of the Disciples' businesses in some capacity. But there was no interview. It was a setup. I've been here for five days. No one knows where I am. My family is probably frantic, my pack worried."

"But your pack is hardly going to come storming into Disciples' territory to look for you," I finished, thinking that they would have the same problem Sebastian had when trying to find Anton.

She nodded. "The others were from packs down farther south. One guy they grabbed when he was visiting friends north of San Diego."

"Tell me about the fights," I urged, wanting to hear the other side of the story.

She shuddered. "Sometimes they're one-on-one, some-times we fight in pairs, other times we're out of the fight cage and in a melee battle with all of us against a dozen or so humans. At first I thought the goal was to incapacitate the human, to win. Then I realized that only meant we'd be facing them again the next night. So, then we tried to kill them." She drew a deep breath. "I'm *not* a fighter. Yeah, I hunt with my pack, but we're not one of those groups that's always duking it out for positions in the hierarchy, or scrap-ping it up. We snowboard, watch television, play Monopoly, cook meatloaf for dinner. We have normal jobs and live normal lives. We don't fight. We don't kill humans. We try to have as little to do with humans as possible, to keep our lives secret, you know?"

I nodded, then remained silent, waiting for her to continue.

"I killed one." Her voice shook. "I don't know how I managed it because they're on that drug and really powerful. I was badly injured. I thought I was probably going to die myself. But I did it. I killed him."

I reached out and put a hand on her knee. "Sometimes you have to do terrible things to survive."

She looked up at me. "Have you ever killed anyone?"

I snorted. "So many I've lost count. It's the world we live in now. I've killed lots of humans. I don't think I've killed anyone who was a shifter—at least not knowingly. I think…I think the one guy I killed was a demon. Or maybe a half-demon."

I was well aware of three demons listening in and watching us from across the room. Admitting I'd killed Navy Seal Guy might make them think twice about attacking me, or it might make them reluctant to side with me if I needed help. I probably should have kept my mouth shut about it, but I felt like I needed to be honest. Isha was being honest. I needed to be as well. And admitting what I'd done…well, it felt better than any confession I'd ever done in church.

Not that I'd ever done a whole lot of confessing in church.

"Killing didn't help either." She pulled away from me and swung her legs up on the cot. "They healed me—or whatever it is that demons do to fix up their broken toys. They healed me so I could fight the next night and the next and the next. Win or lose. Kill or almost be killed. They'll never let me go. I'll fight here until one day I'm too damaged for them to fix."

We needed to get out of here. All of us. And Piers was right. I needed to do something to shut this place down. He wanted the demons out of Inglewood and the stadium because having them here was a blotch on the Disciples' reputation. I wanted them gone for a different reason. Voluntary fights were one thing, but this was far from voluntary. Knowing that these people were being kidnapped and forced to fight for the rest of their lives wasn't something I could walk away from.

I'd been about to leave. I'd been ready to do just that, to gather intel, then walk out of this stadium. I'd promised to help Piers, but in the end, I'd really hoped to drive home, tell Sebastian about his brother, and forget about the whole thing. If I hadn't been nosy, if I hadn't seen the three demons locked behind a gate, would I ever have thought about the people the humans were fighting? Would I ever have even considered them as people?

"What about you?" Isha asked. "What's your story—besides you having killed a bunch of people and a demon, that is."

I winced at that. "I'm a Vulture. I live in the Valley."

She folded her legs up under her. "And you came down for a job interview as well?"

"I came down looking for a friend's brother and sorta got roped into doing a reconnaissance mission. Here's where I found my friend's brother, signed up to fight. I couldn't convince him to leave, so I was going to just nose around a bit, maybe find a place to hole up and watch the fights, then go home."

"And now you're stuck as well because you set us free." She snorted. "Figures. One of the few decent humans I meet, and she's probably not gonna live to see tomorrow. Like I said, I'll do all I can to protect you and keep you alive, but I'm barely hanging on myself, so best say your prayers."

My death was the price I'd pay for setting everyone free, and the demons who paid to watch would be thrilled with the show. But Desiree *knew* I wasn't exactly human. Did she plan on keeping that a secret? Did she want to see whether I'd reveal myself to the humans in a desperate attempt to stay alive, or if I'd die with my secrets?

It would be an awesome time for a rescue, but I couldn't see that happening. The shifters who'd escaped probably ran for home. They didn't know who I was to get word to anyone who cared, and I doubted any of their packs would be eager to drive up here and storm the stadium—especially when the escapees would be bringing home tales of demons, drug enhanced humans, and a fucking basilisk. Telaney knew about the drugs, and that I was going into the stadium to look for Sebastian's brother. She wouldn't expect me back for another day, though.

I didn't have my phone to let anyone else know I needed help. Not that I'd want to risk Bea and the girls, or Bags. HB would help, but the last time she'd come to my rescue, Desiree had almost killed her.

"Bishop, I could really use your help," I muttered. He said he'd appear if I needed him, if I was dying. I wasn't exactly dying, though.

Yet.

"Bishop?" Isha chuckled. "I figured you to be Catholic, praying to God and Jesus, not some shifter legend."

Shifter legend. I thought back on our argument and winced. He'd once been their protector, but now he was just a guy with a bar.

Isha reclined on the cot and stared up at the ceiling. "We've heard the stories from when we were pups. Bishop. The guardian angel of the shifters. He was part of the tenth choir, and he defied the angels in heaven to stay here and protect the descendants of the Nephilim. He's had many names over the ages, and few have ever seen him, but he's supposed to be watching over us. He left the other angels. He renounced them, gave up his wings, his family, and his home, all to keep us safe."

I frowned over at her. "What do you mean few have seen him? The dude owns a bar up in the Valley."

She laughed. "Then that's probably some other Bishop. Angels don't own bars."

Why not? I pondered that for a second. If I were a million-year-old being with wings and unfathomable power, who was living here among humans, estranged from my angel friends and family and unable to return home, I'd need *some* sort of occupation. A hobby of some sort.

"What exactly did the stories say Bishop was supposed to

be protecting the shifters from?" I asked. Up until a few years ago, no one had even known shifters existed. They'd lived as humans, hiding their powers and conducting their shifter-type activities in secret. If a human here and there had seen what they were, he would have been considered crazy. They were stronger than humans, faster than humans, had the ability to survive what for a human would be a life-ending injury. Bishop had mentioned in the beginning it was angels. It *couldn't* have been the relatively weak humans.

Isha shrugged. "Mostly other angels. We used to need to keep our secret from humans because they outnumber us like a million to one, and if they wanted us gone, they have the numbers to make it happen. But in the stories I was told growing up, it was angels we were being protected from. They exterminated Nephilim, at least up until a few years ago. We're descended from Nephilim, so we were under the same danger of genocide-by-angels. The stories say there was another angel who was helping hide the Nephilim, but it was Bishop who gave up his wings to ensure our safety."

He must have metaphorically given up his wings, or he wouldn't have been able to swoop in and save me when I went over the side of that high-rise. Plus, I had that feather in a vase in my living room.

"Are you still in danger from angels?" I asked. Bishop had said they had other, more pressing problems, but if one came across a shifter, would he execute them?

The shifters had come out of the supernatural closet just before the demons had arrived in LA. They'd had a massive PR campaign to portray them as just slightly different beings, who'd lived in peace side-by-side with humans for over ten thousand years. If the angels had wanted them dead, I would have assumed it would have happened then.

"I don't know if we ever really were in danger from the angels. That's the thing about childhood stories, they're not

real. We've never been a threat to *anyone* aside from the occasional deer or squirrel. Even with our existence known, most
of us still try to hide what we are. We just want to live our
lives and be left alone.

Just like me.

"Angels don't seem to give a shit about us," she continued.
"None have attacked us since we went public with our existence. We've got a whole lot of problems, but angels don't
seem to be one of them. And as for those other problems, no
Bishop swoops down to save us when we can't find jobs, or
are going hungry, or get threatened by some human. As far
as I'm concerned, Bishop is in the same category as Santa and
the Easter Bunny."

She rolled over, turning her back to me.

Humans were fighting in this arena for a drug that would
quell their fears of living among beings that could easily
overpower them, could steal everything they owned and kill
them. Humans didn't want to feel helpless, and I completely
understood that need for security. Hell, my whole life I'd
yearned for the same thing. I'd also been helpless, a child
tossed around the foster care system.

Bea had found me, gave me stability. It wasn't just her
love, it was her faith in me, the security of home and family
that had calmed that panicked anxiety I'd had my entire
childhood. Maybe what humans needed was a Bea. Or their
own Bishop—one that actually showed the fuck up when he
was needed.

Anger simmered side-by-side with the warm sizzle of
attraction that came when I thought about the enigmatic
owner of Suerte. He'd sacrificed all to help others, only
to eventually decide he didn't give a shit anymore. Maybe
he was a cast-out, one of the Fallen. Maybe he'd gotten
fed up with his fellow angels and had left Aaru,
becoming a sort of ex-pat living among the humans.

Maybe he had good reasons for his refusal to help the shifters anymore.

Maybe what I and everyone else thought they knew about Bishop was wrong.

But I'd never find out if I didn't get out of here alive. I reached down to where a pocket should have been on these shitty sweatpants and remembered my phone was still in a locker, where it had been since I'd walked into this place.

I needed to stop thinking about him and instead worry about how I was going to survive these fights and manage to get the hell out of here.

$\mathcal{I}$ tossed and turned on the cot, my mind churning through all sorts of impossible plans to escape. Because fight or not, I needed to escape. *We* needed to escape.

Isha was either sleeping or pretending to sleep. The demons were on the other side of the room, chatting excitedly about something. As I watched, the jaundice-eyed Low pulled out his cock and started peeing on the floor. The others cheered. I gagged as the smell hit me, and thought that Isha must really be exhausted to sleep through that stench with her shifter's nose. Jaundice wasn't the only problem that demon had. From the color and odor of his urine, he was clearly on the verge of kidney failure or something. Or maybe that was normal for demons? The Low that had come through our neighborhood burned off vegetation with his sperm. Maybe this guy had acid pee.

Jaundice wasn't just relieving himself in a puddle, he seemed to be attempting some artistic expression, wiggling his dick and shooting urine in arcs and swirls. He finished with a flourish and the other two Lows shouted their approval, patting him on the back as he regarded his artwork with smug satisfaction.

It stank to high heaven, but I was curious enough to get up and approach, wondering what this pee-art was.

"He always manages to write the whole thing." Tufts pointed at the brownish-red streaks of piss. "We try to write our names, but most of us mess up the letters or don't have enough pee to finish in one go. You gotta do it all in one go, or it doesn't count."

A game then—a game where you peed your name on the carpet. I held my breath and took a few steps closer, looking at the entirety of the artistry. I had to admit, the Low's penmanship, or pissmanship, was excellent. The cursive even had decorative little curlicues. I was impressed.

"Gimlet," I read. It was a weird name, but it was better than the moniker I'd saddled him with.

Tufts sighed. "I can only manage to spell out G. A. R. G. before I run out of pee."

I nodded in sympathy. "Your name is Gargoyle?"

"Gargle." He slowly shook his head. "I get close, but I can never manage past that second G."

"The struggle is real," I agreed.

Drool yanked his dick out and before he could begin attempting to replicate Gimlet's success, I walked away. There would be no escaping the smell. The whole place would be disgusting by the time the three of them finished. Maybe we'd all be dead of asphyxiation before they came to let us out for the fight.

Trying to ignore the smell, I walked the floor of the locker room, attempting to get an idea of possible escape options. The door to the meeting room was now gone, but the electrified gate was there, along with the switch to disable it safely on the other side. I walked over and eyed the bars, hoping my resistance to electricity would help. If I could divert the electrical flow, maybe Isha could bend the bars with her shifter strength, and we all could escape.

Reaching out, I grasped the bars with both hands, feeling the electricity slide through my body. Unfortunately, something else accompanied the electricity, flinging me backward to smack against the wall and crumple on the floor.

"Idiot."

I opened my eyes to see Gimlet standing over me.

"If it was just electricity, we would have walked out of here days ago." He reached out a hand to help me up. "The electricity is to keep the shifters in place. The magic is to keep *us* in place."

"How about the other door?" I asked as I got to my feet, refusing his offer of assistance. The guy had just peed on the floor, and I knew full well he hadn't washed his hands.

"The other door is only electrified, but you'd still need to get by the basilisk." His gaze traveled down my body, then back up again. "If I were a betting sort of guy, I'd put my money on the basilisk."

"Thanks." I dusted myself off and looked at my hands that had some greasy black soot coating them.

"Why'd you let us out?" the demon asked. "Was it because you wanted to save the shifters and didn't want to have to deal with the basilisk?"

"I didn't know there was a basilisk." I tried to wipe the sooty grease off on my pants, which only resulted in greasy stained pants and palms. "I don't like anyone being imprisoned and forced to fight for the rest of their lives. Humans, shifters, demons…doesn't matter."

"And which one are you, pretty lady." The demon's voice was an enticing sing-song. "Are you human? Shifter? Demon? Angel? Or something else?"

"Human." It wasn't really a lie. I'd considered myself human for my entire life, and I wasn't going to let the events of the last few months change my beliefs about myself and where I belonged.

"A human who frees captured Lows. A human who risks herself for demons and shifters. My, you *are* an interesting human."

He was mocking me. Not that I gave a rat's ass about what he thought. "And you are a very interesting Low. I've only met a few, but they aren't quite like you."

He grinned. "You're not gonna find a way out of here unless you can figure out how to kill the basilisk, and the demons they probably have right outside in the arena."

He spat at the electrified bars. It sizzled, turning into a rainbow shade of colored smoke. "Your better bet is to try to get out during the fight. Get the humans to focus on that shifter girl over there, and when they're ripping her limbs off, you make a break for it. Everyone will be too entertained by the action to bother going after you."

I felt sick at the idea of sacrificing them to save myself. I'd gotten myself into this trying to set them free, and I wasn't going to leave without them—all of them. Gross Low demons included.

"We're *all* getting out." I didn't say the "or none of us does" part, because I didn't really want to think about that.

"How do you plan on that?" the Low asked.

I had no fucking idea. "We need something to distract the audience."

"And the humans," he added. "It's not like they're going to escape with us. They're here for their prize. They won't leave without it."

He was right. I really didn't want to have to hurt or kill the humans, but they weren't going to care about hurting or killing us. I wasn't even sure what Anton would do tonight when he came face-to-face with me. Would he help me? Or would his desire for the drug be more powerful? Would he kill his brother's ex-girlfriend to get the prize? A woman he'd known for years? A woman who'd risked herself to find and help him?

I was very afraid the answer to that was "yes."

"Do they lock the basilisk up during the fight?" I asked. "Maybe if we can set it free, and get it into the stands, the audience will be too busy running away from it and fighting to deal with us escaping."

"Sometimes they do, sometimes they turn it loose for added entertainment," Gimlet said. "But it obeys Desiree. Well, most of the time anyway. It's fifty-fifty whether she can call it off or not. When that thing gets excited and on the hunt, it doesn't listen to nobody."

"Incapacitate but don't kill the humans," I mused. "Get the basilisk into the stands. Maybe screw up the giant scoreboard they're using so the audience can see what's going on in the arena."

Gimlet held up three fingers. "First problem: we're three Lows, one puny-ass shifter, and a human."

"I heard that," Isha snapped.

"Those other humans will be on that Aries drug," Gimlet went on. "We're not gonna incapacitate them. We're not gonna kill them. We'll be lucky to outrun them. Thankfully Aries doesn't do shit about enhancing their speed."

I thought back to Big Studio Guy, the woman at the market, and the thief. No, they hadn't been any faster than some regular old Joe. Bulletproof skin. Super strong. Super aggressive and violent. Paranoid and delusional. But not particularly fast.

And the drug wore off. I remembered the woman in the market, whose hands had started to bleed, who'd been shot dead before she could dose up again. These guys were only getting one shot with no opportunity for a refill. Wear them out by running them all over the place and having to exert themselves moving boulders and shit, and maybe the drug would work its way out of their system faster. Then we could incapacitate them.

"Second problem," Gimlet continued. "The basilisk has to have a reason to go into the stands. And it's not gonna have a reason when we're running around, giving it all sorts of interesting things to chase."

"What does a basilisk like more than chasing moving things?" I asked. "Bacon? Steak? A sexy male basilisk?"

Gimlet blinked in surprise. "There is a mating call but no one in the audience probably knows it or is stupid enough to use it."

I stared at him. "But you do know it?"

He snorted. "Yes, and even *I'm* not stupid enough to use it."

"What if you broadcast it over the loudspeakers? There's an announcer's booth down near that fight cage. If we deal with the humans and the basilisk, giving you time to get in there and broadcast the mating call over the speakers, will that work?"

Gimlet blinked at me a moment, then burst into laughter. "I like you. I like you a hell of a lot more than I thought I would. Yes. And because there are speakers all over the stadium, the thing will go crazy, racing all over trying to find a mate. If we can manage to pull that off, that basilisk isn't going to be worth shit for the next three days. All it will think about is the fucking harem of basilisk mates it thinks are somewhere nearby."

Good. Finally, something reasonably approaching a plan.

"Once you broadcast the mating call, I'll bring down the jumbotron, and we'll run for it."

The Low nodded. "And until that happens, we only have to stay alive, get away from eight humans doped on Aries, and don't let the basilisk catch us."

"Yeah." It wasn't a great plan, but it was something. And staying alive was always the plan either way.

"We'll be free," Gimlet continued. "And then tomorrow, Desiree will go grab some other shifters and Lows to throw in this arena and kill. But that won't matter, because *we'll* be alive and free."

I scowled because he was right. "First things first," I said, not committing to a plan out loud.

While a demon might not give two shits about anyone but themselves, I wasn't a demon. Nope. I was a human. And I cared. First, I had to get us safely out of here. Second, I needed to figure out a way to shut down this operation. Forever.

I'd already ruined one of Desiree's business ventures. I was bound and determined to ruin another.

I tried to sleep. Really, I tried. It proved impossible to block out the Lows with their loud chatter, their peeing contests, their destroying of a cot so they could chew on the thin mattress and springs.

The humans may have gotten fed, but we didn't. No food. Nothing to drink. The water shut off soon after I'd taken my shower, so we couldn't even drink out of the sink in the adjoining bathroom. I was pretty sure Gargle had lied about not being able to write his name in pee, because judging from the amount of attempts he made, his bladder capacity was substantially more than I would have ever expected.

I finally got up and stared through the magic and electrified bars down the tunnel toward the arena. About a half hour before, the lights had come on, bringing the small view I had into clear, bright focus. I wondered if they ever had electrical blackouts here and what Desiree did if they lost power during one of the events. Although with demons running the whole West Coast, she probably had an exemption from blackouts for the stadium.

Too bad she hadn't asked for an exemption from the water shut offs.

Isha stirred on her cot. I went over, lowering myself beside her as she sat up.

"We've got a plan," I said, ready to tell her all the details.

"I know. I heard." She shot a narrow-eyed glance over at the Lows. "It's not like I could actually sleep with all that going on."

"I need you to handle the humans." She was fast, knew what to expect from her previous fights, and I trusted that she wouldn't get killed. I couldn't say the same about the Lows. "Just antagonize them and keep one step ahead of them. Lead them on a merry chase around the arena."

She ran a hand through her hair. "Right. Eight of them. Fun times."

I grimaced, hating to assign her this task. "Hey, I'm getting the basilisk. Wanna trade?"

"Nope." She glanced again over at the Lows. "What are the other two doing while the beady-eyed one is breaking into the announcer's booth? Can we use them as bait? Demon shields?"

"No." I could tell she didn't think of the demons as human, or even anything worth saving. I didn't blame her. Two years ago, I'd felt the same. Hell, two months ago I'd felt the same. I should *still* feel the same, but knowing I wasn't exactly human myself had me rethinking these beings. That, and a few that I'd encountered in the last month hadn't been *that* bad.

At the end of the day, I had to do what let me sleep at night, and that wasn't throwing two almost powerless Lows at drugged-up homicidal humans, or at a basilisk.

"Gimlet needs their help getting into the booth," I explained.

She drew in a shaky breath and nodded. "Okay. I'm in. It's not like I have any other option."

"Do you think they'll throw us all out there together in a melee?" I asked. If they put us one-against-one in the cage, then my plan wasn't going to be worth shit.

"I'm sure they will. There are eight humans and only five of us. Plus, they usually don't pit one Low against one human. It's over too quick and the audience boos. With the Lows, it's two or three to one at least. With shifters, it's sometimes two to one. They'll want to put on the best show, and that will be tossing us all out there at once." She raised an eyebrow and regarded me. "Plus, you let us out. You got in, and instead of hanging around, getting fed, and fighting for your prize, you threw it all away to stage some shitty jail-break attempt. They know you'll try to protect us, to help us, and that makes for good entertainment."

She wasn't wrong.

"As soon as Gimlet does his thing, and the basilisk is distracted, I'm going to bring down the view screens. Head for the entrance center field. I'll meet you there. If you still have the humans on your tail, I'll help."

She nodded, then frowned. "How are you going to disable the view screens?"

With a huge surge of electricity, but she didn't need to know about that. "I know how to short circuit the system," I said instead.

"And you'll come help me?" She looked over at me, her eyes tight with fear.

"Yes. If you can get out on your own, then go. Don't wait, just go."

It would mean I'd waste precious time making sure she was actually out before leaving myself, but I didn't want her to pass up an opportunity to escape if she had one.

A shadow dimmed the light coming down through the

tunnel. I looked up and saw two demons approaching. One was a lizard with the head of a lion, the other had a human head, a scaled torso, and arms that ended in three hooked talons instead of hands.

Isha stood and smoothed down her filthy, torn T-shirt. "That's our cue. They'll open the bars in a few minutes, and we'll have the choice of either walking out under our own steam, or having those two goons drag us out."

"How big of an audience does this event usually bring?" I asked her.

"Not like I stood still long enough to count them," she drawled.

I rolled my eyes. "Guess. A thousand? Ten thousand? Were the stands packed or half-empty? Was the audience all in one area, or in big groups throughout the stands, or scattered here and there?"

She thought for a second. "Grouped together. Kinda spread out, but all in the midfield seats. There weren't a lot of people out at the edges, I guess because they couldn't see the action as well from there. Maybe a few thousand? This stadium is so huge that I could be underestimating the numbers."

I glanced over at the demons at the gate, wondering how much longer we had. "Any humans in the stands, or just demons?"

She held up both hands. "Some demons look exactly like humans, so I don't know. I could see humans enjoying this sort of thing, though."

"Maybe, but I'm not sure they'd be all that comfortable sitting in a stadium full of demons," I countered.

Gimlet snorted. "You'd be surprised. Some humans are far cozier with demons than you'd think."

I couldn't imagine that, but then again, I'd spent the last two years mostly in the Valley, trying to survive. My neighbors, and co-workers, the gangs and the militia, all worked hard to stay as far away from demons as possible. But the demons who came our way were mainly looking to steal, kill, or vandalize. The demons downtown, like those in the tax office, were different. I'd made a deal with them. I could see some enterprising humans working together with those sorts of demons.

Hell, Desiree had been working with the Disciples. Surely, they weren't the only ones who saw an advantage to partnering with those who'd come from Hel and taken over.

As if reading my mind, a feminine figure appeared at the end of the tunnel, shadowed by the backlighting until she drew close enough to see her features. Even before I saw the reptile eyes and the face I'd come to recognize so well, I knew her. Bishop had said that demons exuded a distinctive energy signature, and Desiree wasn't bothering to even attempt to hide hers.

Sharp. Icy Cold. Bleak contrasts of black and white. The smell of latex paint overlaid with a faint aroma of oxidizing copper and a hint of sulfur. I looked around, not sure if the Lows could read her energy signature as well, or if it was just me. Isha probably couldn't, although her nose twitched as soon as Desiree had appeared at the end of the tunnel, and she'd stiffened, her hands fisting by her sides.

Desiree clapped her hands together. "Are we ready? This should be fun, although not as much fun as we would have had if a certain someone hadn't let all the wolves out of the bag. Lows are so boring. They die too quickly, and while the screaming is very entertaining, it's doesn't have quite the impact of a werewolf fighting for her life."

Her disturbing eyes settled on Isha. I moved to block the demon's gaze, instinctively putting myself in between the two.

"And you. What surprises do you have in store for us?" she mused, tapping a finger against her lips.

Gimlet snorted. "Oh, you have no idea."

I shot him a warning look, not wanting him to give any of our plans away.

She grinned at me, ignoring the Low. "Well, let's get this party started. I'm giving you all a two-minute head start before I let the humans out, and another minute before I let my basilisk out. Don't want everyone dying too quickly. That's bad for business, you know."

She turned around and strode away. At the end of the tunnel, she waved a hand and the bars in front of us dropped along with the electricity and magic. The lion-headed demon stepped inside and growled, gesturing for us to head out.

I took point, and Isha followed me. The three Lows were bringing up the rear.

I had a general idea of where things were from my exploration earlier today, and I knew that both Isha and the Lows had fought here before. Anton probably wasn't the only human who'd also fought in this arena before, and none of these piles of demolition debris looked as if they'd been significantly moved since they'd been deposited here. That meant there really would be no advantage other than a few minutes to prepare ourselves.

"I'll hold back, so I can draw the basilisk away," I told the others. "Isha, you get close to where the humans come onto the field to get their attention. Gimlet, you and Garg and Drool stay close to the fight cage and the announcer booth, but not so close that Desiree gets an idea of what we're up to and sends the basilisk after you instead of me."

We stood for a few seconds, getting our bearings, then Isha took off, jogging at an easy pace across the field to the other tunnel. On her way, she snatched up a long piece of rebar as a weapon.

The Lows moved to the center of the field, Garg and Drool climbing up separate piles of concrete to act as look-outs, while Gimlet hovered near the cage, picking up rocks and stuffing them into his pockets.

I turned and made my way back the way we'd come, stopping in clear view of the tunnel, but far enough away that I'd have a bit of a head start on the basilisk when the thing charged.

A quick glance at the stands told me that Isha's assessment was correct. Demons were clustered in groups, mostly around the midfield area. At this distance they were irregularly shaped blobs, a few bright spots of color in a sea of neutral-colored bodies. I'd never been to this stadium before, but I knew how ridiculously tiny those seats were and wondered how some of the demons in larger forms were managing to squeeze themselves in. Perhaps Desiree had modified the seating to be more inclusive of the variety of demon shapes and sizes.

But spectator comfort wasn't something I needed to be thinking about—not with a monster that spat poison about to be released on me.

A whistle sounded across the loudspeakers. I heard the crowd cheer and bent to pick up a fist-sized chunk of cement as I mentally began the countdown.

Long before I'd reached one, the monstrous chicken-lizard came racing out of the tunnel. Desiree had either lied about the minute gap between releasing the humans and basilisk, had changed her mind when she'd realized we'd left Isha to deal with the humans single-handedly. Or she couldn't count.

Bellatrix spotted me right away and must have remembered that we had an unsolved grievance between us. I didn't even need to use the chunk of cement to get her attention. The basilisk charged.

I turned and ran.

The stadium was a maze filled with piles of the debris, so I thankfully had plenty of places to weave and turn, dodging the fireballs the basilisk was coughing out at me. Occasionally it would spit the nasty green venomous stuff and melt metal, wood, and concrete, but the majority of the thing's attack was fire. Bellatrix was fast on those stumpy chicken legs, but just like before, she slowed down considerably to round corners, and her entire fight strategy consisted of chase, spit fire, and spew venom.

I stayed to the outskirts of the field, not wanting to accidentally lead her to where Gimlet was working on getting into the announcer's booth. Isha must have had the same strategy, because I rounded a corner and barely avoided plowing into her.

She yelped, dancing out of the way, then yelped again and scrambled up and over a pile of steel rods as the basilisk caught up and nearly barbequed her with a mini fireball.

"Hey!" I went to shoot the thing with a bolt of lightning, only to find myself knocked flat on my stomach, something heavy on top of me, pinning me to the ground.

Not something, but someone. Shit, I'd forgotten that of course Isha would be leading eight drugged-up humans on a chase. Panicked that I was about to have my legs and arms ripped from my body, I bucked and squirmed, then shot the guy with the electricity I'd planned for the basilisk.

I'd forgotten to dial the level down, but thankfully it didn't matter. The guy grunted, electricity dancing all along his skin before grounding out. He shifted off me, rolling me over and staring down at me in amazement.

"You're not a shifter. You're one of those demons," he said.

I squirmed under him, not able to wiggle free or get an arm or leg in position to get any leverage at all.

"I'm human," I insisted. "That was magic, a spell I smuggled in. I didn't get any of the drug. That spell was the only weapon I had."

He blinked down at me, clearly not in any hurry to get off, but neither in any hurry to start ripping my limbs off either. Then his grip on my arms suddenly tightened.

"Damned demons," he shouted. "Fucking demons."

I squeaked in panic, but before I could try any last-ditch efforts to save myself from this guy, he stood, yanking me up with him and shoving me behind him with such force that I fell and slid across the ground.

"I'll protect you," he yelled, reminding me suddenly of the woman at the market. "I'll protect you, and when we leave, you're getting two doses instead of one, because this isn't fair. It's not fair."

I got to my feet and ran, not wanting to stay just in case the guy decided I was a demon after all, or he figured that protecting me included hugging me to death. Besides, I couldn't linger. The basilisk was gone. That meant Isha was not only facing the humans, but that monster snake-chicken as well.

A yell from centerfield caught my attention, and I changed course, picking up speed when I saw that the basilisk was chasing the Lows. The fight cage was on fire, part of the supports melted and dripping venomous goo. Garg and Drool might not have been powerful demons, but they were like squirrels scampering around the cage. Bellatrix was dividing her attention between the two of them, which was frustrating her to the point where her fireball shots were wildly off target.

I hit the basilisk with a pulse of electricity. Then another. Then another. Damn, Gimlet had been right. Once this thing was focused on a target, nothing seemed to distract it.

"I'm in!" Gimlet dove inside the announcer booth, running for the mic.

My electricity hadn't distracted the basilisk, but Gimlet's triumphant announcement had. Her chicken-head swiveled, her mouth opened, and another ball of fire set the booth a blaze.

"Gimlet!" I shouted. Was he dead? Barbequed inside the burning building? There was nothing nearby to put the fire out, so I ran, hoping I could at least manage to pull him from the fire before he became a charred corpse.

Suddenly, a horrible noise boomed through the speaker system. It sounded as if someone were dragging a hundred fingernails across a chalkboard while at the same time playing an out-of-tune banjo. Worse, Gimlet must have turned the volume up to eleven, because the sound was so loud that I feared hearing damage.

Bellatrix froze. Her chicken-eyes widened, and her head jerked around. A low warbling noise came from deep in her chest, spilling from her mouth along with a curl of greenish smoke.

Screeeeeech, twang, twang, twang.

The basilisk looked heavenward and repeated the noise. I cringed and covered my ears because her version was even louder than the loudspeaker one.

Screeech, twang, twang, twang. Crack. Sizzle.

Then…silence.

I looked over, realizing that the fire must have destroyed the electronic equipment. Bellatrix squawked, then took off, half-flying as she launched herself across the field and into the stands. Demons scattered, and I could hear their screams even over the noise of the fire.

The fire! I started to run for the booth, only to halt when a figure appeared. Gimlet walked through the flames, patting himself as he exited. His hair and clothing had been singed off his body, and his skin was covered with blisters and red marks. The Low was grinning in spite of the burns.

"Tada!" He bowed. "I do a pretty good coyote impression as well. And Jack Benny, too."

"Are you…okay?" I ran over to him, but I wasn't sure what good I could do. I didn't have any first-aid supplies, and I was reluctant to even touch the guy. Those burns had to be agonizingly painful.

"Pffff." He waved a hand at me. "I'm fine. We better get out of here."

Right. I ran over to one of the cameras mounted on the non-melted, non-smoking part of the fight cage and sent a steady stream of electricity through it. All through the arena I heard the pop and sizzle of cameras. The giant viewscreen began to smoke, and then it abruptly went black.

I jumped down from the side of the cage.

"See you on the outside," I shouted to Gimlet as I took off for the centerfield exit where I'd promised to meet Isha. I was pretty sure the three Lows could manage to get out on their own, but just in case, I planned on doing a quick sweep of the area.

The exit was in sight, but Isha and the humans were nowhere to be found. I hesitated, hunkered down behind a stack of splintered lumber, wondering if I should go search for her or wait a bit.

Concerned that we were running out of time, I got up, turned around, and nearly ran headfirst into one of the humans.

He grabbed for me. I twisted away, ducking down and trying to dart past him. He caught the fabric of my sweat-pants in one hand, and I sprawled to the ground, the damned things sliding down to my knees. Just then another man rounded the corner—this one the same guy who'd pinned me to the ground earlier. He looked at me, then his eyes widened as he saw my pantless state. His gaze traveled from the sweatpants around my knees up to the man behind me who was still holding the waistband.

I'll-save-you man's face turned purple. He snarled, shouted something about demons and rape and protecting the womenfolk, before he dove at the other man. I swear the ground shook as they collided. My attacker dropped my pants.

I scrambled to my feet, yanking them back up around my waist and taking off, leaving the two of them wrestling and shouting curses at each other.

Passing a giant pile of twisted chrome seats and benches, I saw Isha ahead. She was cornered, three men closing in on her. I put on a burst of speed, grabbing the top half of a bent street sign as I ran. Cocking it back, I whacked one man in the head with the sign, and shot a bolt of electricity at another.

Isha's eyes widened as she saw what I'd done, but I was past the point of trying to cover up my abilities. I'd need everything I had to fight these guys, and a werewolf realizing I was more than human was the least of my—or her —worries.

The sign bent around the man's head, the reverberation numbing my wrists. But he bled, a thick red stream running down his scalp and neck. The other guy actually screamed and jerked from the electric shock.

"It's wearing off," I shouted to Isha

I hit the bleeding guy once more with the bent sign and then swung it around like a polearm before hitting the other guy across the lower back. They both turned to come at me, and I danced backward, rotating and spinning the sign in front of me. The Aries might be wearing off, but they were still strong, and I didn't want either one of them grabbing me.

The bleeding guy managed to grab the top of the sign. It

sliced deep into his hand, but he kept his hold, grabbing the pole with his other hand and yanking. I sent another surge of electricity through the pole. The other man dove for me, and on reflex, I threw out a hand, telekinetically flinging him backward into a block of concrete and impaling him on a piece of rebar. He slumped, blood pouring from his chest.

I hadn't wanted to kill these guys, but this had become a matter of survival.

The other guy yanked the sign from my hands, swinging it back and winding up to hit me in the head with it. I stopped holding back, and threw the equivalent of a lightning bolt at him. His eyes bulged, his hair standing straight on end. Lines of red appeared in a spidery network across his body as the blood in his veins burst through his skin.

I spun around and saw Isha standing over the other guy. She was grimacing and rubbing her chest.

"You okay?" I shouted.

She nodded. "Damn, that hurt. Thought I was having a heart attack."

It took me a second to realize she'd meant the lightning I'd summoned to kill the second guy. I'd forgotten she was most likely not immune to electricity like I was. A strike grounding that close had probably darned near killed her as well.

"How did you survive that?" she asked. "Or better yet, how the hell did you *do* that?"

"No time." I pointed to the exit. "Go. Get out of here."

The two guys were still fighting each other, but that left two more. And Anton. She needed to escape before they caught up with her.

And I needed to check on Gimlet, who I hadn't seen leaving the field.

Isha hesitated a second, then nodded and ran for the exit. I watched to make sure she made it out of the arena, and then I ran in the opposite direction, back toward midfield and the cage.

I rounded the pile of steel beams and found Gimlet—at least I found what was left of him.

Skidding to a halt, I stared at the torso that lay on the ground, guts spilling from a gaping wound just under his chest. Gimlet's bulging yellow eyes stared sightlessly at me, his mouth open in what had probably been a scream. His arms and legs had been ripped off and were scattered a few feet from the body. Standing over the whole thing, laughing as if he'd just heard a hysterical joke, was Anton. He kicked Gimlet's torso, launching it a few feet away, then laughed even harder.

My vision blurred, and a primal fury rose from deep inside my chest. My hands curled into fists. I closed the distance between us, reached out, and with my telekinetic abilities, threw him ten feet into one of the concrete blocks.

He slammed into it and slid down, his eyes blinking up at me. "Eden?"

"Fuck you," I snarled. Then I grabbed him once more with my telekinetic strength and threw him another ten feet into a pile of twisted metal. "Fuck you and your ego. Fuck you and your moneymaking schemes. Fuck your selfish ambition, your absolute lack of empathy toward anyone but yourself, and your stupid lust for revenge."

He groaned, scrambling to his feet and holding his arm at an awkward angle. "Eden, what—"

"Fuck you," I snapped, throwing him back into the concrete block. This time when he slid down to the ground, a streak of red painted the pitted white of the stone.

He was slower to get up, his head bleeding, his arm clearly broken. He stared at me, confused, and I held out my hands, ready to bounce him back and forth between the piles until he was nothing but a bag of broken bones and spilled blood.

He deserved it. It didn't matter that he was Sebastian's little brother. It didn't matter that I'd put my neck on the line to save his worthless ass. The world would be a better place without this asshole, without this idiot alive. He deserved to die. They all did.

Then I remembered the woman in the market, her paranoid ranting about how she was going to defend us against the demons. Her neighborhood had been plagued by demons, and one of them had needed to make a stand. One of them had needed to be their defender. And she'd been the one to draw the short straw.

Anton was no hero, no martyr. But in the last two years, he'd seen his heroes become nobodies, weak and helpless compared to shifters and demons. And if his heroes were nobodies, then he had no hope of ever being somebody—not without a miracle drug.

I was a fool for what I was about to do.

"Leave," I told Anton. "If I ever hear of you using Aries again, if you buy it, sell it, even pick a vial up off the pavement, I'm going to kill you. You won't have to worry about the Disciples, *I'll* be the one sending you to your grave, and I'll do it with my own bare hands. Got it?"

He nodded, eyes wide, then ran for the exit.

I watched Anton vanish around the piles of debris. The basilisk was still running through the stands, terrorizing the spectators. I recognized the lion-headed guard demon chasing after it and thought I caught a glimpse of Desiree as well. Good. That would keep them occupied for a while, and with the monitors down, it would be hard for them to see around all the junk to know what was going on down here in the arena.

I walked over and as gross as it was, I picked up one of

Gimlet's dismembered arms. Bloody sinew dangled from the end, along with the shiny white of bone. I looked at the blistered red skin, the stubby dirty fingers, and felt an overwhelming sense of failure.

I'd wanted to save them all. The humans, the Lows, the shifter. I'd wanted them all out of here alive to go home to their families and friends. I'd wanted to save them all, but in the end, the sides I'd chosen meant some lived and some died. I should have somehow made those humans leave and not fight, somehow gotten through to them how dangerous Aries was, and that no drug, no advantage, was worth lowering themselves to fight and kill those who had been kidnapped and forced into this arena.

I'd killed so many in the last two years. I had no right to judge them. When Nevarra had been kidnapped, I would have done anything to get her back, even if it meant murdering kidnapped Lows and shifters in an arena to do it. I didn't know what those humans were going through, why they needed the drug so badly that this was somehow an acceptable means to an end.

I had no right to judge, but I had every right to grieve. I hadn't known this Low more than a handful of hours. He was sneaky, gross, and his pee stunk, but he didn't deserve this.

"I'm sorry." I looked down at the Low's head, at his sightless eyes. "I'm sorry I wasn't here to help you. I'm sorry I didn't get here in time. The others got away, but you didn't, and somehow I feel like that's my fault."

The hand moved, patting me on the cheek. I screamed and flung it away. That's when Gimlet's head made a snort sound. The eyes blinked at me a few times. I backed away slowly, not sure what the fuck was going on here. Was this some kind of zombie demon?

The arms and legs slithered their way over to the torso,

twisting and positioning themselves into place. As I watched, the skin knitted, everything connecting and righting itself in a sickening crunch of skin and bone. I was horrified, but could not look away. As much as I wanted to run, I couldn't. And part of me wondered how the hell I was going to kill a zombie Gimlet.

The undead thing sat up, stretching its arms up high and yawning.

"Well. That really sucked," Gimlet announced.

"Is it…you?" I took another step back. "You were dead. I thought you were dead."

"Oh, it takes more than having my limbs ripped off and my guts dragged out of my abdomen to kill me," the Low said in a cheerful tone. "I was once almost sliced completely in half, and I managed to survive that. Hurts like fuck to reassemble myself like this, but it was worth it just to watch the look on your face."

He laughed, then stood, shaking out arms and legs once more. I stared at him, unable to say anything. Were demons immortal? Because this seemed an awful lot like immortality to me.

The Low eyed me, tip to toe, and nodded. "The fruit *really* doesn't fall far from the tree, does it?"

Then he saluted me and left the stadium, whistling as he walked.

CHAPTER 29

Our distraction techniques seemed to have been enormously successful, so I felt okay taking the time to go into the locker area, dig the combination number out of my bra, then getting my stuff. Shedding the filthy and bloody sweats, I shimmied into my own clothes, securing my shoulder harness with my Glock 43, and my hip holster with the 1911.

As I turned, I saw Desiree standing in the doorway, watching me. With a smirk, she raised both hands and did a slow clap. She hadn't escaped the evening unscathed. There was greenish goo in her hair. Part of her shirt had been burned off. Several of her nails were broken and bleeding. Her makeup was smudged, black mascara smeared under her eyes as if she were a racoon, and red lipstick smeared almost to her cheek.

She grinned wider and walked toward me.

"This has to have been the best show ever," she clapped again. "I'm a bit pissed off about Bellatrix, though. It's going to take me weeks to settle her down. She killed twenty paying customers, and I'm probably going to have to fork out blood money to their households as compensation, but it was absolutely worth it. Even if I didn't make a dime tonight, the entertainment was absolutely worth the trouble."

She stepped closer to me, and I just couldn't move. The basilisk might not have been able to paralyze me, but Desiree was doing a good job with those reptile eyes of hers.

She traced a line down my cheek with a broken fingernail, her pressure hard enough to scratch, but not hard enough to break my skin.

"I like you, Eden Alvaro," she purred. "I like you a lot. I want you for mine. I want you in my household, by my side. I want you to do my bidding. I want you to kneel at my feet."

"I don't do that whole kneeling thing," I sputtered, alarmed at the direction this conversation was taking.

She chuckled. "No, I'm sure you don't. That's okay. Disobedience is so very entertaining, and so is punishment."

I sucked in a breath, backing away from her until my rear hit the metal of the lockers. Would she grab me and take me away? Hide me somewhere I'd never be found? Bea and the girls would wonder what happened to me. Bishop…Bishop would find me. He'd find me and help me.

Hopefully.

Maybe he didn't care whether I lived or died anymore. I hadn't heard from him since our argument. It wasn't like I'd really reached out to him either, though.

Desiree took a step toward me, then halted abruptly, her gaze snagged by something down around my ankles.

Something furry brushed along my lower leg—something furry that was purring.

Mittens.

"Well, well," Desiree said softly. Then she smiled and dug something out of her pants pocket. "I've got your prize, Eden Alvaro."

She tossed something at me, and I snatched it out of the air, not realizing what it was until it hit my hand.

A little brown bottle—a vial of Aries.

"You surpassed every expectation," she told me. "I've got no idea who sired you or who formed you, but I'm absolutely impressed. Now take your little pet and get out of my stadium. I'll be seeing you soon."

She turned and walked out. I watched her until she went around the corner, not truly believing I was once again walking away from an encounter with the demon. Then I knelt down and picked up the kitten. Tucking him into the crook of my arm, I slung my backpack over my shoulder and walked out the door.

No one stopped me. No one followed me. I strode right past the stands, past the vacant ticket booth, and into the parking lot.

Even so, I unholstered my Glock, chambered a round, and kept it in one hand, Mittens tucked under my arm as I made my way to my bike. Two weapons. Only one of which would probably do more than bruise any demon who came after me.

At my bike, I scoped out the area before holstering my pistol and putting the kitten onto the seat.

"How do you want to handle this?" I asked Mittens. "Ride in my backpack? Run alongside my bike? Make your own way back to my house? I'm gonna be a while. I might not be back in Los Feliz until tomorrow sometime."

The kitten meowed, waving a tiny, furry gray paw at me as his glowing green eyes met mine.

I unzipped the backpack and held it open, wishing I had a better way of communicating with this creature. He was clearly intelligent, self-aware, and absolutely deadly in his magical abilities. He might look like an adorable gray kitten, but I was going to keep treating him as if he were just as smart—if not smarter— than me.

Mittens looked at the backpack, and then vanished in a puff of gray smoke. I shrugged, zipping the backpack up and throwing it across my shoulders. Getting on the bike, I headed down six blocks until I came across a twenty-four-hour taco joint. Parking, I went in and bought some tacos and a huge bag of churros. After eating a few and getting my bearings, I pulled my phone out of my pocket and called Piers.

"What?"

"It's me. I've got the information you wanted, as well as an idea of how to get the demons out of here. Our deal is still on, right? I help you out, and Anton gets a pass?"

I had no idea why I even cared anymore. I guess it was because if I was going to all this trouble, I should get *something* out of it, even if that something involved Anton remaining among the living for a little while longer.

Piers was silent for a moment before saying, "Deal. He shows his face south of the Valley, he's a dead man. Understand?"

I nodded, even though he couldn't see the motion. "Good. I understand. So here's the deal, I need you and about ten of your guys to meet me off the El Segundo exit on the 110 at ten o'clock tomorrow morning. Bring as much chrome as you can. I'm talking two or three trucks full of the stuff. I don't care if you have to strip down every vintage Buick and Caddy in South LA, just bring as much chrome as you can."

"Chrome?" His voice was pitched high with incredulity.

I smiled. "Yeah. Chrome."

* * *

AFTER I'D HAD my tacos, I drove past Los Feliz and into the Valley. I pulled into Bishop's driveway, parking my bike beside his old truck before I headed up the stairs.

He opened the front door before I'd even gotten off of my bike and stood in the doorway, just watching me.

I couldn't read his expression, partly because it was dark and he was back-lit through the doorway, and partly because he stared at me with an expressionless face and hooded gaze.

"Can we talk?" I looked up at him, not sure if he was going to tell me to take a hike or invite me in.

"Are we going to talk, or are you going to yell at me then steal my artwork?"

His voice was cool and dispassionate. That hurt more than if he'd been furious with me.

"Talking. I promise I won't yell. And I'm sorry I stole your paintings. I'll give them back."

"And my shirt?"

I winced, because I loved wearing his shirt. "If you want, I'll give you your shirt back, too. And you can have my coffee cup that I stole back, just to show you that I really want us to at least be friends again."

He stepped aside so I could walk in, shutting the door behind me.

I walked into the living room. He didn't ask me to sit or offer me any sort of refreshment. He didn't sit either. Instead, he just stood there, looming over me as if he wanted me to say my piece and get out of his house.

"The demons are running gladiator contests down in Inglewood in the old SoFi stadium. They're bribing humans to fight, awarding them with a dose of Aries if they win. The drug makes humans violent, paranoid, and delusional. It also makes them super strong and impenetrable to bullets, knives, electricity, probably even a fucking nuclear bomb. It wears off in less than a day depending on how much exertion they expend. The demons usually give them a dose before they fight to make the show more entertaining to the paying demon customers who are up in the stands."

He didn't say anything, so I continued.

"Desiree is running the thing. She and her pals are kidnapping shifters and Low demons, keeping them in the locker room, and forcing them to fight the juiced-up humans every night until they die. When they get killed, Desiree grabs more off the street and brings replacements in."

Bishop sighed. "You're here because you want me to go rescue those shifters, aren't you? Our prior argument aside, I am completely outnumbered. There are tens of thousands of demons in the city, and I am one. There's a bit of professional respect going on where I get to run my bar and the demons stay away from what they grudgingly consider my territory, but that's it. I pulled in a favor with Desiree down in the customs warehouse two months ago. I've got no other currency with her that I'm willing to spend. I can't waltz down to Inglewood, confront Desiree, set those shifters free, and forbid her from kidnapping any more of them. I can't."

"You don't have to," I informed him, trying to quell the old anger rising in me. "I already did. Well, rescue them, that is. I went to the stadium and set the shifters and the Lows free. It's kind of a long story, but there was a basilisk and then Desiree showed up... I ended up back in the locker room with the three Lows and one shifter who didn't get away."

A muscle twitched in his jaw. "Desiree locked you up and forced you to fight a bunch of drug-enhanced humans for your freedom?"

Now I felt the anger rolling off him. It reminded me of what Lila said had happened to King. Maybe his death really had been about me, and not Bishop delivering justice for his pack.

"No, she didn't make me fight for my freedom. She intended for all five of us to fight over and over each night until we died. But I came up with a plan, we all escaped, and we kind of screwed up her game—at least for the night. I'm going back down tomorrow, and me and some of the Disciples are going to permanently fuck the whole thing up." I felt kind of smug about that. This would be two of Desiree's businesses I'd destroyed. I might eventually pay for it, but knowing I'd thwarted her twice brought me a ton of satisfaction.

"You rescued the shifters," he stated.

I nodded. "This time. I can't guarantee she won't still mess with them, but she's not going to be able to run these gladiatorial contests on any sort of scale after tomorrow. There aren't any other stadiums of that size still standing, and she wouldn't make enough money hosting them in a smaller venue."

"You rescued the *shifters*," he repeated.

"Well yeah. Someone had to." I couldn't help but get that little dig in there. "And I rescued the three Lows as well. Gimlet kind of got dismembered, but he was able to reassemble his body parts and didn't die. I did kill a couple of the humans, but it couldn't be helped. And they were there voluntarily, trying to kill us, so it was self-defense."

His lips twitched. Seeing that little bit of humor was like the sun coming out from behind storm clouds. We were going to be okay. I just *knew* we were going to be okay.

"Shifters and Lows." He shook his head. "And *Gimlet*? It's been a long time since I saw his ugly face."

It didn't surprise me that Bishop knew the Low. I got the feeling that any demon who could reassemble himself after being disemboweled and having his limbs torn off was one who had been around a long, long time.

"Would you have been able to save me if I had been near

death?" I asked him, suddenly curious. "In Inglewood, where you evidently don't have jurisdiction? Against Desiree and however many demons she had with her at the time?"

His eyes met mine. "I would have come for you. I would have saved you. And I would have paid the price. Any price."

Yeah. We were going to be just fine.

"I should get going." I turned to walk to the door, Bishop beside me. "I've got a busy day tomorrow, ruining a powerful demon's day, making a troll really happy, and paying off a debt to the Disciples. Maybe dinner sometime this week? My house this time? I'll cook."

I'd order carryout, but he didn't have to know that.

He stopped at the doorway "Sure. I'll call you. Hey, Trouble?"

I turned to face him.

"You can keep the shirt. And the paintings. But I want your mug back."

I bit back a smile and nodded. "It's a deal."

CHAPTER 30

$\mathcal{A}$t ten o'clock I pulled off the 110 and saw three pickup trucks loaded down with chrome. Piers was standing outside a silver Dodge Challenger, holding a hand over his nose.

"You get used to the smell," I lied as I pulled up next to him.

"Thank God I don't live here." His voice was muffled under his hand.

"The residents are going to be happy. The Disciples will be happy." I motioned to the overpass. "The troll is going to be happy. Desiree is not going to be happy."

"I take it this thing really likes chrome?" Piers glanced over at the dump trucks. "Think we brought enough?"

"I hope so. The plan is to scatter it like breadcrumbs, leading the troll to the stadium, then inside to the field. There's piles of steel, concrete, and more chrome. It's like a troll candy store in there."

Piers nodded. "How close do we need to put the chrome? It would really suck if the troll got distracted halfway to the stadium and decided to make his home in some building we're currently using."

"It's probably best to drop the chrome within line of sight. Maybe six feet apart?" The only thing I knew about trolls was what Erik at Hook's Catering had told me and what I'd read in my demonology book late last night. "It's probably best if they're smallish, bite-sized pieces. Otherwise, we'll have to keep waiting for the troll to finish what he's eating, and the relocation will take all day."

And with big chunks, there was a chance the troll would get full and wander off before we got him to his destination.

Piers waved over at the guys. "I'll get the guys started. Once we have about eight or so pieces, we'll drop a few closer to the overpass to lure the troll out. You sure this is going to work? I don't want the demons to just incorporate the troll into their fight games."

"It'll work," I assured him.

Trolls were evidently territorial. They had interim spots where they bedded down, but once they found a place with plenty of their favorite food, they marked it and settled in. They also hated demons and would vigorously defend their territory against any demon who tried to drive them away. And they smelled horrible, especially when they started marking their territory. The poop had been eye-wateringly disgusting, but according to the demonology book, the glandular scent they used to mark their territory was worse.

I watched while Piers communicated the plan to his guys.

Two guys got into the bed of each truck with the chrome. The drivers moved the trucks into position, then stopped while the guys in the beds sorted through the chrome, picking out the smallest pieces and placing them along the road. Piers motioned for one truck to pull a few blocks ahead. One remained where it was, and the other pulled up closer to the overpass. One of the guys hopped out of the bed, taking two chunks of chrome from the other guy before walking up and tossing them under the bridge.

The ground rumbled, and the troll jumped out, snatching up a piece of chrome and shoving it in his mouth before running for the other piece. The man on the ground screamed and ran. The truck took off, leaving him behind while the guy in the bed frantically started tossing pieces out.

"Go, go!" Piers yelled.

I caught my breath as the troll moved—and ate—with unexpected speed. The man in the first truck wasn't throwing the chrome fast enough, and the troll caught up, reaching out and grabbing the back bumper of the truck.

The guy shrieked, holding the side of the bed as the driver threw it into four-wheel drive and gunned the engine. For a second, I thought they were going to have to abandon the vehicle, but the troll decided one of the pieces in the bed looked far tastier than the truck's bumper and abruptly let go.

The truck shot forward, nearly throwing the guy in the back out of the vehicle. I turned my bike around, and we all began a mad game of chase through Hawthorne and into Inglewood.

Piers hadn't bothered to clear our path, and a few times pedestrians and other vehicles slowed us to the point where the troll was almost able to snatch up one of our trucks. But Piers used his Challenger to block crossroads and threatened people with his pistol. Ultimately, though, it was the troll itself that cleared our path. Pedestrians got one whiff of the approaching monster and ran. Cars made U-turns when they saw the grayish giant lumbering down the street, and sped away.

Surprisingly it only took us about twenty minutes to make the roughly eight-mile journey to the stadium. The troll sped up once we hit the parking lots, roaring in frustration as it tried to get to the yummy chrome still in the back of the pickups. Piers had been smart enough to have some of his guys here ahead of us, unlocking the gates and giving the trucks a clear path to shoot through into the field.

We drove past the startled ticket agent, who screamed and ran when she saw the troll. Several guards tried to close the gates, but they also fled when they saw what was chasing us. The trucks rolled onto the field. The men in the back frantically threw the rest of the chrome out of the truck beds. Then they got out of the way, waiting for the troll to be focused on the pile of shiny chrome so they could loop around and exit the way we'd come in.

I left my bike by the ticket booth and jogged in after the troll, watching as the thing came to a halt in the middle of the football field, staring in openmouthed fascination at the volume of construction debris.

With a noise that sounded like a teenage girl's squeal, the troll let loose a greenish liquid from its nether regions. I gagged, bent double, and pulled my shirt up to my nose. That demonology book had absolutely *not* prepared me for this. The rotted cod smell had been bad; the poop had been worse. *This*, however, was indescribable.

I wasn't sure I'd ever get the odor out of my clothing. I might just have to burn it all and ride naked on the way home.

The troll began to walk around the arena, squirting the foul green stuff every few feet. Piers's guys fled in their trucks. Piers fled in his Challenger, flashing me a peace sign on the way out.

I wanted to flee, but first I had to make sure that Desiree hadn't kidnapped and imprisoned any more Lows and shifters, hoping to start up her operation again. Keeping as close to the stands and as far away from the troll-liquid as possible, I went to the locker room and was happy to see there were no demons or shifters inside. The basilisk wasn't there either, but I remembered Desiree saying it would take a while for her pet to calm down, so she'd probably taken it to a less stimulating environment.

Just in case, I went to the other side of the field to check where the human fighters had been staying. I was just about to leave when I heard voices in the office where we'd stored our clothes. I froze, recognizing not only Desiree's voice, but Bishop's as well.

"They're *not* yours," Desiree sneered.

"But they are." Bishop's voice was calm, cool. It reminded me of last night when he was still mad at me. Bishop's yelling-mad was scary, but this calm-mad was terrifying.

"Since when?" Desiree snapped. "You haven't bothered with them for thousands of years. They cry and pray and beg, and you ignore them. But now you suddenly decide to claim them? The toys you threw away so long ago are *now* important to you?"

"They're not toys, they're living beings," he informed her. "I claimed them as mine ten thousand years ago. I may not have asserted my claim for a long time, but that doesn't make them any less mine."

"What about the Ha-Satan?" Desiree asked. "The Ruling Council of Angels gave the Nephilim and shifters to her choir."

I frowned, thinking I'd need to look up this council thingy in the book back home. The Ha-Satan must have referred to Satan, who was now a female demon and an imp. If the shifters had been given to her, then God help them.

"I have a prior claim. And even if I didn't, are you really saying the Ha-Satan gave you permission to take members of her choir and pit them to the death against super-powered, drugged humans?"

I clapped a hand over my mouth to hold back a laugh at that.

Desiree sucked in an audible breath. "You better think about what you're doing, Bishop. There are tens of thousands of us, and just one of you."

I frowned, because that was exactly what Bishop had said to me last night.

"That's true," he replied. "But you shouldn't count on every demon in LA supporting you in a fight against me. There are demons who would be on my side."

"Right." She laughed. "You mean Eden? That little thing running around and pretending she's a human? She's young. She's no threat."

"Maybe. Maybe not. But her energy signature is very distinctive, wouldn't you agree? I recognize it. I know you recognize it. Other demons will recognize it as well. They'll know who she is. And those who do will be *very* reluctant to oppose her."

What the fuck? Was he talking about me? He recognized my energy signature? Recognized it as what? He had to be bluffing.

"That's bullshit and you—" She sniffed. "What's that smell? What the fuck is that nasty smell?"

I scrambled up into the stands and ducked behind a nearby row of stadium seats. Desiree and Bishop walked out of the office. Both gagged and covered their noses.

Just then the troll walked around a chunk of concrete and sprayed greenish liquid not twenty feet from where the two stood.

Desiree screamed, her hands in fists.

"Oh, what a shame," Bishop said. "He's marked this place as his. You'll never get him to leave. And even if you managed to, you'll never get the smell out of here."

"You did this." She turned to face Bishop. "You did this, didn't you?"

"You should be careful about what enemies you're making, Desiree." He smiled at her, and then he left.

Desiree took a menacing step toward the troll. It turned and snarled at her. She backed up and then ran as it lunged for her.

I waited for the troll to wander farther into the field, then I left as well, getting on my bike and heading home.

I was still going to have to do something about this Aries drug. I was going to have to ask Bishop what he'd meant about my energy signature. I was going to have to check in with Sebastian to see if Anton had gotten home—and collect my pay. I should also call Telaney to see if there were any good jobs coming up in the next day or two. I needed to swing by to see Bags. And go visit Bea and bring the girls the pictures I'd stolen from Bishop. We'd hang them in their rooms. Then maybe they could spend the night at my place this weekend.

But the first thing on my to-do list was to get a shower and burn these clothes.

CHAPTER 31

*B*efore I drove home I checked in with Telaney, texted Sebastian, then headed for the Valley. I pulled into my driveway with the usual onlookers. As I walked up the pathway, I stopped, staring at all the stuff piled in front of my door. It was like those memorials people put beside the road when someone dies in an auto accident, except next to all the flowers, candles and cards were baskets holding food, bottles of wine, and other gifts.

I picked up a pink zippered bag and looked inside to find it filled with makeup, scented lotions, and a bath bomb.

"They're tithes," a voice behind me said.

I spun around to see Lila standing there, tears in her eyes.

"Thousands of years ago our people would give offerings and tithes of thanks to the Protector. These are all expressions of gratitude."

"But I'm not the Protector, I'm the chihuahua," I insisted. "Shouldn't all this stuff be at Bishop's house? Or his bar?"

"My friend Isha called me last night," Lila said. "She told me how someone she'd originally thought was a human had come to save them, how she'd released the shifters, and then she stayed behind to fight when Isha was caught."

"I couldn't exactly help that," I explained. "The bars were magicked, and there was a basilisk."

"Isha said this woman, Eden, fought with the strength of a lion and with the cleverness of a fox," Lila continued. "You revealed your abilities and what you are to save Isha, who claims she and the others are only alive and free right now because of you."

"It was a team effort," I protested. "None of us would have gotten out without the help of the others."

"She and the others you saved spread the word." Lila gestured to the pile of offerings. "I asked you to intervene on our behalf with Bishop, and instead you were the one who answered our prayers. I underestimated you, Protector. Please forgive me."

"Whoa, whoa." I held out my hands. I was tempted to tell her about what I'd overheard Bishop telling Desiree, that *he'd* stepped in to safeguard the shifters, not me. But I wasn't sure Bishop wanted anyone to know about that. Our relationship was tenuous enough without me spilling his secrets.

"I'm not the Protector," I tried to explain. "I'm the chihuahua. This was a one-time thing. I'm not anyone's angel."

"But you are." Lila bowed. "You will forever be our angel. The descendants of the Nephilim owe you a great debt and our eternal allegiance."

She dashed off to her house before I could reply, leaving me standing in front of my door, holding a bag of cosmetics.

I wasn't about to let all this stuff go to waste, so I shrugged her comments off, opened my door, and took everything inside. It was a pretty good haul. I had enough dried and canned food, and wine for a week or two, and a few of the baskets even held things like eggs, cheese, and baked goods.

A strident meow rang out, and I looked down to see Mittens circling my legs, purring.

"Look, buddy." I showed him the contents on one of the baskets. "Someone gave us tuna and this yummy smoked salmon. Do you like smoked salmon? I know I do."

The kitten made a strange noise, something between a chirp and a squeal, and the packet of smoked salmon vanished from the basket, reappearing on the floor. Mittens snatched it in his mouth, then darted off through the living room with his prize.

Jerk. The least he could have done was share.

I grabbed a bag of homemade venison jerky and headed downstairs, snatching a few bites before taking a luxuriously hot shower. My phone beeped, and I glanced down to see that Sebastian had texted me, wanting to buy me dinner tonight and settle up our debt.

I stared at the text for a moment, trying to read between the lines. Anton had most likely arrived home last night. Had he told Sebastian about the arena? About the fights?

About me using magic to throw him up against the piles of rubble?

I wasn't sure how I was going to explain all of that, but there was nothing in Sebastian's message but appreciation and affability. I took a deep breath, convincing myself that this wasn't a trap.

Got family stuff tonight and this weekend, I texted back. *Can meet for a quick coffee somewhere in Burbank or Sun Valley in the next hour if you're free.*

I'd barely hit send before Sebastian texted back with a location. There was no telling what traffic would be like this time of day, so I quickly finished dressing, and used some of the cosmetics from my gift-bag.

"Don't eat all the food," I called to Mittens as I ran out the door.

I pulled into the coffee shop parking lot right on time, wishing I still had my motorcycle helmet. Well, actually Piers's motorcycle helmet. I'd had to twist my hair back into a tight bun, but I still arrived with bits that had blown loose and were now a frizzy tumbleweed of brown around my head. Quickly taming the mess, I jogged into the coffee shop to find Sebastian at a back table. He held up one of two cups that were on his table and gestured me over.

"Sorry." I smiled at him as I took the coffee and sat down. "Crazy week."

"So I've heard."

I paused mid-sip, tensing. Had Anton told him? Was there a gun pointed at me under the table right now?

Sebastian lifted the hand I couldn't previously see to the table, and pushed an envelope across to me. I picked it up, glanced inside, then gasped. It was full of hundred-dollar bills. I wasn't rude enough to count them, but this wasn't the six hundred we'd agreed upon, it was probably closer to three thousand.

"All I asked was for you to get information on Anton, and you delivered." Sebastian's gaze was intense as he spoke. "But then you went back down to Inglewood, went into that arena, and tried to convince him to leave. When he wouldn't leave, you stayed and made sure he made it out alive, beating some damned sense into him."

"Uhhh." I was frozen in place, the coffee untouched, the envelope of money still in my hand.

Sebastian leaned back in his chair and shook his head. "You acted in my stead. Put the fear of God into that boy. I owe you so much more than what's in that envelope. Anton is only alive because you cared enough to reel him in."

I let out a careful breath. "I'm glad he's home safe."

"Because of you."

Sebastian's eyes met mine, and I wasn't sure I liked what was in them. The respect I'd take, but love?

He broke our gaze and snorted. "The kid was still damned high when he got home. I sent him up to Aunt Natasha in Ventura for a few months to get it out of his system and get his head on straight again. I've got three guys up there with him, just to make sure he doesn't do anything stupid again. Momma isn't in the best of health. She doesn't need Anton putting her into the grave with his shit."

So maybe Anton hadn't told him anything except that I'd beat the crap out of him. That didn't sound like something Anton would admit to, but I had shaken the guy up pretty bad.

"That Aries drug really messes with people," I said. "People on it are paranoid and aggressive. They hallucinate. I know people are desperate and feel like they're eternally the victims ever since the demons came, but Aries isn't the answer."

Sebastian barked out a harsh laugh. "Tell me about it. Anton was shaking and ready to fight everyone and anyone. He had this crazy story that you were actually a demon, that you'd used demon magic to throw him around without touching him, that you'd electrocuted people with your hands."

I forced a laugh of my own. "He said that?"

"Yeah." Sebastian shook his head. "I know, right? Nuts. I told him I've known you since high school. We've dated. We've made love. I know your foster mom, your sisters. Told him if you were a demon, I'd definitely know it."

"Yeah." I tried to laugh again and utterly failed.

"Guy was high as a kite. I just hope there's no lasting damage to his brain or anything." Sebastian sighed. "He was always a difficult kid, but I never expected him to turn to drugs."

I thought of the woman at the market. "People get desperate. Sometimes they think the benefit is worth the cost, that the ends justify the means. I get it. I've *been* there. And if I'd had a drug available that would have helped me get the upper hand, back then I might have taken it."

Sebastian thought about that for a while, then sighed. "What are we gonna do, Eden? If Anton got this drug, others will too. It'll spread throughout the Valley, throughout LA. It's going to be violence and chaos everywhere."

The arena had been shut down, but I had no confidence that the demons wouldn't find another way to distribute Aries. Violence and chaos. That's what demons wanted. And that the body count might include some of their own wouldn't bother them one bit. The Lows pitted against the humans in the arena proved that to me.

"I don't know." I shrugged. "If we can figure out who's manufacturing the stuff, then maybe we can cut it off at the source. Otherwise it's going to be like any other street drug —impossible to stop at the dealer or user level."

"This isn't like heroine or meth," Sebastian commented. "Aries isn't the sort of thing anyone can make in their basement. There's got to be some magic component to the manufacture."

I nodded. "There can't be that many mages skilled enough to create a drug like this. If we do some digging, maybe we can figure out who's making the stuff."

"The demons are getting it from someone. We need someone who knows demons. Maybe we can trace it that way," he suggested.

Desiree would definitely know who was making the stuff, but I had no desire to track her down and ask her, even if I thought I had a snowflake's chance in hell that she'd share that information with me.

I stood, stuffing the money in my backpack and picking up my coffee. "Let me ask around. Keep your ears to the ground, and I'll do the same. Maybe we can grab lunch in a few weeks and swap notes."

"Sounds good." He smiled. "And if there's anything you need, you call me. Anything you want, you call me. I owe you, Eden. And if I owe you, then the Gray Dogs owe you."

"I'll be in touch." I saluted him with the coffee, then downed it on my way to the door.

There was an intimate note in his last words, but I didn't have time to analyze that or begin to worry about Sebastian's expectations.

I needed to get to Bea's. And I absolutely couldn't be late.

CHAPTER 32

Sadie laughed as Bishop picked her up so she could swipe a final bit of paint on the window trim. I smiled over at them, then turned back to the new desk I was assembling.

Bea had arranged for Javier to take Nevarra out on a date so we could redecorate her room as a surprise. Leaving the coffee shop, I'd gotten a text from Bishop asking if I was free for dinner. When I'd told him about my plans, he'd offered to come over and help.

He'd shown up with a new desk in the back of his pickup truck, along with bedding and curtain sets for both girls. Sadie's was a quirky magical dolphin print, where Nevarra's had a cheery sunflower print. He, Bea, and Sadie painted, hung the pictures that I'd stolen from Bishop's house, replaced the bedding, and hung the curtains, all while I wrestled with this new desk. I'd already had to disassemble it twice because I'd screwed something on backward.

"There." I stood and surveyed my work. The new oak desk looked so much nicer than the old chipped one that had somehow managed to survive both Drew and me.

"Finally," Sadie teased. "I was worried you'd be here all night trying to put that thing together."

"Your sister is not all that great at following instructions," Bishop told Sadie.

"Hey. Not fair." I laughed. "Did you *see* those instructions? No? Because there were no instructions, just a bunch of pictures that looked as if they'd been drawn by a drunken toddler. I totally had to wing it here."

"Winging it is something your sister *is* very good at." Bishop was still talking to Sadie, pretending to ignore my protests.

A car door slammed outside. Loudly. So loudly that I knew it was Javier warning us that they were back. The kid was only fifteen, but in New Hell no one cared about driver's licenses. I doubted the Motor Vehicle Administration was even still in business. Either way, Javier had been driving for the last two years, and his family didn't bat an eye when he'd asked to borrow the truck for a date.

I couldn't wait to hear all about it. Javier had taken her to Malibu beach, and then to get some ice cream.

"They're here!" Sadie announced.

"You stall her. We'll clean up," I told her.

She ran out of the room while Bishop and I picked up trash and put away the tools.

"We should take Sadie to the beach for her birthday next week," I mused as I moved the desk to its spot under the window. "Her physical therapist said swimming would be good exercise for her leg."

And I'd seen the gleam of envy in her eyes when Nevarra had announced where she and Javier were going on their date. Sadie was a fish in the water. I remembered taking her to swimming lessons at the community pool when she'd first come here, and marveling at how quickly she'd mastered the activity. That community pool was long gone, neglected and abandoned, but we still had an entire coast-line of ocean to play in. The demons could never take that from us.

I thought of Gimlet, of Drool and Garg. Maybe I needed to stop blaming the demons for all our woes. The demons coming had certainly changed everything, but there was plenty of blame to go around. The angels had abandoned us. Our own country had abandoned us. We'd abandoned ourselves, fleeing the state or hunkering down and focusing only on our personal survival. The demons didn't care whether we had a community pool or not. They hadn't destroyed it or kept anyone from using it. We were the ones who'd drained it and padlocked the gates.

Maybe it was time to open the community pool. Maybe it was time to stand up and take back our lives, not just from the demons, but from our own fears.

"How about a party at the beach," Bishop suggested, pulling my thoughts back to Sadie and her eleventh birthday.

It was a great idea. How long had it been since Sadie had a true birthday party? How long had it been since any of us in LA had a party? I could invite Telaney and Bags and the kids from my neighborhood. Bishop could invite HB and maybe even Bob. Bea would make sure the neighbors here were invited. I had extra money from Sebastian that I'd been planning on putting aside for Bea and the girls to finally get out of here, but some of that could go toward drinks and burgers and decorations.

"A party at the beach." I smiled and walked over to him, wrapping my arms around his waist and snuggling up against him. "She'll love it."

He pulled me tight against him, laying his cheek on the top of my head. Once more, I felt him, that non-human part of him, caressing the non-human part of me. I always felt his presence, even when he wasn't physically nearby. It was a strange sort of awareness, and looking back, I realized it had been going on long before we'd had sex.

"Confession." I pulled back a bit to see his face. "I saw you and Desiree at the stadium."

He chuckled. "She was pretty pissed. That troll was a great idea."

She was pissed at more than the troll. Bishop had reclaimed the shifters, and she'd been furious about his interference. Would he be mad that the shifters were leaving offerings on my doorstep instead of his? From what I knew of Bishop, he'd be relieved not to have the attention, and think it was funny that I had been thrust into the spotlight while he remained behind the scenes.

But it wasn't his reclaiming of the shifters that I really wanted to talk to him about, it was something else.

"I overheard you telling Desiree that you recognized my energy signature, that she probably had as well." My eyes met his. "Does that mean you know who I am? *What* I am? Who my parents, or whatever, are?"

He slid a hand from my waist to my cheek, cupping my face. "I have my suspicions."

I bit my lip, wondering if I really wanted to know. Did it make a difference who'd spawned me? Did it make a difference if he confirmed what in my heart I knew, and put a label on me?

No, it wouldn't.

"You are whatever you want to be," he told me, when I didn't ask the obvious next question.

"But am I?" I wondered.

"You're Eden, and that's more than enough," he stressed.

But I'd almost died a lot in the last few months. The shifters might think I was amazing, but I always felt like I was barely hanging on, like I was absolutely inadequately skilled or prepared for the shit I found myself in the middle of.

"You're more than enough," he repeated. Then he kissed me and all my doubts fled, forgotten in the moment.

Sadie burst through the doorway, Nevarra and Javier right behind her.

"Ta-da!" Sadie stretched her arms out and twirled around, stumbling slightly on her injured leg.

Nevarra's eyes widened. "Oh. Wow." She looked at me and then at Bishop, who still had an arm around my waist—and smiled.

"Do you like it?" I asked. "It was Bea and Sadie's idea, but I'll have you know I did most of the work."

"She put the desk together," Sadie told her sister. "That's all she did. It took her hours."

"It's amazing." Nevarra took it all in. "And I love the desk."

She tugged Javier into the room behind her and the boy made the expected comments about the room being "nice" and the desk being "nice," the whole time keeping an uneasy eye on Bishop.

They were all leaving goodies on my doorstep, but clearly it was Bishop they were still afraid of. I was the one Javier needed to be afraid of, not the dude by my side. But my worries that he might break my sister's heart were alleviated by the way he entwined his fingers with hers, and the adoring looks he kept giving her when she wasn't looking.

"We're still going to your house this weekend, right?" Nevarra asked, turning back to face me.

That would give me two days of Vulturing and some adult activity with Bishop before my hours were filled with games, hiking, and birthday-party planning. I was hoping Bishop would join in on those as well. He'd not hesitated to spend hours painting and redecorating my sister's bedroom. Did he know the way to my heart was through my family?

"Yes. Sleepover at Eden's this weekend." I slid an arm around Bishop's waist, hoping he realized he was included in that as well.

My family was safe and happy. I had an awesome place of my own, even if the neighbors were a bit weird. A kitten from Hel considered me to be his.

And this thing with Bishop was turning out to be far more than a one-night stand. It was turning out to be something amazing.

I hugged him, smiled over at my family, and counted the blessings I had, right here in this house.

* * *

WANT ALL THE IMPISH FUN? Get new release and sale alerts, giveaways, free stuff—and maybe even chicken wand if you're lucky, all by signing up for my newsletter.

Imp Forsaken

Angel of Chaos

Kingdom of Lies

Exodus

Queen of the Damned

The Morning Star

With This Ring

* * *

<u>Half-breed Series</u>
Demons of Desire

Sins of the Flesh

Cornucopia

Unholy Pleasures

City of Lust

* * *

<u>Imp World Novels</u>
No Man's Land

Stolen Souls

Three Wishes

Northern Lights

Far From Center

Penance

* * *

<u>Northern Wolves</u>
Juneau to Kenai

Rogue

Winter Fae

Bad Seed

* * *

<u>The Templar Series</u>

Dead Rising

Last Breath

Bare Bones

Famine's Feast

Royal Blood

Dark Crossroads

* * *

<u>White Lightning Series</u>

Wooden Nickels

Bum's Rush

Clip Joint

Jake Walk

Trouble Boys

Packing Heat (TBD)

ABOUT THE AUTHOR

Debra lives in a little house in the woods of Maryland with her sons and two slobbery bloodhounds. On a good day, she jogs and horseback rides, hopefully managing to keep the horse between herself and the ground. Her only known super power is 'Identify Roadkill'.

For more information:
www.debradunbar.com

ACKNOWLEDGMENTS

Sending a big shout-out to Melissa Marr who read my very clunky first draft, and saw the diamond in the rough. Her suggestions made this book really shine!

Thank you to my friends and family who were my sounding boards and helped me connect with resources as I did my research.

I really appreciate the help of Adam Richardson from the Writer's Detective Bureau who gave me a cop's view on how the police might work in a dystopian LA.

Also, big thanks to my copyeditor Kimberly Cannon, whose eagle eyes catch the typos and keep my comma problem in line, and to Damonza for once again providing me with an amazing cover design.